Passi

By

Book 7 in the Twelve Quickies of Christmas series

What does a prudish, self-proclaimed loner do when a nearly naked man jumps out of an oversized Christmas gift, sings a slightly racy version of the Twelve Days of Christmas, and promises to make her deepest desires come true? She goes for it, of course, and has the best twenty-four hours of her life. But at the stroke of midnight, the spell ends, and her happy holidays take an unexpected turn. Alone again, there's only one thing she wishes for: a little Christmas magic to bring back the man who taught her the joy of giving.

A Christmas Phantasie

By Kit Tunstall

Book 8 in the Twelve Quickies of Christmas series

After a bad marriage, Jakarta finds it difficult to commit to a future with the man she's now seeing. Teague has grown frustrated with her hesitation, believing she doesn't trust him. On their Christmas trip to Castle Phantasie, things come to a head. Jakarta must prove her trust in Teague by submitting to him, or their relationship will end. She loves him, but what he's asking for might be more than she can give.

Snow Angel

By Joey W. Hill

Book 9 in the Twelve Quickies of Christmas series

In her misspent youth, Constance used sex as a shallow substitute for the intimacy and love she craved. Fifteen years later, she whispers her deepest wish into Santa's ear at a Christmas benefit, only to discover he is someone who was part of that unfortunate and embarrassing time of her life.

Mortified, she plans an early exit from the party, but Santa has different ideas. Sam Coble always wanted to get to know the girl behind the reputation, and now that she is an accomplished, independent woman, that determination spurs him to action. Constance is going to discover this particular Santa has a soft spot for naughty girls. He plans to give her everything she ever put on a Christmas list...and then some.

Hot For Santa

By Lacey Alexander

Book 10 in the Twelve Quickies of Christmas series

Amy Finnegan has been attracted to Cole Bradshaw for years, but when he dons a Santa suit at the local mall and asks her to be his elf, her attraction turns into full blown lust. Yet when the entire holiday season passes with no response to her flirtations, (leaving the lacy undies she's been wearing beneath her elf dress untouched), Amy resolves to give up the chase. Cole's Christmas Eve invitation (a thrilling night of eggnog and movies) is the wakeup call Amy needs to get over her crush. Little does she know that Cole has planned a seduction (complete with erotic Christmas gifts) that will turn her into his willing holiday slave. Before the night is over, the sexy man wearing nothing but a Santa hat will prove to Amy that it's more rewarding to be naughty than nice.

Elf Song

By Samantha Winston

Book 11 in the Twelve Quickies Of Christmas Series

Though he is in great demand at the court, Branagh, the Nutcracker Prince, has sought no mate and found no one to fill his needs.

Melflouise Fairnight, once an archer in the elf militia, now a kitchen maid in the palace of the Sugar Plum Fairy, wanted only to catch a glimpse of the secretive Nutcracker Prince. She never dreamed he'd desire her, or that his loving could free the elf song she'd kept caged since her husband's death.

Their unexpected passion forces Branagh to make a terrible choice, between his kingdom and his woman.

Christmas Angel

By Lisa Marie Rice

Book 12 in the Twelve Quickies of Christmas series

Nicole Caron lost the love of her life on Christmas Eve. Now only the Christmas Angel can help her.

Discover for yourself why readers can't get enough of the multiple award-winning publisher Ellora's Cave. Whether you prefer e-books or paperbacks, be sure to visit EC on the web at www.ellorascave.com for an erotic reading experience that will leave you breathless.

WWW.ELLORASCAVE.COM

THE TWELVE QUICKIES OF CHRISTMAS VOLUME 2
ISBN # 1-4199-5072-X
An Ellora's Cave Publication, November 2004

Ellora's Cave Publishing, Inc.
1337 Commerce Drive, Suite 13
Stow OH 44224

ISBN MS Reader (LIT) ISBN # 1-84360-732-8
Passion And A Pear Tree © 2003 Tawny Taylor

ISBN MS Reader (LIT) ISBN # 1-84360-733-6
A Christmas Phantasie © 2003 Kit Tunstall

ISBN MS Reader (LIT) ISBN # 1-84360-734-4
Snow Angel © 2003 Joey W. Hill

ISBN MS Reader (LIT) ISBN # 1-84360-794-1
Hot For Santa © 2003 Lacey Alexander

ISBN MS Reader (LIT) ISBN # 1-84360-735-2
Elf Song © 2003 Samantha Winston

ISBN MS Reader (LIT) ISBN # 1-84360-736-0
Christmas Angel © 2003 Lisa Marie Rice
Other formats available (no ISBNs are assigned)

Cover art by Syneca

Warning:

The following material contains graphic sexual content meant for mature readers. *THE TWELVE QUICKIES OF CHRISTMAS VOLUME 2* has been rated E–rotic by a minimum of three independent reviewers.

Ellora's Cave Publishing offers three levels of Romantica™ reading entertainment: S (S-ensuous), E (E-rotic), and X (X-treme).

S-ensuous love scenes are explicit and leave nothing to the imagination.

E-rotic love scenes are explicit, leave nothing to the imagination, and are high in volume per the overall word count. In addition, some E-rated titles might contain fantasy material that some readers find objectionable, such as bondage, submission, same sex encounters, forced seductions, etc. E-rated titles are the most graphic titles we carry; it is common, for instance, for an author to use words such as "fucking", "cock", "pussy", etc., within their work of literature.

X-treme titles differ from E-rated titles only in plot premise and storyline execution. Unlike E-rated titles, stories designated with the letter X tend to contain controversial subject matter not for the faint of heart.

THE TWELVE
QUICKIES OF CHRISTMAS
VOLUME 2

Passion And A Pear Tree
by Tawny Taylor

A Christmas Phantasie
by Kit Tunstall

Snow Angel
by Joey W. Hill

Hot For Santa
by Lacey Alexander

Elf Song
by Samantha Winston

Christmas Angel
by Lisa Marie Rice

PASSION AND A PEAR TREE

Tawny Taylor

Chapter One

If there was one thing Destiny Doherty knew, it was that her sister, Fate, was up to no good.

Yes, Fate called every Christmas Eve wishing her happy holidays and complaining about the fact that they lived at opposite ends of the continent, but this year something was different. Fate didn't call only once. She called several times, and each time with a different lame excuse. Then she drilled Destiny with questions about her plans for the evening.

What the hell was that troublemaker up to now?

Destiny shoved aside the storm door, ducking against the bitter winter wind cutting through her coat like it was made of mesh, and crammed her key into the lock. She twisted it to the left.

Unlocked? She'd left her front door unlocked? Never!

Scared, not sure what to expect, she pushed open the door, stepped into the warm foyer and scanned it for signs of an unwelcome visitor.

Nothing.

"Fate!" she called out, hoping either she'd summon her sister from her hiding place, or scare away a burglar. "Answer now, or I'm calling the cops."

Not a damn thing.

She grabbed the cordless off the shelf in the foyer and ventured further. "Fate?"

There was a fire in the living room. Flickering light reflected on the far wall.

She glanced at her watch—almost midnight—and stomped into the living room. "If anyone is in here, I'm armed!" She noted the fire first then swept her gaze over the rest of the room.

Nothing seemed to be out of place, but one. The lights and TV were both still on, just as she'd left them. But on the floor, before the sad Christmas tree she'd bought because it suited her mood, sat a huge box the size of a stove. It was wrapped in gold paper.

She swept up the TV remote and turned down the volume. "Fate? Where the hell are you?"

She heard a sound and froze, straining to listen.

There. The box. Had Fate sent her a dog for Christmas? Made arrangements for it to be delivered? That made sense—in a way. After all, how many "I don't need a man. They're nothing but trouble" conversations could Fate endure before doing something to ease her poor little sister's misery?

Sure she'd figured the mystery out, she pulled the ribbon that seemed to hold the box closed.

Holy shit! That was no dog in there!

Nope. No dog. Not even close.

The man sitting inside was the cutest beefcake she'd ever seen—straight out of a Chippendale calendar. Dark, curly hair, brilliant blue eyes, features that were neither too perfect to be pretty nor too rugged, and a body formed by the hand of God.

He wore nothing but a red bow tie and tiny red briefs, and he held a potted plant. As he unfolded a towering frame that would put Goliath to shame, her gaze fixated on his shoulders. *Hot damn, they were broad enough to make her drool.*

She swallowed. "Hello, there." What else does one say to a man wrapped in a box?

"Merry Christmas, Destiny!" he called, then he started singing in a warm baritone voice that soaked into her body like hot chocolate on a cold day, "On the first day of Christmas, my true love gave to me. Passion and a pear tree." He stepped from the box, thigh muscles bunching in scrumptious bulges and handed her the plant.

Despite the tingle in her gut at the sight of his gorgeous body, she took the pot from him and laughed. This had to be the funniest practical joke Fate had ever pulled. "Oh, God! This is good."

He smiled but didn't share her mirth. "What's so funny? Don't you like the tree? Isn't it big enough?"

"Oh," Her gaze swept down his body to focus on the tiny red thing barely containing the huge bulge between his legs-socks, for sure. "I like it. A lot. It's very big...um, bountiful. I'm just a little overwhelmed."

"That sounds promising. Overwhelmed is good."

Oh! What was she saying? Looking at this mostly naked man was wreaking havoc on her ability to think straight. And forming coherent sentences...a lost cause. "I mean, you're not what I expected."

"Why don't you wait to make that determination until afterward?"

"After what?" She swallowed another guffaw at how brainless she felt at the moment.

"After the passion part?" His wicked grin shot straight to her belly, did a few summersaults there and then dropped between her legs. Her lace panties became instantly soaked.

Okay, she could practically hear her body screaming for indulgence, every cell from toe to eye was piping in. But what little was left of her gray matter was making its final feeble call for logic. "As...er, tempting as that is, I don't know you, and I don't do anything more passionate than swapping polite small talk with someone I don't know."

"Easily remedied." He thrust his hand toward her. "Um...Brian...Walsh."

"That name sounds familiar." Where had she heard his name before? Had Fate mentioned him? She took his hand and gave it a quick shake. "Nice to meet you Brian. I'm Destiny —"

"I know." He sighed.

"Oh, yeah." She sighed too. "Uh, how'd you get in here?"

"Delivery van."

"Of course."

"I think your neighbor unlocked the door."

"Oh." She had to admit she was still flustered. What hot-blooded woman wouldn't be? She was shaking hands with a strange, naked man on Christmas morning, and he was propositioning her? Trying like hell to get a handle on the situation, she dropped her gaze to his feet. They couldn't be as distracting as the rest of him was.

Unfortunately, she couldn't let it rest there. As if it had a mind of its own, her gaze climbed north, up long, muscular legs, to those very tight, very sexy briefs.

Hmm...interesting...accepting his proposal was very tempting.

Her gaze halted there for a heartbeat too long, and she wrestled it back into submission and forced it back down to his feet again.

But, her inner slut was winning the battle between naughty and nice. Naughty was simply more fun. Her gaze slid right back up, landing on the red bull's-eye. "So, let me get this straight. My sister sent you here to fuck me?"

"No. Not exactly." His thumb stroked her palm, and she shivered and tugged her hand away.

"Care to explain?"

"Not really. I'd rather do something else first." His gaze slid up and down her body. "Maybe I can offer a couple of suggestions to get things rolling."

Geesh! She practically felt naked — wearing a winter coat.

"I was sent here to fulfill your fantasies for one night."

A blade of heat shot up her spine even as her mind completely rejected the notion as utter insanity. "Only one?" she joked.

"Those are the rules."

"I hate rules."

His gaze meandered down her form again. "Me too."

She gave him a playful shove and brushed past him to the couch. This was all too much. *No, not enough. No, too much. Oh, shit! What did she want?* "Okay, easy Buddy, I was only joking. I don't do gigolos."

"I'm not a gigolo."

She knew what she wanted. She wanted him, sweaty, naked, on top of her. "If you're not a gigolo, then what are you?" She slid off her boots and wiggled her cramped toes.

"Your gift." He dropped to his knees and took her foot into his hands, rubbing the tightness out of the muscles until she sighed with relief. Then he nestled that foot in his crotch and grinned. "Gotta keep it warm or the muscles will knot up again."

She wiggled her toes, keenly aware of the rigid rod they rested against. "Makes perfect sense." She felt a smile busting loose as he pulled off her other boot and massaged the second foot.

"Oh, yeah..." She'd never felt so pampered.

What was she fighting this for? It was Christmas, the man sitting at her feet was ready, and surely able, and tomorrow he'd be gone. No strings. No guilt. Just fun. What the hell? A massage and some conversation would be a start. And later... Where did she put that Nexus Letters Bizarre Sex book she got as a gag gift for her last birthday? She'd always wanted to try a few of those things...

Besides, he was the best Christmas gift she'd received in ages, and she had the sneaky suspicion wherever he came from had a no-refund policy. It would be a terrible waste if she didn't take full advantage of the opportunity.

Not exactly sure how to seduce a man who was already three steps ahead of her, she lowered her voice and said, "You give a good massage. Do you get much practice?"

"Not enough. Would you like one?"

"You bet I would."

"Okay. Strip." He smiled. "The clothes have to go."

As those words penetrated her already foggy brain, more heat zipped through her body. *One step closer...*"Just a second."

Hoping if she acted quickly she wouldn't suffer a sudden case of *second – thoughtitis*, she dashed to her bedroom, shed every stitch of clothing she was wearing, and wrapped herself in a sheet. Then, lying on the bed on her belly, she called out, "Okay. I'm ready." She clamped her eyelids closed and waited.

He didn't respond.

"Brian?"

Nothing.

Shit! Where'd he go? She gripped the sheet in a fist, bunching it just above her tits and shuffled to the living room.

He was reclining on the couch, looking not only thoroughly at home, but also completely, unmistakably turned-on. He wasn't wearing the red skivvies anymore.

And that lump wasn't socks. The man couldn't be human. *What a cock!*

She had no idea what to say or do. She couldn't help staring at his very thick, very long organ. Her throat was dry as hell, every drop of wetness in her body was concentrated in one region. "Can I get you something?" she croaked. "Drink? Food? Maybe a sling for that thing. It has to be heavy. Is it real?"

"Want to find out for yourself?" His gaze was steel-melting hot. Then he smiled, and his expression took on an entirely different mood. Playful. Teasing. "Are you ready for me?"

Was she ever! Parts everywhere were throbbing, and her normally chilled-to-the-bone house felt like a sauna. "Yeah, let's get to it. I mean, I can't wait. I mean... Oh, hell. You're frickin' naked. What did you have to do that for...already?"

He shrugged. "I thought you might be more comfortable being nude in front of me if I was naked too." He bent down and reached for the red garment. "I can put them back on —"

More comfortable? Not unless burning from the inside out was considered comfortable. "No, that's okay." She glanced around the room. "Where do you want me?"

A twinkle shot through his eyes. "On your back, legs spread wide…you moaning my name in ecstasy?"

She couldn't get there soon enough! Her empty pussy clenched tight and a stream of heat shot to her belly. In a last ditch attempt at playing the double entendre game with a man who could put her best friend to shame — something to be admired — she lowered her eyelids and cooed, "Let's take it slow, Cowboy. We're in no hurry, are we?"

He dropped his gaze to that gloriously swollen shaft. "I'm not, but he is."

"Tell him to chill out." She caught his wrist and pulled. "How 'bout we take this to my bedroom?"

"I'd be a fool to turn down an invitation like that." He stood, unfolding his tall, thick frame with impressive grace, and took long strides at her side. As his hip brushed her, her heartbeat shot into overdrive.

She led him into the room and climbed onto the bed, careful to keep the sheet in place. Then she rested her head on her crossed arms and waited, anxiously, for the first touch.

"Do you have any oil?"

Oh, would he ever get to the good part? "What kind did you need?"

"How 'bout some body oil?"

"Oh. Maybe. In the bathroom closet." She started to get up.

A firm touch at her shoulder stopped her instantly. "I'll get it. You stay put."

She lay back down and started humming the first song that came to mind to relax. Unfortunately, *Let's Go All the Way* didn't produce the desired effect. She closed her eyes. Every muscle in her body was wound tight.

"Found it."

"Great." Still a bundle of skittery nerves, she listened to the soft sound of him chafing his hands against each other and mentally prepared for his touch.

"Would you mind removing the sheet? I prefer the feel of skin—though this sheet is very nice." He ran his hand down her length and left it resting on the round of her rump.

Her pussy tingled. "It's good to see a man who appreciates 400 thread count Egyptian cotton." Her head resting on the bed, she pushed the sheet down a few inches, exposing her upper back and shoulders. "Better?"

"More."

"More?" She swallowed. Something was caught in her throat. Her tongue, maybe? "Uh... How about you just go ahead and move it where you need it? I'm a little nervous, and I don't know what you want."

"Please, relax." His hand still firmly planted on her butt, he leaned closer. "What I want," he whispered in her ear, "is for you to enjoy." He pushed the sheet down until it lay at the base of her spine.

His first touch was firm, at her shoulders, and sent an instant blanket of goose bumps over her upper body. "Massage is very therapeutic...and erotic."

He could say that again!

He climbed onto the bed and straddled her back, one knee on each side of her hips, his cock resting on her ass.

Oh God!

"I love this position..."

She moaned, loving the weight of him resting on her, pushing her mound into the mattress. *So do I.*

"I love the feel of your skin, the way your muscles flex and relax under my touch." He inhaled. "The smell of the oil. The sound of your sighs…" He rubbed kinks out of her shoulders with skilled hands, and then shifting his body until he was straddling her thighs, he worked lower, rubbing, kneading until he was at the base of her spine, where the sheet barely covered her ass. "Your body is absolutely exquisite."

"Thanks. Glad you like it…wanna see some more?" she murmured into the pillow.

He smacked her ass. "What was that? Are you falling asleep on me?"

"Me? Sleeping? No way. I just said I hate working out, but it pays."

"That's for sure. I, for one, appreciate the results."

Score one for the inner-thigh machine.

A soft touch replaced the firm one he'd been using, and she realized with heart-stopping glee he was licking her, not rubbing. "You taste as amazing as you look."

Reflexively, she tightened and lifted her ass in the air.

"Now, that's a sight." He slipped the sheet down, and her pussy flamed, throbbing in tempo to her racing heart. "Your ass is scrumptious."

She'd never considered her ass scrumptious. Detestable, a thing to avoid looking at while dressing in fitting rooms, to shrink and tighten, yes. In any way delicious? No. "Really?"

"Can I taste it?" His kisses trailed lower, and then his fingers slipped between her ass cheeks. He found her anus and teased it with a slick fingertip before exploring further.

Her body instantly reacted to his exploration, her pussy producing buckets of juices, her heart skipping along at a pace meant only for hummingbirds, her mouth drying to the point of nearly choking her. With eyes closed, she imagined his face, tension pulling at his mouth. Urgent need reflected in his eyes. She had to moan, she just couldn't help herself.

His finger found home, sliding into her dripping pussy. "Mmm. So hot and tight. Perfect." He pulled his hand away, and she wasn't sure whether she should scream in protest or sigh with relief. "Turn over. Let me see all of you."

No problem! She did a log roll onto her back, and immediately caught his gaze, just before it slipped down to her breasts. She battled the urge to cover herself, since she'd never been very proud of anything north of her belly button. In her opinion, her breasts were much too small.

"Don't." He reached for her arm and stopped it just before it hid her tits from his traveling gaze. "They are absolutely perfect." He dipped his head and traced her nipple with his tongue, then bit down just enough to send a jolt of pleasure-pain down her spine.

She couldn't help herself, she was so eager for more. Like a wanton hussy, she arched her back to lift her breasts high into the air.

With torturous diligence, he licked and teased the second nipple, until she was ready to shout, "*Just fuck me!*" Then he sat up... When had he climbed onto the bed? ...and kneeled next to her stretched out legs.

"Time to get to business," he growled.

"Business? What the hell was that?"

He grinned, flashing pearly whites so perfectly straight they couldn't be natural. "That was only the beginning." He slid his hands under her knees and tickled her. "Are you ready?"

"Oh, yes, yes, yes!"

He couldn't tell? She had to be sopping wet. How ready could a girl be? She nodded, and he lifted and bent her knees, then urged her legs apart.

So exposed, so open. Soft currents of air cooled her flaming pussy as she briefly watched his hot gaze rake over her body. Within two short breaths, she couldn't bear another second. She let her eyelids drop closed and concentrated on the flurry of sensations battering her from all directions. The sound of her own breathing, hard and fast. The memory of his face in her mind's eye, and the fierce hunger she'd seen in his gaze. The way his touches danced over her skin.

She lifted a hand and touched skin, covered in soft down, and then the velvet soft skin of his erection. She squeezed, and relished the groan he relinquished. Encouraged, she slid her hand up to the base, fingered his balls and then slid it back toward the head. He groaned again.

She felt him part her labia, and her legs dropped open even more, welcoming his finger as it found every curve and crevice. The man was a master, leaving no part of her, no matter how miniscule, undiscovered.

Then, dizzy with wanting, she watched him lower his head between her legs. He blew on her cunt, and she sighed. He nibbled her clit, and she tangled her fingers in his hair and gasped. *Good God*!

With tongue and teeth, he taunted, driving her slowly insane. He laved her folds, delved into and out of her slick depths with ferocious hunger and circled over her clit until she could barely breathe. Wild with need, she tossed her arms this way and that. Gripping anything she could reach, sheets, pillows. Anything. Pulling. Clenching. Squeezing. Hugging.

She lifted her hand to find him again, but could not reach him. Then, too weak to keep searching and too lost to care, she let it fall to the mattress. When he stopped his manual slaughter of her pussy, she pried open her eyelids and looked up.

He was kneeling between her wide-spread legs, the head of his huge cock teasing her pussy, circling the opening while not quite delving in and brushing her clit. She longed to lunge forward and bury him deep inside. But as she made her move, he caught her shoulders and pinned them to the bed.

"You must promise me one thing before we continue," he said, his expression an odd mix of emotions she couldn't quite name.

He had to be kidding! A promise? Now? "What?"

"Promise me you'll spend the next twenty-four hours like this, in my arms."

Chapter Two

There was one thing Destiny was prepared to promise at that moment, if she could speak. She'd be thrilled to spend every minute over the next twenty-four hours with the fascinating, sexy, gorgeous hunk of a man hovering over her, ready to plunge his perfect cock deep inside her achingly empty pussy. She wondered why he'd made such a point of it.

His cock pushed against her labia, and all thought of promises faded away. "Sure," she said, trying like hell to move closer. "Twenty-four hours."

The resulting smile that spread over his face was not the picture of innocent glee. It held a hint of wicked playfulness that did nothing to ease her impatience. "Good. You have no idea what you're in for."

She laughed. "Would you please show me? I'm begging here."

"Your wish is my command." He pushed slowly, his thick cock stretching her pussy walls as it sunk in. It was sweet agony. Her skin burned for a brief moment before parting. And he pushed deeper, filling the emptiness inside of her, inch by inch, until he had buried every glorious bit of that shaft inside. The sheer bliss of that complete fullness! She wanted to hold onto it forever.

She let her eyelids fall closed and found herself in a hot world of throbbing, fucking, ecstasy. "Oh…"

He growled in response, slid his cock out until the head rested just outside of her and then plunged deep inside again. "Damn, you're perfect!" Her inner thigh muscles stretched as he palmed her knees and pushed them further apart. She was as open as a woman could be, and loving every minute of it.

And then he found her clit, which was so sensitive even the slightest touch sent her hurtling through the air, thanks to the position she was in, and he traced slow, sensuous circles over it, in time with his thrusts.

Her body was spiraling toward a climax she knew would be earthquaking. Every muscle was clenched, including the one encasing his cock, and steady waves of heat were pulsing from her center out to every distant part. She felt the warmth of his impending climax against her ass, his fingers tensing on her inner thigh, and she heard his short gasps—or were those hers? She couldn't make sense of the sounds, sights, feelings anymore. She was lost in them.

And then she exploded and the welcome rush of pleasure ripped through her body. She gasped, certain she would never take another breath, and succumbed to the climax overtaking her. Her pussy pulsed, drawing him deeper inside, and he stopped thrusting, growled and then came, pistoning in and out of her until both of them were entwined, twitching, sated, weak. He sunk down, resting his length on top of her, and she listened to his racing heart in her ear.

"That was amazing," she said when she found her tongue. "I've never felt anything like that before. Holy shit."

"I'm glad." He dropped a kiss on the top of her head and rolled to his side, drawing her into his arms.

She felt so safe and protected there, snuggled chest to chest with such a powerful yet gentle man. So loved.

Loved? How could that be? This was a one-night thing. That's all he wanted. That was the rule. Where was her head?

"What's wrong?" He ran his hand down her arm and over her hip, tickling, caressing, fingering. She felt the stirring of arousal deep in her belly.

"Nothing's wrong. Thanks to that amazing cock of yours, I can barely keep my eyes open. I'm just thinking."

He slipped that wandering hand between her ass cheeks and poked at her tight hole. "Don't think today. Just feel."

"Is that another rule?"

"No. It's just a suggestion."

"I can't help it, I'm a thinker at heart." She chuckled. "That didn't sound right, did it?"

He caressed her ass cheek. "What do you think about?"

Still foggy-headed, she traced the sexy line down the center of his chest. "Everything, I guess. My work, goals. There are so many things I want out of life."

"Like what?" He cuddled her closer, until she was snuggled tight against his length. "What do you want out of life, Destiny?"

Oh, this felt so right, being with this man, lying here cuddling, sharing her wishes, wants.

If only he could be there when she reached her goals... Celebrated her finest achievements. If only he could be a part of them...

She pulled in a breath and prepared to blurt out her usual list of cars, homes and vacations, but it didn't come out. "I don't know anymore. Sometimes I'm so sure of what I want, and other times... What about you?"

"I know exactly what I want. Unfortunately..." He sighed. "So much of what I want rides on someone else's choices. It's out of my hands."

"How?"

He cupped her ass and squeezed. "Look what you've got me doing! Enough thinking. Time to feel. What do you feel right now?"

She closed her eyes, suddenly aware of the smell of sex all around her. Of him and her. It was a wonderful scent. Musky, sexy. She wanted it to last forever. She wanted today to last forever. "Mmmm. Warm. Cozy. Satisfied. What about you?"

"I feel...starved."

She chuckled. "I thought men were supposed to be dead to the world after fucking."

"Not this one. How about some breakfast? It's almost sunrise. Besides..." He poked at her asshole then slid his finger up to her pussy and plunged it inside. "We need to eat if you're going to make it for round two."

She gasped as he hooked his finger and scraped against the sensitive spot inside. He added a second finger, plunging them in and out. And without thinking, she rolled onto her back and opened her legs, ready to fuck again. "How about round two and then some breakfast?"

"How about round two with some breakfast?" He jumped from the bed and took her hands, leading her out of the bedroom to the kitchen. "What do you have to eat?" Leaving her standing on knees the constitution of warm jelly, he rummaged through her refrigerator, pulling out jars, cans and bottles.

Her gaze slipping from one container to the next, she asked, "What are you going to do with all that?" It was an odd assortment of foods, canned fruits, various condiments, almost all sweet. The man had a real sweet tooth.

"You'll see." He gathered as many of the containers into his thick arms as he could and carried them to the dining nook, then set them on the floor and shoved the kitchen table against the wall. He pointed at the bare spot on the floor. "Lie here."

She eyed the cold linoleum and stifled a shiver. "Couldn't we pick a warmer place? It's December, freezing cold. I'll get frostbite on my ass."

He gave the part mentioned a friendly pat. "Now, that would be a crime. But don't worry. You won't be cold for long. I promise." He took her in his arms and kissed away every thought that had been in her head.

Reeling from that mind-melting kiss, she sat, suddenly thankful for the chill, and waited.

"All the way down, Baby." He kneeled beside her and kissed her again, his tongue doing things she was sure had never been done before by a human being. Slowly, deliciously, it laved her own, performing a wicked, erotic dance in her mouth.

He bit her lip as his hands cupped her breasts and squeezed. He suckled her tongue as he pinched her nipples, rolling them between his thumbs and forefingers. Tension and need rocketed through her body, ripping away her ability to think. He plunged his tongue in and out of her mouth as he dropped both hands to her pussy. She fell back, welcoming his onslaught on her body, as she felt herself taking flight, soaring toward another climax. She smiled against his mouth. "Oh, yeah!"

Then, he stopped, and left her gasping, aching for his touch. "Breakfast time!"

"Breakfast? Now?" He had to be joking. Who could think of food at a time like this? Her pussy was so wet her juices were running between her ass cheeks. Her body was so hot, the floor, normally too cold to walk on without shoes, barely relieved her. And he was ready to eat?

He picked up a carton of vanilla yogurt, ripped off the foil top and turned the container over. The contents fell with a plop on her stomach.

Oh! Breakfast! Slip-sliding fun!

She'd never done food with sex before.

Next, he opened a can of cherries and added them to the mix. He smeared his creation over her breasts and down to her pussy, then, with eyes fixed to hers, he smiled, licked his lips and nibbled at her collarbone.

Hypnotized, she watched his tongue work over her skin, down the valley between her breasts, and then up to each peak. In its wake, her skin cooled, and goose bumps scattered over her arms and stomach. His tongue drew circles over her nipples until they turned to tight pink pebbles, and instead of cold, she felt hot again. Burning need pulsed out from her center. But, before she became lost in it, she relinquished herself to a playful side she'd ignored since puberty, scraped some of the slick mixture from her stomach and smeared it over his tight chest. "My turn!"

He grinned like a boy about to get his first lay, and leaned back, silently welcoming her exploration.

She started at the base of his throat, running her tongue down the deep crevasse between firm, toned pecs that had endured more than a few bench presses. The salty taste of his skin was a pleasant compliment to the sweet yogurt.

Hungry for more, she glanced at the slight sprinkling of dark hair, soft and curly, that arrowed down his chest and stomach, leading to his thick, very erect cock, and it took every ounce of willpower she possessed to take her time and resist the urge to just straddle him and impale herself. His soft moans of appreciation encouraged her to continue nipping and licking his smooth skin, circling each tiny nipple before continuing lower to his washboard stomach and shallow belly button. She poked her tongue into it, and flicked it while giving her hands free rein over his chest, waist and hips.

His fingers tangled in her hair on the top of her head, and he urged her lower and pushed his cock into her mouth. There was no doubt what he was asking for. And that was one thing she did not perform, at least not well. Willing to give it a shot, anyway, she took the base of his shaft in her fist and squeezed as she flicked her tongue over the head.

Louder groans met her feeble attempts, and feeling a little more daring, she tipped her head and ran her tongue down the blue line lying just below the skin's surface to his tight balls and back up again.

Yum. He tasted wonderful, of man and loving. He smelled sexy, masculine, musky. His cock twitched as she flicked her tongue over the head.

Wanting more, wanting to please him, she opened her mouth wide, took as much of him in as she could, and slid her hand up and down to meet her mouth.

She tasted something salty, pre-come, and gleefully licked every bit of the wetness away, relishing the taste.

He sucked in a deep breath, and Destiny felt a twitch shoot from the base of his cock to the head. Not sure if she was doing things right or not, she let him drop from her mouth.

Brian, flush, rumpled and wild-eyed, palmed her cheeks. "Baby, you keep doing that, and I'm going to come. Tonight is about you, not me." He caught her shoulders and pushed them to the floor. "I want to make your every fantasy come true."

Her head swam at those words. So many possibilities! Yet, at the moment, feeling that cock buried deep inside was about all that mattered.

Holding her captive with one hand, he reached for another bottle. Chocolate syrup. "Open your legs."

She dropped her knees open, and watched as he drew a line up one thigh, over her mound and down the other leg.

"Open wider." His shoulder muscles flexing as he leaned on them, palms flat on the floor on either side of her hips, he licked her leg clean, slowly working up to the sensitive skin on the very inside. Then, he skipped the center part...*the tease!* ...and licked his way back down the other leg. When he was finished, he lifted his head and smiled. "How was that?"

"Very erotic. But it wasn't exactly what I was hoping for." She pointed at the chocolate remaining on her pubic bone. "Uh, you missed a spot."

He dropped his gaze. "So I did." He was teasing her, purposefully concentrating high up, far from her aching pussy. Far from her clit, which she swore was so erect he could probably see it. "Better?"

"No."

His handsome face screwed into a picture of confusion. "Why not?"

"You missed the best part."

He visibly inspected her mound and thighs. "Where?"

"There." She pointed at her pussy. "Oh, you know where!"

"Show me."

"I just did."

He lowered his face until his nose nearly touched hers. She smelled the chocolate on his breath and longed to taste it. Her tongue darted out of her mouth and caught his lip, but he didn't kiss her back. "No, show me. Touch yourself where you want me to touch you. I want to watch." His breath dried her lips.

"I can't."

"Why not?"

"I've never… It's too embarrassing."

"It's beautiful. You're beautiful. There is nothing more erotic that a woman pleasuring herself. You dream about masturbating in front of your man, of giving everything you are to him. Raw, open, honest, hiding nothing."

Did he know that for a fact? Did she really have those fantasies?

"Try it." He leaned back and rested his hands on her knees, parting them so wide her inner thigh muscles stretched.

Awkward, yet intrigued, she looked at his face and dropped both of her hands to her pussy. With one, she parted her puffy outer lips to expose her clit. It was a hard little knot of arousal, so sensitive her first touch was nearly electrifying. Oh so slowly, she drew tight circles over her clit. Her eyelids dropped over her eyes, shutting out the world, and enclosing her in a place where sounds shown in colors and touches hummed through her body.

"No, open your eyes. I want you to see me watching you."

She forced her eyelids open, and seeing the hunger in his eyes, gasped. A river of heat flowed up from her clit, over her mound, and pooled in her belly. Another started somewhere around her breasts and rose up to her face.

"That's it, Baby. Touch your pussy. Fuck yourself. I want to see you sink those fingers deep inside."

As she continued torturing her clit with her fingertip, she dropped the other hand and pressed two fingers deep inside her sopping pussy. On the verge of orgasm, she clamped her inner muscles tight around her fingers as she pumped them in and out in time with the motion of her other hand.

He smiled. "Oh, yeah! You're so hot. I'm so ready to fuck you."

She felt the pressure of her impending climax boil up from her belly, but she fought it, slowing her movements. She wanted him inside of her when she came. "Fuck me," she murmured, not even sure if he could hear her. She stared into his eyes.

"What did you say?"

"Fuck me!"

Something flashed across his face. "Can I fuck your ass?"

Her asshole reflexively tightened, sending another rush of heat through her body. "Yes."

"Stand up, but don't stop touching yourself."

This was agony! Why was he doing this to her?

Her body was a quivering mess, barely able to remain upright as she stood, yet she left her hands where they had been, allowing him to both support her and steer her to wherever he wanted to go.

The living room.

He stopped her in front of the couch. "Kneel down."

She knelt and bent over, resting her chest and stomach on the couch seat.

"Don't stop touching yourself!" He left her, and she wondered where he'd gone. She didn't have to wait long. He returned in a couple of heartbeats.

Her eyelids refused to stay open, so she let them fall closed again. She felt him parting her ass cheeks and a slick fingertip teasing her asshole.

Good God, she was going to come!

"Don't come yet."

She stopped touching her pussy. What he was doing to her was more than enough to drive her over the brink.

"Don't stop that, either. Get those hands back down there."

"But I can't."

He thrust his finger into her ass, and she bucked against him, feeling full and exposed all at once.

"Oh God!"

He slid his finger in and out a few more times then pulled it away. The wide head of his cock took its place.

Damn, it felt big. Would it fit? "I'm scared. Won't it hurt?"

"A little. But you won't care. We will take this slow and easy. You'll be so hot, it won't matter." His cock strained against the skin around her asshole. "Trust me. Touch yourself."

She was tearing, burning. "Oh no!"

"Touch yourself."

She felt some wetness, cool and soothing on her asshole, and then more pressure. And trying like hell to concentrate on relaxing her muscles to allow him in, she caught some of the juices pouring from her pussy and dragged it up to her clit. His cock breached the barrier and slid slowly deeper, filling her ass until she couldn't breathe. The pain was nothing compared to the pleasure as he buried himself to the hilt. She slid a finger into her pussy, moving in and out in tempo with his cock, and in three swift strokes, she lost all control, her body caught in the convulsions of a powerful orgasm. Her ass muscles and pussy pulsed, and she cried out in ecstasy.

Brian gasped, froze in place for a brief instant, and then slid his cock deep as he spurted his come inside. She felt the warm trickle as some escaped when he pulled out. "That was amazing." He sagged over her, his chest pressed against her back, his breathing fast and hot in her ear. "Damn!"

She was speechless, overcome by what she'd done. What she'd felt, and more than that, what she wanted to do.

Did this really have to end after today? This was unbelievable, the way Brian made her feel, the way he touched her, the way he encouraged her. She wanted more. She wanted him every day, every night, every moment.

Couldn't Christmas last forever?

Chapter Three

Destiny Doherty was the one.

Brian glanced at her, watching her sleep. He had to have her. He would die without her. And she needed him.

But would she give him the one thing he needed to be free of the curse that would lock him away for another three hundred sixty five days? Or would his transformation shatter her fragile heart?

After nearly twenty-four hours of lovemaking and talking, he hadn't had nearly enough of her. Not even close. He thought she felt the same. Her easy smile and eager lovemaking sure suggested she did.

If only he could know for sure.

He pulled her closer to him, eager to make her a part of himself. He swallowed his apprehension and spoke into the darkness, "Destiny?"

"Hm?" She sounded sleepy, sexy.

"It's late. I have to leave soon."

"No. Please don't go." She tossed a heavy arm over his chest and squeezed. "Stay here with me."

"I must leave. I have no choice."

"This is America, you have a choice. Please. I want you to stay."

He wished it were that simple! "It's the rule."

"To hell with the rule. Stay here. My sister won't hate you for it. It's probably what she wanted all along."

"Your sister?"

She lifted her head and a worried expression spread over her face. "My sister, Fate. She arranged for you to come spend the day with me, didn't she?"

"Perhaps indirectly."

That woke her up completely. She propped herself on her elbow. "Can't you tell me?"

"I can't explain it all."

"You're speaking in riddles. Why can't you be straight with me? After everything we've done and said to each other, I think I deserve to know what's going on. My God, I...I touched myself in front of you. I told you things I haven't told another human being."

He glanced at the clock. One full year, eight thousand, seven hundred sixty hours, of cold nothingness was mere minutes away. Damn! How could he explain thousands of years of hell in minutes? Would she believe him? "How did you like your Christmas gift?"

"It was the best damn Christmas gift I can ever remember getting." She smiled. "Even better than the bike I got when I was ten."

"What did it mean to you?"

"Mean?" She fluffed a pillow and leaned back on it. "It meant I didn't spend Christmas day wishing I was someone else for once, or traveling from party to party swapping empty holiday greetings and ugly Christmas cards. Christmas is always a drag because I'm single, and I hate being alone during the holidays. Someday, I want to have a husband, kids, a houseful of chaos during Christmas. You know?"

"Anything else?"

"Isn't that enough?"

"I'm not sure. I don't think it is." He swallowed a sigh and glanced at the clock. Time was running out in a hurry. Damn it!

"What do you want from me? Just tell me. I thought we were starting something really special here. Was I wrong?"

His heart grew heavy. She was so eager to be whatever he wished. So attentive. She deserved more. More than he would provide her, one day a year. "Nothing you can't give freely." Choking back bitter disappointment...no, more than that, aching sorrow...for the shock she would face shortly, he ran his finger along her jaw. "Let's just enjoy the last few minutes we have together, okay?"

She pulled his finger into her mouth and sucked. "If you stay longer, you won't turn into a pumpkin, you know."

"I know." He closed his eyes, feeling the beginning of the transformation starting. It always started in the same place, in his heart. The stone cold spread outward like a cancer, cutting off life, shutting out all sensations but sound. He struggled against it but knew it was senseless. It happened the same way every time.

Except this time he didn't want to go for an altogether different reason.

She needed him.

If only he could take back his actions on that one fateful day. The day he'd proven how cold-hearted he was by thoughtlessly shunning the woman who loved him. The daughter of a powerful sorcerer.

Her enraged father's curse, the stone that had encased his heart would encase his entire being for three hundred sixty four days a year. Until he learned the true meaning of love.

* * * * *

Something was wrong. Brian was cold. Stone cold. And so still.

"What the hell?" Shocked, scared, Destiny dropped his hand, reached for his chest, and shook it, but it didn't budge.

She pulled on his arm. It didn't bend. She touched his hair. It was hard too.

Cement?

She glanced at the clock...one minute after midnight...and blinked away her swelling disbelief. There was now a statue lying in her bed. A statue where there'd been a living, breathing man! It was all a bad joke. Or...a trick. "Brian?"

Silence.

"Shit!" Panicking, she leapt from the bed and flipped the light switch so she could get a better look at him. As her gaze wandered over the face she'd grown so fond of in such a short time, her heart broke. "This isn't fair! He was real." Suddenly overcome by shivers, she studied every detail of his body, anxious to find a hint of life. His face was gray and still, his shoulders and chest, his stomach, legs... His feet were still slightly pink. She touched one. Warm! "Brian! Tell me what to do to make it stop. I want you here with me. For good. For always. It's my fondest wish. My only wish..." Her gaze traveled over his body, the one that had spent the past twenty-four hours doing nothing but giving her pleasure. It had been all about her. He'd given, freely. What was the one thing she could give him in return?

"I..." Oh God, could she actually say what she was thinking? After one day? It made no sense.

But, wasn't that what love was? Senseless. Illogical. Of the heart, not the mind. She glanced down. His feet were turning gray, only his toes remaining slightly pink. She had the feeling this was her only chance. She couldn't wait another second.

"I love you, Brian."

Her heart stopped for a split second, and her breathing hitched. She watched his chest for movement. Nothing. She looked at his feet. They were entirely gray, like the rest of his body.

It was too late. He was gone.

"Damn it!" She dropped on her knees and pounded her fists against his concrete-hard chest, wishing she could shatter the cocoon that sealed him from her. "Damn! Damn! Damn! I finally meet a man who doesn't think about himself all the time, who wants nothing more than to give, and what is he? A fricken sculpture!" Her stomach tied into a knot and her eyes burned. Tears slid from them, down her cheeks and pooled on his still, cold chest.

The phone rang and she jumped at the unexpected sound. It was after midnight.

Curious to see who was calling her so late, yet reluctant to leave Brian, she ran and caught it on the last ring. "Hello?"

"Hey, sis! How was your Christmas?"

"Fate?"

"Yeah. Did you get my package?"

"Did I ever. Where the hell did you find him?"

"I bought him at an estate sale. Figured you'd put him in the yard this summer. I know he's huge, takes up a lot of space right now, since you don't have a garage, but I just couldn't pass him up. He was so gorgeous. And I thought the baby pear tree was a cute compliment to the garden theme, since you love pears so much."

"The yard?"

"What's wrong?"

He was a garden statue. Was she going insane? Had she spent the last day hallucinating about a chunk of stone? "Nothing."

"So, you didn't tell me. What do you think? Isn't he a hunk?"

Destiny sunk into the couch cushion and covered herself with the afghan Fate had given her last Christmas. "He sure is." She wanted to scream, she was so confused.

"What's wrong?"

"I don't know."

"Didn't you like him?"

She glanced at the bedroom door, wishing he would walk through it. "I did. I really, really did." *More than you'll ever know.*

"Oh, there was one thing I didn't tell you because it was so stupid, and I knew you wouldn't believe it. The woman who sold him to me said he's cursed. Isn't that funny?"

She wiped away another tear. "Yeah. Funny."

"Well, you're not very talkative. Should I call you later? Are you busy?"

"Sorry. No, I'm not busy. Just tired. I'll call you tomorrow."

"Okay. Bye, D."

"Bye, Fate."

"Oh, and Merry Christmas."

She glanced out the window and watched white flakes drift slowly past. "Yeah. Merry Christmas. I love you."

"You too, Sis."

Too exhausted to move from the spot, she hung up the phone and closed her eyes.

She had no idea how long she'd been sleeping when she woke up to a soft touch on her cheek. Eyes still closed, she brushed a stray strand of hair off her face, but that didn't stop the tickling.

What the hell? She sighed, disappointed at having to leave the quiet peace of her dreams, and opened her eyes. "Brian?"

He was sitting on the floor, next to her, smiling. "Yep. It's me."

She swallowed a sob. "You came back. How?"

"Your love brought me back."

She sat up and hugged him, grateful for his warm embrace, his masculine scent, the steady beat of his heart in her ear. Thankful just for him. She tipped her head back so she could see his face. "So, do I have a time limit?"

"Not anymore."

"Thank God!" She glanced outside. Still dark. "Though I've learned one thing from this strange series of events." Standing, she took his hand and pulled, leading him back to the bedroom.

"Oh yeah? What's that?"

"I learned not to waste time, not even a minute. I've learned I need to enjoy people when I have the chance, because I just never know when I'll lose them." In the bedroom, she shoved him onto the bed. "So, without further ado, I say we fuck. I want to give you your Christmas gift."

"You already have." He sat up and pulled her on top of him, and then flipped her onto her back in a stealth wrestling move.

Overwhelmed with emotions she couldn't even name, she giggled, but her laughter came to a quick halt when Brian parted her legs and buried his head between them. His tongue did things that could be deemed lethal, it did so much damage to her ability to function. That agile organ danced over her clit, darted in and out of her pussy, and teased her asshole until she was a mass of superheated, overwrought nerves. Her stomach muscles tensed, tipping her pelvis up, as her pussy pulsed with the need to be filled. Her face flamed. Her pussy dripped.

He lifted his head and quirked a playful smile at her, and her heart grew a dozen times bigger. He licked his lips and delved in for more, and she groaned.

"Please, stop. I can't take any more of this teasing."

"If you insist." He sat up and jammed her knees together so abruptly she howled in shock.

"Why did you do that?" she asked between panting breaths.

"You told me to stop."

"Teasing me, you sexy goof! I wanted you to stop teasing me and just fuck me."

"I'm not ready to do that yet. And neither are you."

"Not ready? Me? I'm a quivering mess, so wet down below I could use a towel, and you say I'm not ready?"

He nodded. "Yep."

"Well, how more ready could I be?"

He crawled on hands and knees over her. His face hovered a fraction of an inch over hers. His breath, which had a very pleasant musky-sweet scent, warmed her face and dried her lips. "You're still speaking."

Her eyelids were heavy. She let them fall closed. And her back tightened, lifting her breasts up until they brushed against his chest. "Believe me, that's no easy task at the moment."

After sealing each eyelid with a kiss, he left a trail of gentle kisses over her face and down her neck. A crop of goose bumps blossomed over her whole body, and she smiled and shivered.

"I won't stop teasing you until you can't utter a sound."

Welcoming his nips and kisses, she tipped her head to the side and groaned.

"Still not ready yet." He worked lower, his tongue taunting one nipple to aching erection while he pinched and pulled the other.

It was as if there was a direct line from her tits to her pussy. A steady current blazed down her stomach, ending between her legs. She let them drop open, wishing for the feel of his cock at their juncture.

She watched him as he continued his onslaught on her breast. He kissed her stomach, licking, biting, his tongue probing her belly button. Then he slipped lower, gave her pussy a few tantalizing laps and stopped.

Damn it, he was going to drive her crazy!

"Do you have a scarf?"

"What?"

"Do you have a scarf," he repeated.

"Out in the hall closet, I think." Her head still in a fog, she sat up and watched him exit the room. Where was he going? Nude? Wearing only a scarf?

Before she had enough strength in her shaky body to stand, he returned, carrying a string of foil Christmas garland.

"I couldn't find the scarf, so this'll have to do."

"What are you going to do with that?" A skitter of excitement shuddered through her body.

"Tie you up, of course."

She swallowed, not so much because there was something in her throat, but more because she didn't know what else to do. "Of course."

He crawled up on the bed and kneeled in front of her. "Have you ever been tied up?"

"No." She wasn't scared. Nervous, yes. Intrigued, excited, horny. All those things too.

"Lie back."

She positioned herself in the center of the bed and watched him tie one ankle. Then he pulled on the garland until her leg was lifted up high, her spine curled, her pussy open. With a nod of appreciation, he looped the garland around the bedposts a few times and then tied the opposite end to her other ankle, which was positioned in the same way.

Wow! She'd never felt so turned on. Her ass and pussy couldn't be more exposed.

"Now, that's better. Are you okay?"

Her tongue was stuck to the roof of her mouth, so she nodded.

"Speechless?" He grinned as she nodded. "Good. Time to fuck now." He kneeled down, teased her clenching, soaking pussy with the head of his cock until she was ready to beg for mercy. He traced tight circles over her clit and slid two, maybe three fingers inside, hooking them and stroking the sensitive walls. Another finger teased her asshole.

She was so close to coming, she could feel the flush spreading up from her belly. The steady throb in her pussy was changing, becoming more of a burning feeling than the pleasant warmth it had been.

She watched as he parted her folds and in a swift motion, thrust his cock deep inside. Dizzy, she closed her eyes and relished the way he filled her, leaving no part needing. His hands were everywhere. They kneaded her breasts and tugged on her nipples, sending bolts of biting pleasure up and down her spine. She gasped. She groaned. She cried out, "More! Please, more!"

His taunting touch dropped to her stomach, tickling her skin and giving rise to more goose bumps. Then his fingers traveled lower, parting her pussy and drawing smooth, rhythmic circles over her clit.

He pumped his cock in and out in time with the motion over her clit, and her mind, body and soul took flight. Soared into the heavens, into the stars and then dove back to earth and fused with him.

They were one. His smell filled her mind. The sound of his breathing echoed the sound of hers. She felt their hearts beating as one.

As Destiny found herself once again in the grip of a powerful orgasm that made her teeth chatter, she clung to Brian, digging her fingernails into his back. After the mind-blowing pulses eased to pleasant twitches, she opened her eyes and laughed.

She wasn't surprised by his scowl and stroked his chest, hoping to salve his wounded ego. "Sorry, it's not what you think. It's just that I've hated Christmas since I was too old to believe in Santa. I can't tell you how many times I've wished the damn holiday would be outlawed. But a little bit of Christmas magic...and I'll never doubt that again." She laughed against another round of tears. "Magic brought you to me. I'm so grateful! I love you."

"I love you, too." He gathered her into his arms and hugged her close. "But if you think this is great, just wait until you see what happens next Christmas."

The End

About the author:

Tawny welcomes mail from readers. You can write to her c/o Ellora's Cave Publishing at 1337 Commerce Drive, Suite 13, Stow OH 44224.

Also by Tawny Taylor:

A Christmas Phantasie

Kit Tunstall

Chapter One

Jakarta stumbled when she and Teague entered the lobby of Castle Phantasie. If not for his supporting arm cradling hers, she might have fallen over in shock at the sight that met her eyes. She couldn't help gazing with childlike wonder at the Christmas tree dominating the lobby. It must have been twenty feet tall, but the arched ceiling of the room easily accommodated its height.

Even more stunning than its stature were the tree's decorations. Real candles in brass holders, numbering in the hundreds, dotted the branches. Interwoven among the lights were thick bunches of white garland, along with antique ivory and brass bulbs. The angel at the top was too far up to distinguish its features, but it wore an intricate scarlet and ivory dress. To show up as well as it did, the tree topper must have been at least three or four feet in height.

She turned to Teague, giving him an impulsive hug. "This is fabulous, darling." When he had promised to give her a Christmas to remember, he hadn't taken the oath lightly.

He put his arm around her waist, pulling her closer. Strands of her ebony hair brushed his cheek when he bent his head to kiss her. "Wait until you see the room. It's their Deluxe Phantasie suite."

A surge of excitement filled her at the prospect. As she walked with Teague to check in, in her mind's eye she envisioned yards of soft carpet, decadent fabrics, and antique furnishings.

The process went quickly, handled by an efficient blond German man who spoke English with a crisp accent. After taking their pertinent information, he entrusted them to a bellhop. The young man took Jakarta's carry-on bag and led them up the stone staircase.

Jakarta admired the castle with wide eyes. It was obvious the owner had made every attempt to restore Castle Phantasie to its original splendor wherever possible. The details were exquisite, down to the candleholders mounted on the wall flanking the staircase complete with red, holly-scented candles, wreathed with real holly leaves, and currently not lit.

The climb up the stairs seemed to take forever, and she became aware of the chill that had settled into her bones during the drive from the airport in the van. Even her new ski jacket didn't do much to warm her.

She slanted a look at Teague, noting the flush of color in his wind-kissed cheeks. His hair was damp from the snow that had melted on it. The light cast by the crystal chandeliers spaced every few feet on the vaulted ceiling brought out red-gold highlights in his honey-brown hair. He looked cold too, but she easily thought of ways they could quickly warm each other up.

"Just this last flight," said their bellhop several flights of stairs later. "There's an elevator, but this is the best way to see the castle."

Jakarta breathed a sigh of relief, knowing the trek was almost over, and that she could use the elevator from now on. Apparently, even chasing after a classroom of forty-two six-year-olds all day hadn't given her the stamina to tackle all these stairs.

A couple of minutes later, she decided it had been worth every single step to arrive at their room. The young man had swiped an electronic card through the box mounted beside the ornately carved wooden door and now stood back to let them enter. "There are only two tower rooms," he said, as they slipped past him. "These suites are always booked, sometimes years in advance."

Jakarta lifted a brow in Teague's direction. "How long ago did you make this reservation?"

He squirmed, appearing embarrassed. "Last Thanksgiving."

She flinched, abruptly remembering that last November had been the first time he proposed to her. Had he booked this room with the anticipation of honeymooning here?

The thought was uncomfortable, and she allowed the room's beauty to distract her from it. It was a circle, complete with two tall windows that would have been without glass when the castle was first constructed. The stone walls could have been original, but they were well maintained if they were.

While Teague tipped their attendant, Jakarta wandered deeper into the sitting room, paused by the roaring fire to strip off her heavy gloves, which she stuffed into her pockets, and brought her hands closer to the flame. A white fur rug—appearing soft and inviting—draped strategically in front of the fireplace, was the perfect contrast to the black carpet. The furniture wasn't the antique style she had anticipated, but modern, covered by gleaming white fabric, and didn't detract from the aged atmosphere of the annular room.

Sliding glass doors, set directly into the rounded side of the outer wall, caught her attention. Jakarta walked over to them, taking a moment to figure out how they worked. The doors opened like any other sliding glass door, but curved around the orbicular shape of the room, instead of sliding straight.

Beyond the glass doors was a balcony. She stepped outside, immediately huddling deeper into her jacket as the cold wind tried to burrow inside. Her bare hands instantly felt chapped by the temperature, and fat snowflakes stung her cheeks. She walked to the thin metal rail and looked down.

She stepped back when vertigo seized her. They were at the highest point of Castle Phantasie, and the ground was a long way down. From this vantage point, the mountain framing the castle seemed accessible merely by reaching out to touch it.

She turned around and went back inside, just as Teague closed the door behind the man and dropped the electronic key on the gleaming black table by the door. She went to him, putting her arms around his waist. "This is fabulous, honey." Tears welled in her eyes, thinking about the trouble he must have gone to in planning this trip.

"It is beautiful, isn't it?" He stepped away long enough to unzip his coat and pull it off. "Let me take yours too."

She shrugged off the damp ski jacket and handed it to him. He hung both on the black coat rack by the door before turning back to her. She smiled. "Let's see what's behind curtain number one."

He nodded, and they walked together over to the partition that divided the room. It wasn't so much a suite as it was a studio, with only one wooden door, which must conceal the bathroom. Teague slid back the fabric partitions separating the sleeping area from the sitting room space to reveal the bedroom. It was sparse, with only a large dresser in the same gleaming black wood as the rest of the suite, and a rack for hanging clothes.

Only the bed saved it from being mundane. An image of the two of them rolling on the snowy white fur coverlet draped over the massive round bed caused her breath to catch in her throat. She looked at Teague, noting his flush had deepened, and his breathing was ragged. She knew he was sharing her thoughts, but that didn't surprise her. After two years together, their minds were often in accord. "I've never slept on a round bed before."

Teague gave a husky chuckle. "You won't be doing much sleeping for the next few days, my love."

No, she didn't imagine she would. A sigh escaped her, as she found herself wishing they could just stay in the bedroom. Their rapport was perfect there, unlike other aspects of their lives. Did he feel it too, that they were drifting apart? Was this trip nothing more than a last-ditch effort to salvage their relationship?

A knock at the door interrupted her morose thoughts. "Who's that?"

"Probably dinner. I requested it be brought to our room tonight, since I anticipated we would both be tired from the long flight." He frowned. "I hope that was okay with you? I wasn't trying to make the decision for you."

Jakarta smiled, and her dark-brown eyes softened. "That's fine." She searched for a way to express how touched she was that he would worry about making such a small decision for her, but the moment passed when he walked to the door to admit room service. Again, tears welled in her eyes, and she brushed them away, impatient with her melancholy thoughts and tendency to cry tonight.

Besides, Teague wouldn't be expecting gratitude. For him, offering her a choice in everything was an essential part of helping her heal. She knew he held the hope that if she could completely get beyond the past with Darien, then she could move onto a future with him. Thus far, she hadn't been able to convince him that she didn't want any sort of permanency in the future. A sinking sensation filled her stomach, because she suspected when he accepted that, he would end things. Teague wanted more, deserved more, than she could ever give him.

Chapter Two

Jakarta trailed a finger of her left hand across the china plate, getting the last bit of cream. "Those pastries were to die for," she said, bringing her finger to her mouth to lick off the topping.

Teague intercepted her hand, taking her finger to his mouth. A quiver of delight ran down her spine when he drew the digit between his lips and cleansed her finger with his tongue. He drew out his strokes, licking her finger with small swipes long after when it would have been clean. Finally, he removed her finger, but held her hand, pressing it against his chest. "Delicious."

She pretended to pout. "I know. That's why I wanted the last bite."

His blue eyes took on a smoky tinge, and his voice lowered an octave. "I wasn't talking about the cream."

Just the timbre of his voice and that look in his eyes caused her pussy to flood with moisture. Her nipples beaded in her bra, and the lace was suddenly abrasive. She was ready for him to make love to her.

He felt in his pocket for something, and her pulse skyrocketed. He must be looking for a condom, which meant he planned to fuck her right there before the fire, on the white fur rug, where they'd had their impromptu carpet picnic. She couldn't wait to feel the soft fur against her back, Teague against her front, and his cock sliding deep inside her.

Her erotic thoughts fled when he removed his hand from his pocket, and she saw the familiar diamond ring between his thumb and middle finger. She tried to tug her hand away, as he poised the band over her ring finger. Why did he persist in pushing this issue? "Teague," she said in a steely tone, meant to act as a warning.

He looked up from the ring and her finger. "Why don't you just try it on, to see how it fits? You might like it."

She succeeded in pulling away from his hold. Jakarta shook her head. "No. I already know how I'll feel about wearing any ring again. It's a prison, Teague...maybe symbolic, but it's still a sign of ownership, of possession. I won't be bound again."

His eyes darkened further, but not with passion. He dropped the ring on the floor. "Fine. You don't have to wear a ring. I don't need that. I'll take you as my wife, any way I can get you."

She shook her head. "Why is the piece of paper making it all official so damned important, if the ring isn't?"

"Because at least then I'd know you want more than the moment with me." He got to his feet. "I love you, Jak, you know that."

She nodded. She did know that. Unlike her, he was free with the words. The few times she had managed to express her emotions, the words came out stilted, lacking even a hint of the depth of love she felt for him.

He paced a small circle around the rug. "I want to spend my life with you."

"I want to be with you too."

His mouth twisted. "But you want an escape option, should things not go as expected."

She bowed her head, not meeting his eyes. Her voice was stiff when she said, "I do love you, Teague. It's just—"

He sighed. "I know what the problem is. Don't you think it's time to let go of the past?"

Her eyes widened. "I have! Do you know how hard it was for me to start seeing you? I wanted to call off that first date, but I didn't." She lifted her head, trying to convey her earnestness when their gazes locked. "I was terrified to move in with you three months ago, but I did it. Why do you have to keep pushing me? Why can't you be happy with what we have?"

Her heart broke when she saw his shoulders fall. He turned his back to her, and she knew the argument was over for now. It wasn't gone though. The issue hovered between them all the time, tainting every moment they spent together. Half the time, she was so tense about another impending proposal that she couldn't relax. She had trouble sleeping now, and she knew it was the same for him. Until he brought up the future talk, and kept bringing it up, her sleep had finally been nightmare-free for the first time in years.

"I think I'll go to bed," he said with an utter lack of emotion. "We'll want to hit the slopes early tomorrow."

She forced her voice to sound pleasant and polite. "Yes, I'm sure we will." She winced at the stiff exchange, sensing the chasm opening between them had just widened a few more inches. Castle Phantasie might be a dream come true for a vacation, but it might also be the last stop at the end of their relationship's road. Why couldn't he be happy with the moment and forget about the future?

He lay beside her, casting a glance at the luminous hands of the clock on the dresser every few minutes. The numbers seemed to change with infuriating slowness. Jakarta's even breathing indicated she was asleep, but she had required the aid of a Valium to get there. She had claimed jet lag and the time difference prompted the medication, but he knew it was because his proposal and the subsequent argument had troubled her.

Teague balled his hands into fists around the thick fur cover. He had promised himself he wouldn't ask her to marry him the very night they arrived, but the moment had felt right. Holding her hand to his heart, feeling the connection that sizzled between them, he had assumed she couldn't possibly deny him yet again.

He sighed, finally rolling over onto his side, with his back toward her. He knew her refusal wasn't about him, but her rejection still hurt. At the heart of the matter was her lack of trust in him and in the strength of their bond. She couldn't make the next logical leap-of-faith that would take them to the future he craved. He wanted to know she would always be there by his side. He wanted to watch her belly swell with his children, and to grow old with her, while she seemed content with living moment-to-moment.

That wasn't enough for him any longer. If she couldn't trust him, their relationship was doomed. That's why he fervently hoped his plans for tomorrow night would work. If she felt threatened and left him, he knew he wouldn't get her back, because she would never trust him again.

But then, did she really trust him now?

Chapter Three

Her muscles ached in places she had forgotten she had. A day on the slopes, skiing down the Alps, had shown her just how out of shape she was. Jakarta shot a glance at Teague, as he stripped off his outer coat and hung it on the coat rack. He didn't seem more than a little winded. Obviously, his tri-weekly trips to the gym and weekly squash games with one of the partners in his law firm had prepared him adequately for a day of rigorous activity.

It had been fun, of course. It was heady to plunge down the mountain, knowing she was at the mercy of nature, with only her own wits and two ski poles to save her if something went wrong.

Still, that was enough adventure for her. It was the day before Christmas Eve, and they were due to fly out in the early hours of Christmas Day, to make it back in time for dinner with his parents. She would be content to spend the next two days sipping hot chocolate in the lobby by the huge fireplace that dominated one whole wall, basking in the candlelight from the tree.

Better yet, she'd rather spend the rest of their time in this fabulous room, making love in front of their smaller, cozier fireplace or on the round bed that was surprisingly comfortable and similar to a normal bed.

She hesitated to suggest that plan, not certain what his reception would be. From the time they woke that morning, he had acted as if last night hadn't happened, but she could tell by his bleary eyes that he hadn't slept, and by the way he sometimes studied her peripherally that he hadn't forgotten her latest refusal.

"Are you hungry?" he asked.

She shook her head. "Not really. I'm too tired to be hungry."

He nodded. "Why don't I send for a bottle of wine and a plate of cheese, and we'll relax for a while? Maybe later, we'll want to have dinner in one of the three restaurants."

"That sounds like a plan." She rolled her tight shoulders. "I think I'll have a hot bath while we wait for the wine."

Teague waved his hand. "You have plenty of time."

When she emerged an hour later, freshly bathed and still warm from the Jacuzzi, wearing only a white silk robe, she found Teague sprawled across the overstuffed sofa. Two glasses of wine were on the table in front of him, as was a medium-sized gift box, wrapped with a green satin bow. She frowned. "What's that?"

"Scharzhofberger Auslese. It's not the most expensive wine Castle Phantasie stocks, but it's a respectable vintage — "

Jakarta rolled her eyes. "Not the wine. I'm talking about the box."

He smiled. "Oh, that's a present for you."

Her frown deepened. "I thought we agreed to exchange our gifts Christmas night, when we get home?"

He shrugged. "So I smuggled along a tiny one. Shoot me." He patted the cushion beside him. "Come on and open it. You know you want to."

She couldn't resist the allure of the package, or the teasing glint in his eyes. Jakarta went to the sofa and sat down beside him. She frowned when she realized his lighthearted façade hid a deeper layer of tension. His gaze was watchful, and his hand wasn't quite steady when he lifted a glass to sip the pale Riesling.

She had a stirring of unease when she pulled off the bow and lifted the lid. His indrawn breath of anxiety was barely discernable over her gasp when she peeled back the tissue paper to find a pair of white furry handcuffs. Stricken, she looked up at him. "What the hell is this?"

"A gift." All trace of teasing was gone. He sounded deadly serious, and grim lines bracketed his mouth.

She dropped the box on the table, anxious to rid herself of the sight of the cuffs. They were too much like the pair her ex-husband liked to confine her with, right before he had sex with her. Of course, his had been the real thing, strictly police issue, to accompany his job as a detective. "Why would you ever get me something like this?"

"It's a gift," he said again, no less somber, "but more for me than you."

She shook her head, bewildered. In two years, Teague had never once given her any indication that he liked to play the sort of perverse control games Darien had enjoyed. She started to get to her feet, feeling the need to escape. His hand shot out quickly, clamping around her wrist. She struggled to pull free.

"Don't fight me, Jak. I won't hurt you." He looked sad, rather than demented.

She cast a wild-eyed glance at the cuffs. "Oh, yeah? Then why did you bring those?"

"Desperation," he said quietly.

His tone caught her attention, and she stopped struggling. "What?"

Teague's eyes captured hers, and the pain in them cut through her. "I can't keep going like this, not knowing what tomorrow will bring, knowing you don't trust me."

She shook her head. "I do trust you."

He grimaced. "No, you don't. You trust me more than you trust any other man, which I know is difficult for you, but it isn't enough." His grip eased on her wrist, and he lifted her other hand, pressing hers between his. "I need to know you trust me completely, Jakarta. If you can't commit to a future right now, I need to believe there's at least a possibility that you can someday."

"I..." She trailed off before uttering a reckless promise.

"You say you love me."

She nodded, but he ignored her.

"Love and trust go hand in hand. I'm asking you to give me one night to show you can trust me. I need more than the verbal assurance that you do. I need proof."

"What kind of proof?" Her stomach churned with nausea, and the cuffs drew her eyes once more.

"I want you to surrender control to me." He dropped one of her hands and leaned forward to pick up the cuffs. "These are flimsy, meant only for lovers' games. It's the symbolism that matters, Jak. I want you to wear these for the rest of the night and let me do whatever I want to you." He closed his eyes briefly, as if gathering strength. "And I want you to do this because you trust me, not because you want to placate me."

Her eyes burned with tears. "What if I can't do that?"

He looked down. "As I said, I can't keep doing this." Teague straightened. "It all comes down to tonight, Jak. The decision is yours. I know how bad things were for you, and I know what he did to you. Hell, I was there beside you in the courthouse hall when he threatened to kill you after the judge granted the divorce." He squeezed her hand. "I know what I'm asking of you, but I *need* this."

Yes, he had been beside her. From the first day she had gone to his office to hire him to handle her divorce, she had always been able to count on Teague. Jakarta frowned, realizing how much she had relied on him, especially in the first few months after her divorce was final. Darien had never made good on his threat, but Teague had hovered beside her, protecting her, and giving her his support.

As their relationship changed, she became emotionally stronger, and his support hadn't wavered. It had only changed to accommodate her newfound independence. He had never tried to stifle that. The only thing he had ever asked was for her to trust in their future, and she couldn't do that. It brought a lump to her throat to know he thought she didn't trust him, just because she didn't trust in marriage any longer.

It was easier than she expected to take the cuffs from him and fasten one around her wrist. "Just because I don't want to attach a label to us and be bound to a future that might not turn out as we expect doesn't mean I don't trust you." She swallowed. "If you need this to prove I do trust you, then I'll do my best to give it to you."

He nodded, reaching for her other wrist. Jakarta surrendered it to him, squeezing her eyes shut when he snapped the fur manacle around her other wrist. She had a momentary recollection of the bite of steel cutting into her flesh deep enough to bruise, but that faded when she pulled on the cuffs. They were loose, hanging more like bracelets than handcuffs. The chain holding them together was plastic, and she could break it with little effort.

She looked up and met his eyes, licking her lips. "Now what?"

He put his arm around her, pulling her closer. "I just want to hold you for a little while."

She scooted closer, trying to remove some of the tension gripping her body. The brush of *faux* fur against her wrists was meant to be sensuous, but it was a forceful reminder that she had surrendered total control to her lover for the night. If she changed her mind or panicked, their relationship would be over.

Slowly, she turned her head to rest her cheek against Teague's chest. The soft cashmere of his blue sweater was comforting, as was the way he stroked his hand up and down her arm. Her mouth was still dry, and she attempted to swallow. "I'm thirsty."

Teague leaned forward to retrieve her untouched glass of wine, bringing it to her lips with deliberate movements. She tilted her mouth to drink, as he brought up the base of the glass.

She sensed the wine rushing forward and jerked away without thought, fearing she would choke.

She knew she had made a mistake when she looked up to see the sadness in his eyes. She wondered if he would end things right then. He studied her for a moment before leaning forward. Wine dripped down her chin and into the cleavage of her robe. His tongue traced a path from her lips, down her neck, and to the V where the robe gapped.

Jakarta shivered at the light touch, and her nipples pressed into the silk when he flicked open the lapels with one hand and burrowed his face between her breasts. His tongue swiped away the last of the wine before tracing lazy circles over her skin, moving ever closer to her right nipple, without making contact.

She longed to bury her hands in his hair, but when she tried to lift her wrists, his other hand grasped the chain between them, preventing her from moving. His tongue continued working toward her nipple, finally arriving at the nut-brown peak. He drew it into his mouth, and she moaned with pleasure. Teague bit down gently, and she squirmed. Her hands tried to rise again, but he applied enough pressure to keep them in place against her stomach.

He traced her nipple with the tip of his tongue, pausing to flick rapidly over the tip. As she shifted her weight, his free hand moved under her left breast. He cupped it, rubbing his thumb across her neglected nipple. It responded immediately by hardening further, seeking more of his light touch.

He lifted his head to meet her eyes, while lowering her hands from her stomach to her lap. "Do you know how much I love that robe?"

"Yes. I wore it for that reason." It had been a gift from him last Christmas.

Teague squeezed her breast once more before letting his hand drift lower, to span her soft stomach. "The white is such a stunning contrast to your beautiful skin." He moved his hand in a circle over her stomach. "Your creamy, milk-chocolate skin."

A grin twitched at her lips. "Are you going to eat me or make love to me?"

He leaned closer to her face, rubbing his nose against hers. "Both, my love, but first..." He trailed off, getting to his feet, much to her disappointment.

She eyed him uncertainly, longing for him to continue what he had started. "First what?"

His eyes raked from her shoulder-length tight curls to her bare feet, tipped with light-pink toenails. "I'm going to play with you, and you're going to sit there, without moving."

She lifted a brow. How difficult could that be? "Okay."

He grinned, but his smile wasn't entirely cheerful. It held a hint of something indefinable that lifted the hairs on the back of her neck. "I'll be right back. I have to get a few things."

As Teague went to their luggage, Jakarta changed her position, easing back against the thick cushions in an attempt to get more comfortable. She had a feeling she would be sitting there for a while. Her muscles were stiff, but it was impossible to relax without knowing what he planned to do to her.

He returned quickly with a green plastic case, which he set carefully on the cushion beside her. He didn't open it. Teague turned away from her to push aside the coffee table, but brought back her glass of wine, which he placed on the floor.

When he lifted his hands to her face, she realized he held a white scarf. "What's that for?" Even as she asked, he was placing it over her eyes and knotting it at the back of her head. "Teague?" She couldn't hide the panic in her tone, and her first instinct was to get away.

He put a hand on top of her head. "Shh, just relax."

She tried to, but it was difficult just sitting there, not able to see what would come next. She flinched when something touched her lips, until she realized it was her wine. She opened her mouth and dipped her tongue inside the rim, to gauge where the level was. The crisp, fruity wine welcomed her tongue, bringing with it a slight tang. It flowed into her mouth in the perfect amount. She swallowed, and he withdrew the glass without her choking.

His hands disappeared from her body for a moment, and then they were untying the sash of her robe before pushing it off her front. It pooled on either side of her legs, leaving the front of her body naked to him.

She stiffened when she heard him open the mysterious case with a click. Seconds later, something cool touched her chest. It was small and metallic. Jakarta gasped when it raked over her nipple. "What is that?"

"No questions," he said in a firm tone. He didn't sound angry, but he was clearly establishing the rules. "In fact, there won't be any talking at all, unless you need me to stop. If so, I want you to say 'fantasy.' If you do, I'll stop right away, to ask you if you want to continue with something else, or if you want to end this completely."

She knew he meant the game they were playing, but her heart read the more ominous meaning he could infer. If she stopped him, she might as well pack her bags and leave without looking back. It was over between them. Considering how aggressively she had fought the notion of establishing something more permanent, the idea of never seeing him again frightened her more than she would have expected. "I understand."

His fingers were gentle as they tweaked one of her nipples. "You're allowed to moan and make breathless cries of pleasure, of course."

She almost giggled at his silliness, but caught herself. She didn't know if that was an approved sound. "Okay."

He touched her lips. "Shh." Then his fingers were back at her nipple, along with the metal thing. As he slipped it over her sensitive flesh, she recognized a nipple clamp. Her stomach churned when she remembered previous experiences with similar items. Darien had delighted in tightening it to the point of agony, despite her pleas for him to stop.

Just like the handcuffs, Teague barely tightened the clamp. It was just to the point where she could feel pressure, without any pain. He did the same to her other nipple, and she relaxed slightly.

He dipped his head, and his tongue laved one of the swelling peaks, eliciting a moan. Jakarta pressed her hands together, striving not to move as he worked her nipple with his mouth, before grazing it with his teeth.

The sensation was short-lived. Teague took something else from his box, and she jumped with surprise when many thin quills brushed over her thigh. She almost asked what it was, but held back.

He must have decided to reward her restraint with an explanation. "This is a bamboo whip." He brought the bristles to her hand, brushing the tips against her fingers. "It can be sharp if I poke you with it, and it stings when used the old-fashioned way, but it has an interesting texture."

She had to agree when he drew the ends down her left breast, pausing to brush the bristles against one of her supersensitive nipples. It almost hurt, without crossing the line into pain. She didn't know if she was relieved or disappointed when he brought it lower, down her stomach, and back to her thighs.

She stiffened when he slapped her across the thigh. The bamboo bristles left a sharp sting behind. That didn't surprise her, but the way her pussy creamed did. She squirmed without thinking, earning another strike.

"Stay still, Jak."

She nodded, and then wondered if that was a forbidden movement. He didn't acknowledge it, but she decided not to push his rules.

The bristles went lower, and his hand slipped between her thighs to push them wider. Then the bamboo strands feathered across her mound, catching curls and tugging them lightly. The tips stung just a bit, especially when they slid down her slit and brushed against her clit. She let out a startled yelp, even as his finger followed in the wake of the whip to soothe her clit.

He caressed her with small circles, while the whip forged ahead, tracing a line down the inside of her thigh. It paused at her knee, and his fingers left her pussy. She felt him get closer as he knelt on the floor and lifted her leg. The sting of the bamboo tips carried down her leg, to her ankle. She stiffened when it went across the arch of her foot. Jakarta couldn't hold in a cry when he brought it against the sole of her foot with a resounding slap. The sting lingered, even as he withdrew the whip.

Her stomach quivered when she felt the spines brushing up her other leg, but the tips didn't rake her skin. She dug her nails into her hands when he brought the whip against her pussy. Her eyes widened when he pressed the smooth wooden shaft a couple of inches into her opening. She was wet and more aroused than she could believe, and the handle had easy entry. He teased her by thrusting it into her a few times before taking it away.

She heard him rummaging in his case and hoped that was the last of the bamboo whip. Her foot still stung from where he'd swatted her. She didn't want to imagine how her butt would feel if he chose to spank her with it. To her relief, he grasped her breast and removed the nipple clamp from her right nipple. Blood flow returned with a vengeance, and it stung, but in a pleasurable way. He released the other clamp too.

Before she could bask in the relief, he took one nipple into his mouth, sucking forcefully. Spasms shot through her pussy at the increased sensitivity. When he bit her with gentle force, she cried out. The feeling was intense, but more pleasurable than painful. While his mouth devoured her nipple, his fingers alternately squeezed and released the other, working her into a frenzy. She arched her back, and he pressed a hand against her stomach, reminding her to return to her appointed position.

She leaned back, gritting her teeth to withstand the sensations overwhelming her. Just when she thought she couldn't take any more, Teague lifted his head and released her nipple. She whimpered, not sure if she protested his withdrawal, or if she was thankful for it.

She cocked her head slightly when she heard a buzzing sound. The origin of the sound moved lower, until something muffled it. She stiffened when a cool object pressed into the opening of her pussy, before gliding up to tease her clit.

"The batteries in this vibrator should be good for a long while," Teague said softly. He circled her clit with the tip of the vibrator, chuckling when she groaned.

Jakarta couldn't keep her thighs from trying to close, but he refused to let them. With a sudden movement, the vibrator left her clit and entered her pussy, as deep as it would go. Her pussy immediately convulsed in sympathy with the vibrations.

"That might be set too high," he said. The vibrations lessened, until they were barely noticeable. "I just want you to feel it, love. I don't want you coming yet." He cupped her pussy, bringing her lips together around the vibrator. "In fact, you aren't allowed to come until I say so. If you're about to, I need you to let me know. Since you can't talk, you'll have to lift your hands. If I see you do that, I'll stop what I'm doing until you've regained control."

Jakarta nodded to show she understood, and he didn't reprimand her for the movement. It was all she could do to manage the action, as the low buzz of the vibrator sent shockwaves through her. There was no ignoring the way it increased her arousal and tried to coax an orgasm from her. Since he had it turned so low, all it succeeded in doing was torturing her into a fever pitch. She ached for release, and the vibrator had been inside her only a few minutes.

"Now, stand up, slowly. We don't want the vibe falling out."

Jakarta responded to his hands as he helped her gain her feet. She pressed her thighs together and took small steps as he led her to the side of the couch. She didn't resist when he bent her over the arm at the waist. He pushed her robe over her left side, exposing her buttocks and thighs.

"Is the toy still in tight? Raise your hands above your head if it is."

The position was awkward. She braced herself against the armrest with her stomach, while raising her arms over her head. The vibrator was still deep inside her, providing its never-ending erotic torture.

"Good. Put your arms down across the armrest and stand here, just like this."

Jakarta stayed in the position he had assigned. He moved past her, and she heard the rustle of clothing, followed by the noise of him searching through the box. Her legs shook with the effort to stand while simultaneously holding back her orgasm, and she leaned most of her weight against the arm of the couch.

When he returned to her, he pressed his body against hers briefly, to show her he was now naked. She shivered when his lips brushed her lower back, as he licked the line of her spine, stopping at the indent of her buttocks. His hands slipped lower, to part her cheeks.

"You're doing so well, Jak. I'm proud of you." There was a squirting sound, and then his index finger was probing her anus. It was slick with lube and slipped inside easily. She moaned with pleasure. He knew just what to do to get her aroused. She wriggled her ass, earning a light smack for moving.

"I know how much you like this." He caressed one of her buttocks with his free hand, while a second finger ventured into her anus. "Do you like having that vibrator in your pussy, while I play with your ass?" He chuckled. "No need to answer, love. I know you do."

Convulsions rippled through her pussy when Teague began thrusting his fingers into her anus. He stopped much too soon, and she groaned in protest. He continued to hold her cheeks open, and she stiffened when she felt the head of a plug probing her anal opening. Judging from the feel, it was larger than any she had ever tried before, and she took a deep breath as he carefully pushed it deeper into her. Her body adjusted much faster than she had expected, but it was used to accommodating Teague's cock.

She was stretched to her limit, and with the vibrator thrumming inside her, she could feel her orgasm approaching. For a minute, she was tempted to let it happen and try to hide it from him, but imagining his disappointment had her raising her arms.

"Is it too much? Poor darling." His voice was little more than a harsh exhalation as he caressed her buttocks. One of his hands traced the line of her cleft, pausing to push against the butt plug, forcing it in deeper, and making her moan.

She gritted her teeth, trying to fight the pleasure. A sob of relief escaped her when Teague extracted the vibrator from her pussy. The sense of fullness immediately eased to a manageable level. She sensed him moving away from her, but didn't shift positions.

The vibrator fell into the box with a thunk, and the couch dipped as Teague got on it. His hand tipped up her chin, and his mouth claimed hers. Her lips softened against his, and a new sense of calm filled her. He nibbled on her lower lip, and she sighed. When he drew the lip into his mouth to suck gently, she tried to reach up to cup his face. Right before touching him, she remembered she wasn't supposed to move and lowered her hands again.

In punishment, he nipped her just forcefully enough to sting, and then soothed the sore spot he had created on her lip with his tongue. It swept over her upper lip, tracing its contours, before plunging into her mouth. The tempo of the kiss changed from light to earnest, and she responded in kind. His hunger might have frightened her, if she hadn't sensed the underlying tenderness in his touch.

She longed to reach out for him when he drew away. The couch made a low squeaking sound when he changed positions. Seconds later, her eyes widened behind the blindfold when he touched his cock lightly to her mouth. She obeyed the unspoken command and parted her lips. His cock slipped inside, and she ran her tongue around the corona. He was hard and throbbing. She didn't think it would take much to make him come. She sucked lightly, and Teague groaned.

He cupped the back of her head, bringing her closer, so she could take in more of his cock. She relaxed her throat and let him enter. She bit lightly, and his hands tightened in her hair. She smiled around his cock, knowing he was the vulnerable one at that moment, despite her blindfold and handcuffs. She gloried in holding his cock in her mouth. He trusted her implicitly not to hurt him, and she appreciated how difficult that could be, which made pleasing him pleasing for her.

"I love it when you do that." He stroked her hair, as he thrust into her mouth.

She didn't verbally respond. Instead, she obeyed the parameters he had set and replied by drawing his cock as deeply into her mouth as she could and sucking forcefully. He stiffened at the sensation, and she expected him to find release any second.

"Not yet," he said with a grunt. It was impossible to tell if he was talking to himself or her.

She wasn't surprised when he withdrew his cock from her mouth, but she felt a flutter of disappointment. That abated when he came around behind her and removed the plug. She waited for him to take its place or surge into her pussy, but he didn't. Instead, he gripped her shoulders and straightened her gently.

"Turn around, Jak."

She turned, finding his commands easy to obey. She didn't know what tonight was supposed to prove. She felt no different about the future than she had when they started this game. She only hoped it would satisfy him for a while. She didn't want to lose Teague, despite her reluctance to commit to him.

He kissed her on the cheek. "You've been incredible so far. I want you to know I appreciate how much trust it took to bind yourself with those handcuffs. I know it must be frightening to not know what's coming next, so wearing the blindfold is a big step."

She relaxed against his chest, sensing he had finished playing games. Now, maybe he would just take her to bed and make love to her properly, allowing her to touch and please him in return.

But he wasn't done yet. "What I'm asking of you now is the real test, Jak. You have to trust me. Consider everything else a warm-up."

Chapter Four

Her stomach churned, and she wanted to ask what he meant. She held back, not knowing if the rules were still the same. The chance to ask him anything disappeared when he left her. She turned her head when she heard the glass doors sliding open, followed by a chill wind sweeping into the suite. She shivered. "Teague?"

"No questions," he reminded.

She bit down the urge to speak and strained to hear what he was doing, hoping to get an idea of what to expect. She heard him move to the fireplace, but that was the only sound she identified.

When he came back to her, he didn't give her a chance to ask questions. She gasped when he lifted her into his arms. Teague was only a few inches taller than she, but he apparently had no trouble carrying her. The cold increased when an icy wind blew up her robe. Her teeth chattered as they stepped outside. What was he doing?

He started to lower her, and she braced her feet, ready to stand. Instead, her buttocks collided with the fur from in front of the fireplace—and it was barely supported on the rail. She couldn't help breaking the rules. "Teague, what's happening?"

"Trust me, Jak."

Her balance felt precarious, in spite of his arms locked around her. She knew she was perched on the rail of the balcony, high in the air. If he dropped her, she would fall to her death. She whimpered with fear and tried to fight the handcuffs. They were stronger than they had appeared, and she wasn't able to break them. "Let me down."

He sounded sad. "I will, if you're sure that's what you want. Just say the word, and it all ends."

She started to confirm she wanted to stop, but the safe word he had established wouldn't pass her lips. She trembled with a combination of cold and fear, but still couldn't say 'fantasy'. She had every right to end this ridiculous game now, before one of them got hurt, but she couldn't do it.

From somewhere, she summoned a surge of strength, pursed her lips, and leaned against him. He remained stiff for a moment, but then relaxed against her, shifting her balance again. She clawed for support, but her cuffed hands found nothing. One of his arms remained around her back, as the other slipped between her thighs. She never could have imagined she could get aroused under the circumstances, but her pussy responded to his caress by supplying more moisture.

"You're doing great." He circled her clit between his thumb and finger. He applied more pressure, and his pinkie flirted with the opening of her pussy.

She fought back the urge to thrust against his finger, knowing she could fall if she did. The temperature was in the lower-twenties, and her nipples ached with the cold, but she burned inside. Part of her still had the urge to demand he stop, but the other part surrendered to his passionate ministrations. She tried to block all thoughts of her precarious position from her mind and concentrate on his hand working its magic. Soon, an orgasm built, and his encouraging, "Come for me, Jak," was all she needed.

Her body shook under the onslaught for several seconds, and she couldn't seem to draw in a deep breath. He continued to stroke lightly as convulsions swept through her. The orgasm took the edge off her desire, but wasn't fulfilling enough to satisfy her. Her heart raced, and it was several minutes before she regained any awareness of her surroundings.

Slowly, she realized his arm was no longer around her back, and she was perched on the rail just by her own balance and his hand between her thighs. She stiffened and felt herself inching backward. She reached for him, breaking the silence rule once again. "I'm falling."

"I know." He sounded calm. "The question is, do you think I'll let you fall?"

Her brain raced. She tried leaning forward, hoping to drop onto the balcony if she slipped, but he wouldn't let her. His hands prevented her from moving toward him. Her only options were to stay erect or lean backward. Fear stirred in her, and she couldn't help remembering the times Darien had hurt her, threatened her, and pushed her beyond her limits. Until tonight, she never could have pictured Teague having the same sadistic tendencies. It didn't fit with his personality. So, how could he do this? Was he getting off on her fear? Did he want her to fall?

It was almost as if he read her mind. Considering how well he knew her, he probably didn't need to be clairvoyant to know her thoughts. "Do you think I'll reach out and save you before it's too late, or do you think I'm like your ex-husband? Will I watch you suffer for my own enjoyment? Tell me what kind of man you think I am, Jak. Do you trust me?" He asked the last question with intensity, as if everything depended on her answer — which it did.

His point couldn't have been clearer. As she perched on the rail, feeling gravity struggling to assert itself on her, with only his hand between her thighs keeping her steady, she understood what he was trying to tell her.

She had automatically assumed he was doing this for his own sick pleasure, had even compared him to her ex-husband, who had been the most sadistic bastard to ever live, and it had been second nature to do so. She *didn't* trust him enough, not as she should.

She whimpered, but not with fear. It was pure mental distress. After two years of knowing him, of seeing what kind of man he was, she hadn't been able to move past the lessons she had learned at the hands of her ex-husband during a three-year period of Hell. Everything about Teague proclaimed he was a decent, trustworthy man, but she couldn't see that. All the times she had told him she trusted him, she had been lying. She couldn't trust anyone but herself.

She was going to lose him if she didn't change that. She had to trust in Teague and their future, or she would be alone forever. If she couldn't have faith in him, she would never trust anyone.

Knowing she had to trust him and doing it were two different things. It took every particle of courage she had to relax her body. With her hands bound, she had no hope of grabbing onto anything if he didn't catch her. She took a deep breath and leaned backward, feeling herself slipping from the rail, along with the rug.

She was surprisingly unafraid. She didn't think for one minute he would let her fall, and her trust in Teague proved well placed when his arms wrapped around her, arresting her descent. He lifted her from the rail, holding her close. She was surprised to hear him sob, and one of his tears splashed on her cheek when she lifted her head. This time, she knew the game was truly over, and she didn't hesitate to speak. "I love you." The words sounded completely natural, and they felt liberating to utter.

"I'm sorry." His voice shook slightly, and his arms tightened around her. "I shouldn't have forced you into that, but I didn't know what else to do."

She pushed her bound hands up between them to slip off her blindfold. She blinked at the light filtering onto the balcony from their room. It was a sharp contrast to the clear night skies of Lasënbourg, dotted with millions of stars. "You wouldn't have let me fall." She spoke with conviction, knowing it was true, because he had proved it. But if she hadn't trusted him enough to let herself fall, he never would have had the chance.

Awkwardly, she cupped his face with her cuffed hands. "I trust you, Teague. I trust you with my life." The wind increased, and she shivered in reaction. "Are we done outside?"

"Yes." He put his arm around her waist. "We aren't done inside yet." He lifted her into his arms and carried her inside. Teague put her on her feet long enough to close the balcony door, and then he lifted and carried her to the bed.

"I'm cold."

He smiled down at her, and his eyes were smoky-blue. "You won't be for long."

He laid her in the center, propping her head on a pillow. Jakarta buried her fingers into his chest hair, forcing him to come down with her. Teague took a second to undo the safety release catch on the handcuffs, and her hands were free to roam over his body as she pleased.

"I can't wait for you any longer. It was just as much torture for me as it was for you tonight." He pushed strands of hair off her face before leaning forward to kiss her.

She opened her mouth and thrust her tongue inside his as she parted her thighs and locked her legs around his.

Teague barely had time to sheath his cock with a condom he must have left on the bed earlier. He tossed the wrapper over his shoulder without looking to see where it landed.

She broke the kiss long enough to voice her demands. "I need you now," she said, writhing impatiently.

His hand moved between their bodies, and he parted her lips. His cock hovered at her entrance, and they both moved simultaneously, with her arching her hips as he sank his cock into her. She'd had one orgasm, but it hadn't been enough to satisfy her, not after everything he had done to stimulate her. She arched against him frantically, but his thrusts were equally fervid.

One again, their mouths met and dueled, with their tongues matching the actions of their lower bodies. Jakarta moaned when Teague sought out her clit with his fingers, pinching it lightly. She tightened her thighs around him, urging him deeper.

Spasms started in her womb, and she knew she wouldn't be able to hold out much longer. When she felt Teague's cock stiffen inside her, followed by tremors as he came, she let go of her resistance and let the orgasm sweep over her. Just having him inside her, with her, made the climax much more intense and gratifying. She dug her fingers into his shoulders and milked his cock with her convulsions of satisfaction.

Their orgasms seemed to go on forever, although only a few minutes could have passed. Eventually, Teague relaxed against her, careful to brace his weight so he didn't crush her. His tongue swirled around her ear before he spoke. "That was incredible."

"Yes." She snuggled closer, letting the delicious warmth spread through her. She was so relaxed that her eyes were drifting closed.

"Jakarta?" He sounded hesitant.

She forced up her eyelids to meet his gaze. He looked troubled. "Hmm?"

"What does this mean for us? Do we have a future?"

She smiled. Before answering, she brought a hand up to push damp strands of honey-brown hair off his sweaty forehead. How could they have gotten so hot after being out in the cold? She almost giggled at the answer. Easy, they had been together, and that was instant combustion. "Oh, yes, you're stuck with me. I have to warn you, if I'm like the other women in my family, I'll probably get fat and wrinkly when I get older."

He grinned, and his relief at her commitment was obvious. "That's okay. My granddad went bald by forty, and you've seen Dad's paunch."

She clicked her tongue. "I guess we'd better take each other. In a few years, no one else will want us."

His eyes grew somber. "I'll always want you." His expression cleared. "We're doing it tonight."

She lifted a brow. "I thought we just did."

He chuckled. "No...well, I'm sure we'll do that again too. I meant we're getting married tonight."

She shook her head. "How?"

"There's a chapel in Castle Phantasie." A tinge of color flushed his cheeks. "I, um, made a midnight reservation, so we could get married on Christmas Eve."

Before that night, she would have been angry at his presumption, but she couldn't muster the energy to care. She wanted to marry him, so why wait? They could always have a real wedding when they returned home. Their families would understand. "I do."

He frowned. "What?"

Jakarta laughed. "Just practicing for later."

About the author:

Kit Tunstall lives in Idaho with her husband and dog-son. She started reading at the age of three and hasn't stopped since. Love of the written word, and a smart marriage to a supportive man, led her to a full-time career in writing. Romances have always intrigued her, and erotic romance is a natural extension because it more completely explores the emotions between the hero and heroine. That, and it sure is fun to write.

Kit welcomes mail from readers. You can write to her c/o Ellora's Cave Publishing at 1337 Commerce Drive, Suite 13, Stow OH 44224.

Also by Kit Tunstall:

SNOW ANGEL

Joey W. Hill

"So what do you want for Christmas, little girl?"

Constance Jayne Bradwell looked over her shoulder, startled and then amused to find Santa looking directly at her.

The Children's Home Benefit Party was one of the city elite's most popular Christmas Eve events. The organizers had wanted some of the hands-on volunteers here tonight to mingle with the wealthy attendees and answer questions about the shelter. She was told she had a pleasing appearance that would fit in well. She'd done her duty, mixing, mingling, making conversation, all the while wondering if any of them had the slightest inkling what it was like to face Christmas alone in the world, belonging to no one but yourself.

She hated this holiday, with its pounding messages of family, love and togetherness, a scream so strong there was no escaping from it. Another hour and she could go home, put a pillow over her ears and sleep until it went away. She tried not to watch the dancing couples, one woman's elegantly manicured hand resting on the shoulder of her husband, his hand around her waist. What would it be like to have that casual intimacy? Any intimacy at all?

It had been a long time since she'd had sex, and she was lonely enough to long for even the artificial intimacy it could conjure. Wouldn't it be nice to find a safe guy to take her home, let him inundate her with mindless physical desire, and make her forget what she really wanted? What would it be like to have a man guide her to the dance floor with a protective, possessive hand to the small of her back? Get an aspirin out of the medicine cabinet if she had a headache, rather than having to stumble there by herself, blinded by the pain? What would it be like to have someone else hold the reins for awhile, not because it was his job or volunteer shift, but because he'd made a willing commitment to make her his, to cherish and care for her?

It was a confusing yearning, as if she wanted a parent and a lover both. She'd always been terrified to let go of control of her life, and yet tonight she had an overwhelming desire to do just that.

"You can't tell me a pretty little thing like you doesn't want anything for Christmas. Come here."

Santa held out his hand. On an impulse, she set her rum punch on a nearby table and took his offered hand to help her up to his throne. Some of the wrapped packages around his feet had gotten scattered, so she had to pick her way carefully through them with her heels. Santa's other hand touched her waist to steady and guide her, then she was up the step. He sat back down, using their clasped hands and the hand on her waist to guide her onto his knee.

Well, they always said "knee", but it was really a man's thigh you sat upon, a very intimate posture. There was no doubt the person on whose leg she sat could feel the shape of her bottom, the division of her thighs, perhaps even the small apple-sized area of vulva and labia, the dress being a typical formal, thin silken cloth that hugged her curves and sparkled.

"Let me guess." She arched a brow. "It's getting late, so you decided to make a play for the only other person at the party without a date."

His lips curved into an appreciative smile. Hazel eyes tipped by dark lashes looked at her from the framework of the curly white wig and beard. Putting that together with the muscular thigh that felt capable of accommodating her as long as she wanted to sit there, Constance realized with some surprise that this Santa was in his late thirties.

It made sense. Ironically, there were no children at this event, so his efforts were geared toward adults, exchanging quips with the men as he handed out presents, and encouraging ladies young and old to take his knee for a moment's flirtation.

"Not necessarily. You looked sad, and I thought you might like to tell the one person at the party who's supposed to grant wishes what would make you happy."

He had a compelling voice, with the smooth, rich tones of a late night radio talk show host. It was a voice that inspired confidence and comfort, and Constance felt something in her chest tighten, as if his words had the ability to wrap around her heart and squeeze out thoughts she would normally have no intention of saying out loud.

"So, is this like a confessional? Nothing I say will be repeated?"

"What's spoken in this ear," he tapped it with one finger, cocking his head, "is only repeated to elves and angels."

She'd asked it half joking, but his response was serious, and her attention clung to those beautiful eyes. She had an urge to reach out and touch his mouth, and decided she needed to go home before she embarrassed herself.

But the shallow, harsh noise of two hundred impersonal voices pressed against her, and his touch, kind and strong against the small of her back, his expression attentive, steady, roused things in her she couldn't ignore.

He was Santa, and she had a very special wish. Maybe wishes whispered into the ears of a symbolic Santa *would* get to the ears of an angel and, if she'd been very, very good, some small part of her desire would be answered. She'd believed it once.

Constance leaned back, her shoulder pressing into his chest so she was speaking into his ear, not to any party guests standing too close. He tilted his head closer and when she spoke, she inadvertently brushed his ear with her lips, her jaw line pressing against the silky cotton sideburns of the beard.

She closed her eyes, shutting out reality, giving herself the same courage that the screen of the confessional provided. A safe place to voice her sins, her fears, her deepest wants. His hand tightened on her waist, holding her to him, and the words tumbled out of her mouth.

"I don't want to be here. I want to be home with someone who cares about me. I want to wake up tomorrow with someone's arms around me. I want to hear someone whisper 'Merry Christmas' in my ear, and be able to believe, if just for that moment, that I'm the most important person in his life. I want to be swept away, taken over. For one night, I want to believe I can trust my happiness in someone else's hands."

She straightened up, looked into those golden green eyes. "Pretty tall order, hmm, Santa? Bet you don't have anything in those little boxes at your feet to cover that."

She pushed off his lap before he could respond and walked away, already feeling like a fool.

* * * * *

For the next half hour, she was caught in a conversation with the owner of the city's pro basketball team and his wife. When she dared a look around, she saw she'd finished off Kris Kringle, because the dais had been removed, the packages cleared to make more dance room. Poor guy. Paid to do a Santa gig and got a load of crap dumped on him.

She made her goodbyes to the hostess and then stopped in at the restroom. With only a small twinge of guilt and a relieved sigh, she flipped the lock to keep everyone out. It wasn't the main restroom, but a two-stall facility so the party attendees wouldn't have to walk down to the main foyer. She just couldn't take the risk of one more conversation. It was ridiculous, she knew. She worked with children who'd come from the most horrible of circumstances, who had a wide range of emotional and physical problems, yet tonight's glittering party easily qualified as the hardest volunteer task she'd worked all year. Next year she was taking the children's Christmas party, even if she had to bribe someone to get it. Or maim them.

"Would it help if we nailed some boards over it? It's soundproof, if you need to let out a primal scream."

A man stepped out of the second stall. He wore jeans and was sliding a shirt over his broad shoulders. The Santa suit hung on a rack on the open stall door. The beard and wig were gone, leaving dark hair raked back by his fingers and a smoothly shaven jaw. A jaw she recognized.

"They...they *pay* you to be Santa?"

Her Santa was S. Coble Whitney III, or Sam Coble, as he'd preferred in high school when she'd last known him fifteen years ago. Now he was a wealthy manufacturing CEO, recently divorced. She'd tutored him in math through her junior year, and had had the kind of heart-aching crush on him only an awkward, geeky foster kid could have for a boy who was handsome, funny and kind to her when others laughed at her unpolished table manners or the way she dressed.

Sam smiled, and she found it could still bump her heart up a few beats. "They're predicting a slump for manufacturing first quarter, so I figure it would be good to rack up a few extra dollars at Christmas."

The last thing she wanted tonight was to see someone from high school, someone who remembered her.

"I'm sorry about the Santa thing. I just...it just..." she stopped short, baffled when he took two steps forward, caught her nervous hands in his.

"It's the best request I've had all night. One I think this Santa is going to handle personally."

His hands moved to her hips and Constance found herself trapped between a warm, solid body and the cool surface of the door. "Sam, what are you —?"

"Going on impulse," he said. "If you're going to stare at a man's body with that much hunger in your eyes, you're going to have to take the risk of being eaten yourself."

Heat overpowered shock and mortification as he moved in, pressing her body against the door with the strength of his. His lips touched hers, opened them with insistent demand. A shiver swept up from her knees, like an electric shock passing through her muscles and nerve endings. Locking her bones into a paralysis she couldn't shake as his mouth explored hers, his tongue teasing hers to play with him. His fingers dug into her waist, her hipbones. His cock, leashed in the tidy, civilized constraint of his jeans, swelled against the denim, pressed between their thighs in blatant invitation.

Her body ignored all rational protests to this astounding turn of events. She was kissing back, perhaps too greedily. One of his large hands captured her nape, controlling her movements, his fingers caressing the back shell of her ear, the dangling earring.

The sensitive pressure points of her neck screamed in response, and the reaction rippled outward, tightening her breasts, her loins, her buttocks.

She'd never had the feeling of safety a parent could evoke, and knew when she was too old to continue hoping she'd be adopted into a family. About that time, she'd gotten hooked on romance novels, transferring her desire for parents to a desire for the protective alpha males within their pages. The emotional and physical yearnings the characters stoked to a fever pitch had grown so excruciating she'd submitted to the eager gropings of a slew of boys happy to find someone upon whom they could relieve their own overwhelming glandular urgings.

It had taught her that sex didn't come with the emotional fulfillment it promised. Like the best sales force, her hormones would tell her anything to get what they wanted.

Now she maintained a careful understanding of what was sex and what was more, and had indulged in lukewarm relationships that dwindled into tepid friendships. She was an adult, beyond the need for the parental bond, but she knew she yearned for something indefinably similar in a lover, a sense that he was in control but with her best interests at heart. A fantasy. No. A fantasy suggested something exciting, whimsical. What her heart ached for was a miracle.

It was Christmas, she was lonely, she wanted to be taken. If it was empty lust, so be it. She'd take lust over simple emptiness. Her body was so ravenous for a man's touch, a man's loving, that even if it was for five minutes in the bathroom, she'd accept it. She might even convince herself he cared, because Sam had always been a good person to her, the one boy who hadn't taken advantage.

Only now he was a man, a gorgeous male specimen with a warm body and taut muscles that her hands were grasping just above his waist under the unbuttoned shirt. Her thumbs were at his waistband, feeling the curve of his back, the narrowing to his hips. The look in his eyes was pure primal dominance driven by desire, a male ready to sweep her off her feet, overpower her.

"Hold onto me, baby," he murmured, and it was her only warning to clutch his shoulders before he turned them toward the sink counter. The edge pressed into her ass as his teeth scraped over hers, then he pushed her back, breaking the connection. He turned her so she faced the mirror and he stood behind her, those hazel eyes fired with desire. He slipped off the spaghetti strap of one side of her dress and caught her hand in his, holding it by her hip. He reached across her, his forearm pressing against her breasts, and dropped the other strap. She made a helpless noise, mesmerized by their images as he tugged gently at her waist, and the dress tumbled, pooling at her waist, revealing her curves, held up and together for display in the black strapless bra. The straps, lying loosely just above her elbows, held her arms to her sides unless she wanted to rip the dress.

"Beautiful," he slid his thumb across the top of one breast, her flesh prickling with need at his lightest touch. "Constance, you have always had such lovely breasts."

She wanted to tell him it was the clever engineering of wires and side pads, but anything more complicated than a whimper was beyond her just now. His hands moved back to her waist, then he was gathering the fabric of her snug skirt, inching it up over her hips. The palm of one hand pressed the small of her back, bending her forward so her cleavage was propped up on cool formica.

He's going to fuck you like some feudal lord with a castle serving girl, her mind screamed. *You're going to feel degraded, cheap, worse than when you started. Remember the boys in the back seat, who wouldn't even buy you a Big Mac when it was over? Cheapest little whore at school, that's what they called you, because you never asked, never demanded more. You just wanted them to take care of you. But they never did. They didn't care. You're not sixteen anymore, Constance.*

"No." She started to rise, and found out how much stronger he was. His hands slid down her bare hips, and he grasped her thighs above the lace top of her stockings. He went to one knee and lifted her as she might lift a pillow, putting her knees on his shoulders, balancing her there, still facing the mirror. She rocked forward as he raised her hips just above the line of her shoulders, making her completely helpless. It was a terrifying, exhilarating feeling to be submissive to a man's overwhelming strength. His mouth closed over her pussy, his lips separated from her flesh only by the black strip of the thong she had worn to avoid panty lines.

He wasn't fucking her like some rutting beast. He was offering her pleasure like a gift.

"Oh, God…" It had been too long since she'd let her body feel this, and now suddenly everything was pressurized, like a bottle of soda that had been tossed around and now lay in his control to turn the top and let what was churning inside explode. She didn't have the reins. He had simply plucked them away.

"Sam, I can't…"

"Yes, baby. You can."

His tongue licked, licked, pulled satin across swollen, wet folds, the friction rubbing again, again. His teeth closed over her clit, pressing down, urging her on. His nose was against her, nuzzling the enervated crease of her buttocks, his hair brushing the inside of her thighs, forced open a fixed width by his head being there. Her feet kicked the air uselessly in her slender heels, her knees pressing into his shoulders as he worked her with his mouth and his arms banded over her thighs. He gripped each of her ass cheeks, spreading her open with his thumbs and moving the strap of her thong against the opening of her anus. As rhythmically and relentlessly as the passage of time, he licked her pussy some more.

"No, no…"

She threw her head back, saw herself in the mirror, eyes wild, moist lips parted, her breasts overflowing the bra, sliding against the smooth surface of the counter as he kept fucking her from behind with his mouth. Her hands caught the edge of the counter below her hips and pressed against it, instinctively seeking the rhythm to send her over, pushing her harder against his mouth.

As the orgasm descended upon her, she turned her head and tried to press her mouth against her shoulder to keep her screams from reverberating.

He caught her fingers, pulled them from the edge of the counter, his grip shifting to hold her arm behind her back in a way that increased the spiral of reaction in her belly. Her other hand lost its purchase on the counter. Now she had no anchor. Like foam, she moved on the ocean of his mouth, only able to travel where it took her.

"It's soundproof, sweetheart. I want to hear you scream."

He replaced his tongue working in her cunt with his thumb, sliding it down from where it had been busy at her anus with the thong strap, to rub her clit in light, perfect circles. At the same moment, he sank his teeth into the meat of her left buttock. The counterpoint of pleasure and pain sent her surging forward. Only his relentless grip on her arm and thighs kept her from slamming face first into the mirror as another orgasm exploded through her. She flailed, tossed ruthlessly on the tempest of her climax, the sensation rolling her psyche over and over, stretching every muscle and tendon to the breaking point. That explosive center he continued to manipulate served as a repeated detonation area, wringing every ounce of response from her straining body.

Moments later, she discovered the faucet pressing against her cheek where her head had come to rest after the tidal wave of sensation had passed. Her thighs trembled against his jaw as he pressed gentle kisses along the skin inside them. Her body quivered, jerked at each touch of his lips.

"Easy," he soothed her. "Easy."

He moved back, lifting her knees from his shoulders, guiding them down so the heels of her shoes made a controlled descent to earth, which was more than she could say for the rest of her. He smoothed her skirt back into place, his palm fully appreciative of the shape and weight of each buttock, and then he slid the same hand under her, his palm flat against her rib cage, raising her up so her back pressed into his chest and she faced him and herself through the reflection of the mirror.

Her skin was flushed, her shoulder-length dark hair mussed, her lips full and parted, eyes gone deep green with confusion and desire. His thumb played idly over the front clasp of the strapless bra, and the hard steel of his erection pressed between her buttocks, through the tough fabric of his jeans and flimsy substance of her skirt, underscoring the differences between male and female. Hard, penetrating. Soft, yielding.

He bent his head, pressed his lips against her temple, a tender gesture that had her leaning the weight of her skull into his palm as he caressed the side of her face.

"I'd like to come home with you, Constance. Be that person who wakes up with you on Christmas morning, my arms around you. I want to go to your home, drink hot chocolate in front of a fire, watch the Christmas tree lights reflect off your face. I want to fuck you senseless. I want you to belong to me tonight."

She put her hand over his at her waist, felt the shape of his long fingers. She didn't lift her head from his touch, wanting to at least savor the fantasy another moment before she had to embrace her reality.

"I'm sure there are plenty of women who would give you a cup of cocoa and an easy lay."

She gasped as he lifted her under the elbows and turned her. He rested her hips on the counter and moved himself between them so the stiff cock beneath his pants was pushed against her still rippling pussy. "Don't, Constance. Don't play Jayna, not tonight."

"Do...do what?"

"You know what. That person you pretended to be in high school. The wise-ass bad girl, when everyone who mattered knew you were just a sixteen-year-old foster kid desperate for love. We can be together tonight without wrapping it up with a bunch of baggage, don't you think?"

"Sure, no-strings-attached sex. A really novel concept." She tried to wrench away from him, settled for crossing her arms over her chest when he kept her pinned, and jutted her chin out. "I had enough of the give-everything-to-a-guy-so-he-can-ignore-me-tomorrow strategy in high school. Why would I want to go back to that?"

"Because my ex-wife and son are in Aspen this week, skiing with her new boyfriend. A boyfriend she efficiently discovered just a few days after our divorce was finalized. We split my son, just like Solomon, but she gets the two weeks of Christmas, because that's the date of the great Aspen getaway. I supposed it makes sense, because how can you spend Christmas together as a family together, anyway, when you're no longer a family?"

The words cut harsh lines into his handsome face, but she had her scars, too. "I don't want to be your consolation prize, or a warming blanket for you to stave off the cold of being by yourself. There are women out there you can buy for that."

"It's not like that. Would you please stop trying to get away?" He set his hands to her shoulders, keeping her in place. "Yes, I want to bury myself in a woman tonight, Constance. A woman who knows what it's like to go through the holidays without a family. But if it were just that, I'd have kept my distance."

He cupped her chin, made her face his gaze. "It was really, really good to see you here. When I saw you, I knew I wanted to find out more about the woman you'd become. I wasn't going to ask you out tonight. I knew if I did, you'd think it was just the desperate come-on of a lonely divorced guy, and I'm not desperate. I'm interested."

Her cheeks warmed, but he wasn't done. "Then you whispered in my ear and made me think, this is a Christmas wish I can grant, because it's my Christmas wish, too. To be with someone who's not just lonely for a quick fuck, but something deeper. And you felt good on my knee. *Right.* Can't it be that simple?"

No, it couldn't. She knew what it was to indulge in the illusion of intimacy for one night to stave off the demons of loneliness. They came snapping back twice as hard the next day, which is why she'd learned not to fall into the trap of casual sex. There was nothing casual about it for her, no more than one drink could be a casual thing for a reformed alcoholic. But he'd hit her on a night when she was vulnerable. She could despise him for it, or let him take her home, fuck her to exhaustion, and have him slip away in the morning.

"Constance—"

"Yes. Okay. I need my arms free to get my dress back up on my shoulders, unless you want me to walk out like this."

"It has its appeal, but I think I'd rather keep you all to myself. There were too many guys eyeing you as it was." He drew her hands through the straps, slid them back up on her shoulders, lifting the gathered neckline so it hung properly over the swell of her bosom.

"Maybe I should return the favor," she said. If she'd made her choice, then she was going to enjoy the full measure of it. She reached out to button his shirt. When he drew in his breath when she touched him, she found herself a little short of oxygen, especially when he bent, and bit her neck. He gathered her in to him, his arm about her waist, his face buried in her hair. Her arms crept up around his neck, and she marveled at the scrape of his rougher chin against the soft skin of her cheek. It had been a long time since she'd held a man.

"Are you sure you don't tell all the Santas what you want for Christmas, to get them to go home with you?"

She curved her lips against him. "Yes, but you're the first to fall for it. I thought I had one at the mall earlier today, but he said he couldn't give up his bingo night with the boys down at the Lions Club."

Sam laughed, lifting his head. He sobered when he looked into her face, traced her lips with a finger. "I'm not going to hurt you, Constance. Okay?"

Yes, you will. It's never as simple as sex. "Okay."

She finished buttoning his shirt and watched him tuck it in the loose waistband of his jeans. The shirt stretched across his upper torso as he did it and she suppressed the urge to touch.

"So why did you do Santa? I imagine someone like you would be one of the partygoers. I don't think anybody even knew it was you."

"That's the point. I don't want them to know it's me. I usually work events with children, but I'm glad to work a dinner party that benefits them as well. You run a good organization, Constance. My company gives about fifteen percent of our charity budget to it."

"I didn't know that."

"I know you didn't." He gave her a steady look. "I didn't tell you that to make this about that, in any way. I just want to make sure you know I think you run a good place."

"Thank you."

He nodded. "I hate these events. Particularly at Christmas. Playing Santa is a way to get out of doing the dog and pony show and put my energy where it will do some good. You're the brave one, sweetheart. You came as yourself, and held up your end of the bargain." His fingers touched her face. "When you spoke to me, it was the first time tonight I wanted to be someone real, not pretending to be someone else. So here we are. Let's take you home."

* * * * *

Her patio home was clean and cozily decorated in warm tones of blue, soft greens, pale yellows. It was a place she always felt welcome, which reflected herself. But as she let them in, she couldn't help wondering how it looked to him, a man whose address covered five acres, with a ten thousand square foot home, stables and an Olympic-sized swimming pool.

Her Christmas tree was in a corner of the living room. He stopped her from turning on the overhead light, his hand covering hers. "Just let the Christmas lights do it."

She put down her purse and turned to him, twisting her fingers. "Hot cocoa?"

He nodded.

Constance heard him behind her as she went into the kitchen. What on earth could she talk about? Inspired, she reached out to the countertop CD player. The instrumental strains of *Silent Night* filled the room.

"Music always makes things seem more special, doesn't it?" she commented, moving to the cabinet and taking down the canister of cocoa. "A person stops, looks at a chair. Put it to classical music, or to funny music, and people will get choked up or laugh at the way that person is standing there, even if they're standing exactly the same way. Take the music away, and it's just some person standing looking at a chair, no big deal."

His hands closed on her shoulders. She stopped, flushing. "I'm babbling."

"Yes. I like it. I want you out of this."

He pushed her dress off her shoulders again, and Constance held still as he worked it off her arms, loosened her grip on the canister so he could slide the straps over them, then his touch was back at her hips, guiding the dress down, molding the shape of her ass with his hands, bringing the dress to the floor. He bent, looped an arm around her thighs and pressed, causing her to take a half seat on his shoulder so he could lift her feet off the floor and neatly clear the dress from the snag of her heels. Then he moved her into a standing position again and stood. She made to turn in his embrace, but he held her there.

"No," he said against her ear, his fingertips playing over her exposed skin. "Make us hot chocolate, Constance. I want to see you move around the kitchen in nothing but your heels and stockings, your panties and bra. I like how your breasts jiggle with every little movement, and that swatch of panties, not covering your ass, barely covering your pussy. I'm going to watch and get hard as iron, and never feel the same way again about having a woman fix me a cup of hot chocolate." He reached past her, turned off the CD player. "And the music we make will give this moment its true meaning. We won't play head games with ourselves. Okay?"

She nodded, and he moved back from her, but his body's warmth remained.

When she heard the creak as he settled into one of her chairs, reaction swept through her. What was he seeing as she maneuvered around her kitchen? The stretch of her torso as she reached up to pull down two mugs. Goosepimples rising on her flesh as she opened the refrigerator. The plump curve of her pussy as she bent low to retrieve the saucepan from the cabinets. She deliberately shifted her thighs a little apart.

Pleasure skittered up her spine at the combination of a moan and growl behind her. She took the saucepan back to the stove and noticed he was right, that her breasts swayed attractively as she moved. Heat built in her kitchen, and it wasn't coming from the burner.

A phone tone split the quiet, the only other noise the escalated rate of breathing from two intensely roused bodies and the hum of the refrigerator.

Sam muttered something. Constance turned to see him having some difficulty retrieving the cell phone from his jeans pocket, due to the constriction of the fabric across his crotch. He worked it free.

"Sam Coble. Yeah, hey there buddy. How's Aspen?"

His son. Constance went to recover her dress. With a smile at her modest gesture, Sam reached out, drew her onto his knee. He settled his hand on her hip, his fingers hooked into the band of the thong, his thumb rubbing her hipbone. He pressed a kiss to her shoulder, reassuring her both with the affectionate touch and the obvious warmth in his voice.

"Second-level slope. That's something else. Yeah, he sounds like he's a pretty darn good skier. You're really lucky, sport, getting to spend Christmas in a place like Aspen."

The love in his voice never diminished, but the hand on the phone whitened, and the grip on her hip convulsed with every word exchanged about his mother and the accomplished skiing boyfriend.

Sam Coble had married Tracy Whitline, an obvious money and looks match, but Constance had always thought Sam had much more character and depth. Watching his pain, she wished she had been wrong.

"Okay. You be careful, son. I love you. Merry Christmas." Sam broke the connection, laid the phone carefully down on the table.

"Sam, I'm so sorry."

"You know what you said about music?" He rubbed a hand over his face. "Right now there'd be some goddamned ballad playing, extolling the pain of fathers ripped from their kids by divorce, something that would hammer its way into your brain and torture you throughout the holiday season."

"Sam." She put her hand out to give him gentleness, but he stopped her.

"Tonight's not going to be about that." He hooked his other hand into her strapless bra, ripping open the front clasp so it fell away from her body, pushed away by his impatient hands. Gripping her around her rib cage, he yanked her forward, thrusting her right breast into his open, eager mouth, clamping down on the nipple, suckling it, flicking it with his tongue.

Constance grabbed onto his shoulders, her belly curling with each pull of his mouth against her stiffening nipple.

"Sam—"

"No." He caught his fingers in her hair, took her head back so they were eye to eye. "I need to take you, Constance. Take you hard. I told you I need to bury myself in a woman. That woman is you. Tell me you're on birth control, because I've no intention of separating myself from the heat of your pussy with anything if it can be helped. I want my cock driving into your sweet cunt, and I want it there *now*. Will you take it?"

"Yes," she whispered, overwhelmed by his brutal need. How could she deny him when she understood the raging pain she saw in his eyes? Only maybe it was worse for him, because he was the outsider in his own family, whereas she had never had a family.

She rose off of him, bent and laid her upper torso on the table surface gracefully, her ass tilted up because of the height of her heels. Keeping her eyes on his, she reached back, slid her finger under the thong back, moved it aside so her pink, wet labia was clearly visible. "You can fuck me as long and hard as you need to, Sam. But it doesn't help you forget. It just makes it hurt less for a little while."

He stared at her. Her heart thundered against the table surface. He rose abruptly, and she saw the length of one long thigh as he moved behind her. She heard him unfasten his jeans, and her pussy contracted, wanting him even as her heart drew in on itself, protecting her against what was to come. The pounding of flesh against flesh, where her soul would be left out in the cold, unneeded and unwanted because the simple act of lust to escape pain only needed a pussy and a cock to satisfy it.

She tensed as he put his hands to her hips. The silence of the kitchen drew out, the ticking clock on top of her refrigerator and the appliance's low hum the only noise.

"Constance, you really need to learn when to throw a guy out for being a jerk. You're worth more than that." He lifted her, turned her to face him.

She raised her hands to his face. "So are you. You're a good man, Sam. Most dads wouldn't have been able to stop themselves from saying something nasty."

"He and I have a good relationship. I know and he knows I'll always be his dad. It just rankles the hell out of me that some asshole gets to play Daddy to him just so he can fuck what used to be mine. Sorry," he shook his head. "I'm a little territorial. I've no regrets. It was way past time for Tracy and me to split. We never should have gotten together in the first place. We defined the term 'marriage of convenience'. But, God, I just feel so mad when I think of her with someone else…"

"That you feel like you need to go pee on some bushes or fuck a woman to assert your dominance again?"

He didn't quite manage the smile. "Something exactly like that."

"All right, then." She brought his hand to her breast. "Take me, Sam. I want to feel that. I've never been taken, swept away. Give that to me. Prove to me that I'm yours, that I belong only to you and no one else will ever have me. Fuck my heart and soul when you fuck my pussy."

"Jesus, Constance," he muttered, his hand closing over the nipple that grew stiff and longer under his touch, fueled by the illusion her words were constructing.

"Please, Sam. Please."

Civility had compelled him to rein back animal instincts, but she knew it was still there, simmering behind that control. At her words, it broke free.

He lifted her under the arms, shoved her to her back on the kitchen table and tore the thong away with a rip of fabric that scraped her skin with his brutal need. He gripped her hips, tested her waters with the head of his cock, and finding her ready, drove in with the strength of a stallion in full rut.

Constance arched, cried out. He filled her tight passage to the point of pain, yet she wanted it, wanted the closest thing to intimacy she could have on this Christmas Eve. She raised her stockinged legs, wrapped them around him, driving the points of her heels into his buttocks.

"Oh, sweetheart. Be still, girl. You're tight as a virgin. You've not done this in a while." He bent, bracing one hand over her. "I like knowing that. How long has it been?"

"Since high school," she managed.

With a muttered oath, he stopped. He would not let her move, kept his hand pressed down on her as he shut his eyes, fought some battle within himself. Her pussy quivered around him, wanting to hold that part of him forever.

"No. No, we're not doing it this way." He withdrew from her, groaning at the retreat, but he took both her hands and brought her to her feet. "You were making me some hot chocolate, and that's what you're going to do." He sent her toward the counter with a light smack on one bare buttock. By the time she had turned to look at him with a confused expression, he had his jeans up, fastened and buckled.

"I don't understand. What... Did I do something wrong?"

Sam cupped her face, brushed his lips over hers. "You reminded me of something. A soft voice whispering in my ear what she wanted for Christmas."

"But—"

"What I was about to do wasn't even close to what you wanted, Constance, and we both know it." His fingers slid down the side of her neck, her shoulders. Touched the side of her breast. "Don't settle for being Jayna. You did that in school. You should have outgrown it, but from the tight fit of that sweet pussy of yours, I'd say you just gave up on finding it."

"I thought you went into business, not psychology."

"Don't." He caught her hands. "I'm sorry, Constance. I wasn't trying to make you feel bad. Those phone calls make me unlivable. Sometimes it just seems like everything in the whole world goes wrong and we can't do a damn thing about it. Why should my son be spending fifty percent of his life with some asshole who just wants to get into my ex-wife's pants? Why did you have to sleep with every insensitive jerk in high school just to figure out you were never going to find love that way? Why do we fuck up our lives in ways we can't possibly anticipate?

"Ah, hell." He wrapped his arms around her, brought her to his warmth and strength, cloaked her with the hug, his fingers wrapped around her bare back and waist, holding her with undemanding intimacy.

"I didn't...I didn't agree to this because..."

"I know, ssshh...I know. I'm an idiot, Constance. Forgive me."

He held her for awhile that way, his hands just stroking her back, and after the aching in her throat went away, she wanted it to go on forever, that glide of fingers up and down her bare spine, the closeness of him, his clean smell, the brush of his breath against her temple.

"I'm sorry you had to go through that, Constance. I'm sorry I wasn't a better friend."

Her brow furrowed. "It wasn't your doing, Sam. We barely knew each other."

He shook his head. "I had ten times more fun in our tutoring sessions than I did on one single date with Tracy." At her arch look, he chuckled. "Okay, not counting the sex. Hey, I was seventeen. Give me a break."

"Sam, it was fifteen years ago."

"That would make it a year ago in Mind-Life."

"Oh, God. I can't believe you remembered that."

"You do," he pointed out. "What you said about music earlier? You were always saying things like that. You said that for every decade of time that passed in our adult lives, our minds and hearts would only be one 'Mind-Life' year away from the memories of our adolescent lives, because the things that happened then are so strong inside us." He reached out, touched her face. It was a reverent, appreciative touch that startled her, made her suddenly not so aware that she was nearly naked.

"So, Miss Constance Jayne Bradwell, that means you were tutoring me in math all of eighteen months ago. And that is also why," he tipped her chin up, "you're still hurt and embarrassed by the mistakes that lonely teenager who called herself Jayna made, even though you're now a beautiful, accomplished woman who's made an impact in her community and a home for herself, and feels pretty good about life all but these two lousy days of the year."

"You always called me Constance, even then."

"Because you always were Constance to me. Now finish that cocoa, and then we'll go sit in front of the Christmas tree, just like you said."

"You didn't mention me being naked was part of the plan."

"Well, the best plans allow for a little flexibility." He flashed her a grin. "I'm going to go back to sitting in this chair and watching your beautiful ass."

"It's nothing special," she said, embarrassed.

"You weren't staring at it half the night."

Constance chuckled. "So it wasn't my pickup line, but my ass that got you here tonight?"

She turned from the counter, holding the hot chocolate and found his heated gaze focused on the movement of her bare breasts. He lifted his attention to her face and there was no more humor in his eyes, but something far more potent. "If you were mine," he observed softly, "I'd make you walk around the house like this all the time."

"Well, I guess for tonight, I am yours, aren't I?"

She'd meant to be light and facetious with it, but it came out quiet, direct. Inviting. His eyes flamed hotter at her words.

"Yes, you are. Come here, sweetheart."

She obeyed, and leaned forward to set the mugs down on the table.

"No, hold them. I like having your hands occupied." His hand slid up her belly, his thumb sweeping over the top of her mound. "I'd shave your pussy myself, keep you smooth so I could see it, though you have some pretty hair there now, like goose down."

Constance trembled under his touch, as much from the feel of it against her skin as from watching his fingers, their tanned color moving over her. "I can smell you." His hazel eyes lifted to hers. "It makes me want to eat you out all over again."

"I've never known a man who liked doing that," she said. "It was...incredible."

"Most men don't know what they're missing. Look here." His finger brushed her thigh, came away with moisture. "Am I making you hot for me, little girl?"

"You know you are."

"Then let's go in the living room," he rose, "and see what gifts we have for a good girl."

She'd never been with anyone with Sam Coble's sexual confidence. Her body responded to his physical dominance like she was spoils of war and he was the conquering general. Her heart was opening to his gentle touch, his smile. Her soul was terrified of being so out of control. All three parts wanted this Christmas Eve never to end.

If she'd been in her clothes, she would have sat down on the couch, settled a hip comfortably so she was facing her guest, her elbow along the head rest, forming a comfortable position for conversation, but in her current state of undress and the current mood, something else seemed more appropriate.

When Sam sat down, she folded her legs beneath her and sat down on the carpet between his knees. She put the mugs on the table, and then put her back against the brace of his calf and thigh so she could look up at his face, bathed in the soft light thrown from the Christmas tree. She liked things that moved, so her tree had a variety of little electronic ornaments that made soft clicks and slides, whirs as angels turned in joyous celebration. A tiny train ran the gamut around and around to the base of the tree, and then back up again.

She found him studying her with an unreadable expression. "What?"

He lifted a shoulder. "Tracy and I were combatants, in a way. It sounds strange, but she never would have sat this way."

She flushed. "I like feeling protected and safe, and you like making a woman feel that way," she said simply. "The way you acted in the kitchen, taking control, I can tell you like it."

"And what about you? Tell me the truth, Constance. It won't change my desire for you either way."

"I like it," she admitted. "I mean, I'm not saying I'd like a man ordering me about, but for this...this way, I like it."

"I like it, too." He touched her hair, curled a lock back behind her ear, offered a smile that didn't quite reach his eyes. "I'm fairly alpha when it comes to sex. A chauvinist pig down to the bone. I like to overpower a woman until she's screaming with pleasure, begging me to fuck her. I like her to obey me in the bedroom, accept and submit to me for our mutual pleasure. Do you understand what I'm talking about?" He wound the lock around his fingers, taking a firmer grip on her hair, tilting back her head so their eyes met. He leaned forward, bringing his energy closer to hers. "Tell me if you like what you're hearing, Constance."

She'd respond if she could breathe. She did know what he was talking about, though no man had ever cared about her enough to want to overwhelm her, be her master in the bedroom. It took a level of caring and possession no one had ever been willing to offer her, even if it was just for a night.

"Yes. I like it," she whispered.

"I thought so, the minute I took you over in the bathroom. I could sense it in you. I think that helped me make the move I did." He leaned down further, resting his hand along the side of her throat, and reached with his other hand. She parted her thighs and he passed his finger over her clit, testing her wetness, making them both aware of how aroused she was. His expression reflected how her actions were affecting him. She could feel the heat building around him, drawing her into it.

"I've been a remiss Santa," he straightened, turned his attention to the mostly empty skirt beneath her tree. "A pretty little thing like you deserves more gifts." He rose, swinging his leg over her head, making her giggle.

"It's not this pitiful. I've got gifts the children gave me, I just prefer putting them out on Christmas morning."

"Well, we have one more gift to wrap. You." He had zeroed in on the canister on her fireplace, whose half open top revealed tools and materials for decorating the tree and the room. Extra tinsel, ribbon, scissors. Multi-colored satin nylon cords for hanging Christmas cards over her valances.

Sam removed a spool of gold cord and one of deep pine green. He measured out a length of each over twenty feet, withdrew a pocketknife from his jeans and made a clean cut with the sharp blade.

"This isn't where you tell me your Boston Strangler fantasy, is it?" she asked, eyeing him.

"No." His sensual lips curved, reminding her how they felt on her. "In one of my brief hiatuses from my relationship with Tracy, before we were married, I dated a girl who was a fan of Shibari. Are you familiar with it?"

"No...no." But her heart was beating faster, as she watched him shake out the cords.

"Come stand out here, in the middle of the floor."

His voice was low. It wasn't a request. Constance swallowed, rose and moved around the table.

After she came to a halt where he motioned to her to stand, silence drew out in the room, and she became exponentially more aroused as he simply sat there on the hearth, studying her. She was aware of how he watched her breasts as she moved toward him, the track of his gaze now over her hips, her thighs, damp with her arousal, the soft furred mound of her pussy. She was aware not just because she watched him with her eyes, but she felt his attention press upon her flesh like a physical touch stroking her in all those same places.

"Shibari uses sensual pressure on the skin and the psychological impact of being restrained to arouse," he said at last. "As well as some very clever knots and arrangements. Even suspension. I could suspend you from the ceiling like a Christmas angel, and stroke every part of you at my pleasure. Feed you when you're hungry, let you suck water from my fingertips."

He stood up and came to her, his broad shoulders and greater height taking up all her senses as he approached. His hands slid up her rib cage, spanning it with the spread of his fingers, as if he was learning her shape and size. Then he took up the green cord, doubled it, and passed it around to the back of her body. He moved behind her and she felt him pass the ends through the loop of the double end and tighten it on her rib cage, just under her breasts. The slack dangled down her back, the rope end brushing her buttocks, the back of her knee, her ankle.

"This," he put his fingers beneath the point at her back where he had passed the ends through the looped end, "is the first cinch. Each one will increase the sense of constriction and restraint and can be adjusted for more or less of the same. It's called a lark's head, since it looks somewhat like a bird's head and you," his fingers whispered down her back, caressed her buttocks exposed by the thong, "are as delicate as one."

His body pressed up against hers as he passed the rope forward and back, creating another cinch. She felt a perceptible tightening, and her breathing rate went up, but the trouble didn't lie with the constriction, but her response to it. "The first series I'm doing is *shinju*," he said. "A breast restraint. Shinju means pearls, and that's how your breasts are treated. Jewels placed in a setting, displayed to their best advantage to a man's eyes. My eyes."

He brought the rope around, and now the cord ran in two parallel lengths above and below her breasts. He moved back behind her again. His unexpected touches made her dizzy, his movements, the spinning and twirls of the sparkling angels on the tree, the shine of the Christmas lights in her eyes. Her whole body quivered with a strong emotional, as well as physical, reaction to what he was doing.

Now he was in front of her again. He brought the two pieces of the green cord over her shoulders and passed them under the lines above and below her breasts. He turned a loop in the rope beneath them, his fingertips brushing her curves, and then threaded it back up, making a knot that drew together the two parallel lines, constricting her breasts, causing them to swell and distend before his appreciative gaze.

"Oh..." Her breath left her in a shudder, and he took the ends back over her shoulder, securing them to the lark's head in back, lifting her breasts higher at the same time, increasing the sensitivity caused by the constriction, creating the sense that she was wearing a silken harness on her upper body.

"Clasp your hands together behind your back, palms facing, sweetheart."

She did, overcome by her arousal as he wrapped more cord around the wrists, clothing them in a coil, working the last of the two strands between her clasped fingers, then tying them off.

"After a few minutes of this, I could put my lips to your nipples, and they'd be so sensitive, you'd scream at the sensation. It's wonderful, isn't it?" He put his hands on her shoulders, dropped a kiss into her collarbone, then slid his hands around, cupping her.

She did cry out, though he did no more than caress her, lightly pinch the pink tips.

"Hang on, sweetheart, there's more." He bent, picked up the other rope, and attached it to the back of the harness she wore now, at the point below her shoulder blades. "You can wear the *shinju* under your clothes, as a reminder of your lover's claim on you."

"How about as a reminder of my claim on him, by him knowing I'm wearing this?" She looked up at him, her nose brushing his jaw since he stood right behind her.

"You're learning, baby."

He pressed her back against him and she arched her neck, giving him better access to sink his teeth into her. His hand, still holding the loose end of the rope, came around to caress her nipple again, and Constance whimpered, brushing her ass against the hard length of him. He groaned and managed to draw back, putting some distance between them.

"I'm not through decorating you, sweetheart. You're just going to have to wait."

Her body was turning into liquid heat, needing him inside her. He created another double wrap at her waist and now came in front of her, going to one knee so she could gaze down at the broad shoulders, the dark strands of hair that fell over his forehead. The movement of those large, capable hands as they worked the cinches. He tied two knots, one right after the other, then slid his hands between her legs, reaching under her to the back, his fingers probing her anus. She gasped, caught his shoulder for balance. He slid his fingers forward again, away from her, used whatever he had been doing to determine where to tie the next knot.

"Spread your legs a bit for me."

She opened trembling thighs and he passed the length of knots between her legs, moved around back to take up the slack.

"Sam, I want you."

"I know, sweetheart. I want you, too. But I want you wild for me. I want you to soak your bindings. Feel this, sweetheart."

Abruptly the line of knots tightened against her flesh and pressed perfectly against her clit. His fingers opened her ass cheeks, made an adjustment, and the other set of knots settled against her anus. He tightened the cinches again and she made a small whimpering noise of need. When he tied the rope ends into the fulcrum of the shoulder harness and modified it so that every movement of her upper or lower body tightened the ropes in the opposite region, she had to fight the urge to simply roll her body with the sensations. She felt completely bound and yet she still had a wide range of mobility, with every movement telegraphing a sensual message to her body.

"You look gorgeous," he said. "And look at this." His hand slipped between her legs, where the two lengths of rope between the lowest knot at her clit and the first knot at her rectum allowed his fingers access to slip between them inside her pussy, which clenched around his fingers in fervent welcome.

"Sam, I'm...my knees."

Constance swayed, her breath coming short, and Sam caught her at the waist. "Easy, sweetheart. It's a bit overwhelming, isn't it?"

He caught her just as they buckled, and lifted her over his shoulder, so her ass was under his hand, her head hanging down. He retrieved a straight-backed chair from the kitchen and brought it into the living room, then slid her back over his shoulder and put her gently into the chair in one easy movement that made her heart lodge in her throat. With her hands bound, increasing her sense of helplessness, and the bending of her knees and body rubbing the bindings against her, she felt almost...

"It's...it's magic."

"You're magic." He thrust his fingers into her gently, mimicking the motion of a cock, and she gasped, bucking against him.

"Try holding still, sweetheart," he suggested. "It makes it much more potent."

"Command me," she whispered, her green eyes flickering up to his startled ones, eyes that went from surprise to flame in the next blink.

"Be still," he told her, his voice rough. "I want you wet and panting for it, but don't you move a muscle unless I give you permission."

If it was possible, the quivering in her body doubled. He withdrew from her slowly, brought his fingers to his lips, tasting her as she watched him, wanting to beg him to fill her, wanting to wait and see what he did next. He went to her tree, removed several items. His jeans hugged his ass and she wanted to grip it under her fingers, feel his buttocks clench and release as he thrust into her. Just the thought made her want to squirm her clit and anus against the cleverly placed knots, but she was frozen by his command, and by the certainty that the slightest movement might send her into orgasm.

He brought back a handful of items, and set them on the table next to her, sat himself on the coffee table before her, spreading his legs so they were outside her clasped ones.

"Open your thighs for me, sweetheart," he said. "Just until your knees touch the inside of mine."

The silk knot slid up higher, pressing upward on her clit, pulling the knot deeper into her ass. Her constricted breasts jutted out further for his regard.

"I can smell your cunt, Constance. I like it." He lifted two small icicle ornaments, done in delicate blown glass that caught the lights of the Christmas tree. "These are beautiful," he observed, fingering the wire hooks on them.

She could tell what he was going to do, and the anticipation was excruciating, so that she made small plaintive noises as he leaned forward, cried out again as he worked the wrap of the wire hooks over her nipples and tightened them. The tips responded to the pressure of his fingers as well as the wire and the weight of the glass.

He picked up a handful of tinsel he'd plucked from the branches then and scattered it over her shoulders, the crown of her hair, smiling at her, bending forward to kiss the side of her breast in a gesture that was oddly tender. She battled back laughter and tears both. She'd never been so aroused and happy at once, even as her body strained for more of his attention.

"Look at this." He plucked her digital camera off the table by her purse.

"Oh, Sam, don't—"

"You, Miss Bradwell, aren't in a position to make demands." With a wicked grin, he stepped back, went to one knee. The flash was a quick, blinding moment that obliterated her view of him.

His hand touched her shoulder as she blinked, and he knelt down next to her.

"Look."

The view screen showed a woman decorated and bound in gold and green silken ropes, her breasts high and proud, the sparkle of tinsel on her shoulders and her fall of hair. There was a soft smile on her lips, her lashes fanning her cheeks, head slightly tilted away. In most pictures, Constance made a funny face or came off looking self-conscious. She liked this picture. Ironically, by stripping away everything on the outside and decorating her as he wished, he had brought forward something from within her. In that picture, for once, she saw some of her true self.

"Quiet. Intense. Passionate. The real Constance Jayne at last."

She lifted her gaze, amazed he spoke her thoughts. Sam pushed her hair from her cheek, threading his fingers in the softness of it with the tinsel, and laid his lips over hers.

If he had kissed her roughly, demanding her body's response, it would have obliged. But this kiss was more, rousing an emotional reaction that swamped the physical, so that she shivered within and without, wanting him in ways that surpassed the simple desires of their bodies, as if everything was being reduced to raw need.

She knew the illusory danger of intimacy, making her believe more was there. But tonight was about magic and miracles, and suddenly she truly believed anything was possible, the way a child at Christmas was supposed to feel, even if that same child was an adult who knew that Santa Claus might or might not be the figure she had been raised to believe he was.

For tonight, she chose to believe he was.

"I think I need to have you now, Constance," Sam observed, raising his lips only the necessary amount to speak the words. His green eyes filled her vision so there was nothing but the grey, gold and green color, a mix of all the colors of the earth, wind, sea and sky.

"Please," she whispered. "Take off all your clothes. I want to feel you everywhere."

He rose and unbuttoned the cuffs of the shirt, then the front of it, showing her the smooth muscle of a man in his thirties who took good care of his body. He shrugged out of it, and she relished that motion, that beautiful roll of powerful shoulder muscles, the slide of cotton down firm skin. The shirt dropped, drawing her eyes to his waist, the way the jeans fit even more loosely there with the shirt gone, but tight over the crotch, almost level with her gaze.

He unfastened the button, eased down the zipper. He left it open that way as he toed off his shoes. Her fingers itched to slide into that gapped area, reach in and down, cup his heat through the thin cloth of his underwear, run her thumb over the broad head she could see straining and wetting the threads of the fabric. She wanted him in her mouth, to taste the meat and power of him.

"Sam," she strained against the bonds. "Let me taste you. Please."

"I think you could make me do anything with those hungry eyes of yours." He pushed the pants down to his thighs with the underwear, took them off his long legs with his socks and stood before her in nothing but the fine flesh he had been blessed with.

His pubic hair was dark like the hair on his head and the light covering of it on his arms, legs and chest. It was very fine, gleaming hair that lay against his body like fur rather than curling. She wanted to touch it, rub her face against him, and she groaned in approval as he guided his cock to her waiting lips.

She had to bend forward a little to take him and she worked the fingers of her bound hands into the back slat of the kitchen chair to give her balance and an anchor point to steady her as she slid her lips and teeth down the full length of him. She wanted to get all the way to where her bottom lip would touch that sensitive base against the scrotum, but there was too much of him. She took in as much as she could and then flicked her tongue over him, licked, bathed him, sucked hard on him as her head moved up and down.

"You are too damn good at this," he muttered.

How could she explain that it was the first time she'd actually enjoyed doing it as much for the man as for herself? Always before, in high school, the act had been between her and the cock, as if the organ had possessed the sentience its gland-driven teenage owner had not. It seemed to understand the energy of the connection between her mouth and the pulsing power she was drawing from it. In a way, the boy hadn't even been part of it. This was the first time her emotions remained linked to the man's response, so that every groan and tightening of his touch on her head heightened her own fevered reaction, the fervor of her mouth working on him. Each hard thrust into her mouth made her body roll forward in proportionate response. The knot caressing her became more insistent.

"I'm going to come," she gasped around his cock.

"Come, baby," he urged. "I'll make you come again tonight. I don't want you to hold any of it back."

He wouldn't let her resist, used the strength of his hand and arm to keep her going down on him, rocking her body back and forth on those devilishly clever knots and her thighs sliding on the fluids slicked there from her pussy.

He also wouldn't let her draw back, so her jaw trembled with the effort not to bite down as the orgasm rolled over her, rippling out from her cunt, tightening all the motions of her body so that she was helpless to the rhythmic movement he kept forcing her to make, making it unbearable, unbelievable, glittering. It was a volcanic explosion, the heat and power shaking every structure on its foundations. Her hands lost their purchase on the back of the chair and his cock shoved into the back of her throat. He forced her to stillness there, her mouth full of his erection as she shuddered and screamed, jerked and twisted against her bonds until her vision teared.

She came down to earth, making soft whimpers like the cooing noises of a dove, an instinctive lullaby. The sounds were an antidote to the adrenaline, the body bringing all the organs back to a normal cadence with the soothing noise.

She tried to resume her movements on him with her mouth, but he pulled back, taking his glistening, hard cock away, and cradled her chin with his fingers as he did so to ease the removal.

"I'll hold out a little longer, baby," he said. "When I come I want to be deep in your cunt." He bent down, brushed a kiss on her soft lips. "It will be the last thing you feel before you fall asleep in my arms, knowing someone is with you, holding you close throughout the night.

"Now," his tone lightened before she could respond, "I don't know about you, but I need a cool down. First, let's take the top part off. Don't pout," he touched her lips before she could protest. "I'm glad you like it, but it's not supposed to be too tight for too long."

He loosened the cords around her breasts and removed the *shinju* arrangement, unwinding it from her rib cage. Her breasts tingled with the release of tension, but he quickened the blood flow by tracing the path where the ropes had been with his tongue, the sensitive undercurve, the delicate pale slope at the top. Constance watched him, her head bent attentively over his, and touched soft kisses on his hair, the curve of his ear. He smiled, rubbed his cheek against her mouth, then put the cord aside. He did not remove the lower piece that girded her loins, but he did make an adjustment to compensate for the release in tension from the removal of the top. The friction of the knots rippled an aftershock from her orgasm through her, and he anticipated it, catching her nipple in his mouth as she arched.

The feel of his tongue and lips over the encircling wire of the icicle was as breathtaking as the true touch of heated flesh against cold. She moaned, lifting herself up higher, deeper into his mouth, and he tugged, flicked, let her feel the edge of his teeth. He reached behind her as he did it, with one jerk loosening the knot holding her hands tied and the coil so it dropped away, freeing her wrists.

She ran her palms down the bare slopes of his shoulders. Her gaze fixed upon his cock, still erect from his unsatisfied need. Incredibly, her pussy responded to the sight, as if it had not just been sated beyond anything it had ever known before. But this was more. She wanted to be filled, joined, and he was holding that back until the end, knowing that.

He bent, scooped her back up in his arms before she could reach for it, and headed for the kitchen.

"Where are we going?" she asked, winding her arms around his shoulders and gratified when he picked up on her need and held her closer, a mid-air hug.

"Outside. Your backyard. It's snowing again."

"What... What?!"

He balanced and held her struggling body easily with one arm and opened up her door to the back courtyard. She kept a cottage garden out there with a small bench next to a fountain. It was a quiet secluded niche she enjoyed for reading, unwinding, sipping her morning coffee. Surrounded by a ten foot high privacy fence, there was no easy view into it by her neighbors, but it was the principle of it, being naked, outside, in snow. The cold shocked her warm, stimulated flesh.

"You like to make snow angels, Constance?" He let her feet down but kept a firm grasp on her when she would have dashed for the door. "Come on, let's make two of them, before we freeze our asses off."

He tugged her off the stoop, swinging her down into a clear spot in the fresh snow. She squealed as her feet sank into the half foot coverage.

"You're nuts. You're—"

"Crazy about you." He turned, caught her in his arms. Lifted her off her feet. "Hold on."

He fell backwards, and she was laughing by the time he landed, straight as a tree falling to earth.

She held on tight so she wouldn't slide and ruin his impression, and because it felt so good to hold his body, his heart pounding beneath her racing one, his legs tangled with hers, rough male hair and firm skin against her smoothly shaven calves. His genitals pressed against her thighs, semi-erect now due to the cold and the change in their focus, but she felt his response grow as she slid her thighs around him, squeezed.

It was so incredibly warm between their bodies, but the air was so cold in contrast around them she could not stop a shiver from running through her shoulders and back, tightening her buttocks beneath the firm clutch of his hands on either cheek. "You're a temptress," he growled, curling his fingers in the rope and giving her pussy a swift, tart burst of sensation. Then he lifted her in the air like a figure skating move, bringing his own body straight up from the waist to set her between his calves, a feat of strength that clearly displayed the ripple of upper body muscles and made those in her own abdomen weaken beneath

121

the beat of butterfly wings. "Do a little hop leap over there, sweetheart," he pointed to the patch of snow just past his armspan. "And show me what kind of snow angel an angel makes."

She wanted to just stand there and look down at his body, the fine lines of thigh and torso, the cluster of his cock lying against the nest of testicles. She wanted to explore every inch of him, as if he were the one Christmas gift she'd been allowed to open the night before Christmas Day.

"You've no idea how beautiful you look," he gazed up at her. "Your pussy all tied up, those icicles sparkling on your nipples, your hair soft around your face. You're a sugar plum fairy, baby. Make an angel for me."

She hopped over, a good three foot jump, fueled by exuberance like that of a well-loved child who didn't know how to be self-conscious, and lowered herself to the snow. Constance gasped as she lay back. The cold ice of the snow flakes burned into her skin and she immediately stretched her arms out to either side of her and began to make wings, sliding her arms through the sugar spun snow, feeling the disturbed and newly fallen flakes on her lashes and lips. It was painful and exhilarating at once, and she laughed out loud, hearing him snorting and doing the same, a furious cloud of snow coming from her right as he put his considerable male strength to it while she flowed through it like she lay in water.

She remembered the skirt part, and began to open and close her legs. She immediately discovered that to be a pleasurable sensation, the arch and press of hips communicating itself to her delicate silken restraint, the diamond crisscross of the ropes tightening over her hips, the knots rubbing against her, all reminding her that she was bound in sexual restraints, and rousing her the more she continued the movement. If not for the cold, she could have just lost herself in the building heat of renewed arousal, the undulation, cold to heat, friction to pleasure, over and over, not really able to build to climax, just riding wave after sweet wave of sensation, as if she were an angel in truth, floating over air currents.

She bared her throat, opening her mouth to take in the flakes, seeing the faceted jewel pattern as they collected on her lashes. The world was a soft swirl of white, gray and black, icy cold and yet ringing with the passion and heat of life all at once. She was happy. It was Christmas Eve, and for the first time in her life on this night, she was happy.

Constance brought her legs back together. The backs of her calves were losing feeling. They closed on Sam's ankles, and she tilted her head down to gaze upon another miracle and wonder of nature.

He stood above her, looking at her body against the snow, his hazel eyes glinting with the same sparkling light that rippled over the white ground. She wanted him to touch her, could almost feel the way those hands would feel on her, and she lifted her own hands, molded them over her breasts, let the nipples slide through her fingers, tugged on the icicles. As he watched, she drifted down, found her pussy, caressed it. Her nipples were tight with cold, her legs spread, opening herself to him, her pale body dusted with flakes and the icicles glittering at her nipples. She knew her cheeks were flushed with her excitement and the reaction of her body to the cold.

"I think I've found a snow angel in truth," he observed, his voice gruff. "Are you cold, baby?"

She nodded, and when he bent to her, she wrapped her arms around his shoulders, her legs around his hips. He lifted her out of her angel silhouette, turned and carried her back into the house.

The blast of warmth shivered through her skin and his arms tightened around her. She kept her cheek pressed against his neck as he moved through the house, past the living room, and down the short hallway into her bedroom.

She'd painted the walls a tranquil blue and hung chimes of metal stars from the ceiling fan, so they sang softly with the slow level air currents. He laid her back on the quilted comforter, her knees crooked over the side so her hips were on the edge and he stood between her knees. His chest filled her vision in that moment, and then slid back as he took her arms from his neck and laid them over her head so they draped, relaxed against the soft fabric. The only illumination was the hall light, so every feature of his body was defined by the interplay between shadows and shafts of light.

He raised and shifted her to ease the remaining cords from her waist, thighs and crotch. His fingers caressed her clit as he eased the knots away from them, and her hips lifted, responding to his fingers, wanting more.

"Hold on a moment, sweetheart," he said. "I want this off so there's nothing to keep me from burying my cock all the way to the hilt in your cunt." But when he got the ropes off, he did not move immediately to do that. He stroked her, his hooded eyes becoming more intent as her movements began to work in a rhythm with his stroking, and she turned her cheek to the cover, biting it as he manipulated her clit between his fingers, worked it in tiny movements and light squeezings of his fingers, lazy long caresses with his knuckles and finger tips.

"Sam, please…"

"That's right, Constance. Remember, I want my woman wet and begging. I love to watch you get hot. See how hard you're making me?"

She did, and it made her want him all the more. The numbness of her cold backside, thighs and back had become a tingling that meshed with the coiling sensation of his fingers. She was losing her mind, losing everything but an intent focus on everything he was doing to her.

He removed the icicles, one at a time, leaving her completely naked, just her and him now.

"This moment is about more than sex, Constance. When I fuck you, it's just going to be you and me."

She wanted to believe him, but was so afraid to do so that she did not respond. He kept his fingers on her clit and pussy, kept her moving restlessly beneath his touch, her body open and eager for him. She thought he might move to take her then, but then his gaze flicked up to hers and she knew before he said it that he wanted to drive her up even higher.

"Hold completely still for just a minute. One full minute, don't move a muscle. Not until I tell you that you can. If you can do that, all the waiting will be over."

She gave a savage moan, but she obeyed, though it was like reining in a chariot of wild horses. Her body wanted to buck and twist, only instead of trying to throw a rider she was trying to entice one to mount her.

He traced a path down between her breasts, drew a fingertip under the crease of one. "Be still. Not a single movement, or we'll start over…"

She became aware of the ticking of the bedroom clock like the countdown of a bomb, and she was eager for the explosion, the shattering of the world around her. All the nerves in her stomach and thigh muscles tightened, like an orchestra waiting to begin a piece of classical music. Her senses, every part of her body attuned to his cock like the sections of winds, percussion and bass to the raising of the conductor's baton.

"Sam…" She almost wailed it.

"Constance. Beautiful, sexy, shy, Constance. Do you want me, sweetheart?"

"Yes. Yes!"

"Only half a minute more."

She cursed him colorfully, and made him smile down at her, a playful, sexy smile.

Her body shuddered a response she couldn't control and she had a moment of panic that he'd count it as a movement, but he did not. He leaned closer, closer to her body. She almost clenched her fingers to remind herself she had to stay still, remembered just in time that would be *movement*. Air left her in a soundless scream as his mouth stopped, hovering just over her breast, his thighs brushing the inside of her immobile ones. The head of his cock brushed her pussy.

"Don't move. I mean it, baby. Twelve more seconds…"

She registered it, marked it on the first tick of the bedside clock at the same moment he closed his mouth over her nipple and the breast around it, suckling her, gently for a moment, then harder, pressing his tongue over the swollen tip, teasing it, nursing it, all while she shook in the throes of his imposed command.

Unbelievably, she was able to make her body stay still through that, though she could not control the trembling, the reaction of her nerves to the friction between her taut muscles and emotional arousal. His hand clasped that same breast, squeezing as if he were getting the sweetness from an orange into his mouth.

Five, four…

Her legs quivered harder. She wanted to spread even wider for him. His hands slid down and he lifted his head, looked into her eyes, only inches away.

"Two, one…" he whispered. "Don't move, baby. Not yet." The lips covered her, as gentle as the kiss of an angel, silencing the futility of her protest, and then she cried out in his mouth as his cock eased into her, slowly, slowly, stroking her, teasing her. Sliding into a wetness so complete she could feel it lubricate him as he made his slow, sweet way in, pushing himself into her like the slide of a plow's shaft into a furrow of rich, moist earth.

"Sam…" It was a whispered plea because she had strength for nothing more. "Please let me move. Please. You said one minute. I can't bear any more."

"You're so sweet, baby. So obedient." He nibbled the corner of her mouth and she felt his muscular body shudder, wanting her. "You want to move."

"Yes," she hissed. "Yes."

"Okay. Move, sweetheart. Fuck me."

She lifted aching, needy arms to him and he came down to where she could curl her arms around his shoulders, draw her body halfway up to his, pressing heart to heart, mouth to mouth. She was as greedy for that intimate kiss as she was to lift her hips, take him deep within her, clutch him with her silken walls and make him drag himself through her snug lubricated tissues.

She wasn't sure why her subconscious had capitulated so easily to him, why it had been so easy to fall under his command, obey him, let him bind her. She'd never had any inkling that she enjoyed bondage games, but then she'd always equated it with the maneuvers in a cheap S&M flick. She had never realized the term could mean something like this, a complete sexual trust that spilled into the emotional, a mastery where they both served what the other needed. A fulfillment, the discovery of a bond where there'd been none just a handful of hours before.

His hands slid from her waist to her hips, his large hands curling under her, cupping her ass, lifting her up, lifting her thighs, so when he rammed back in again, it was all the way to the womb, stirring places in her that spun at the same high intensity as her clit, not toward a finish, but a completion.

Constance let go of his shoulders, her arms falling above her head, and gave him her complete surrender, using her stomach muscles and the drive of her hips to take his every stroke, match it, suck him deep within, hold him tight as he pulled out. She watched the changes in his handsome face, the gathering of flames there, the awareness of the pinnacle they were reaching, civilized things that were overwhelmed by the power of the male animal charging toward climax. Muscles rippled along his chest and the strength increased as he drove in her again and again. If he did not stand next to the high tester bed, holding tight to her thighs, they'd have been sliding across the mattress with the propulsion of a battering ram against a gateway.

"Sam."

"Come for me, baby," he growled.

"You too," she gasped. "Please…you go, too. This time. I…want…to…feel…you…"

The last syllable was lost as the climax overwhelmed her, exploded down her channel, clenched her pussy hard on his cock. Her fists tangled in the covers and her body bowed up impossibly, her thighs and calves clutching him to her. She heard him groan, felt the hot fluid of him, and her cries escalated with the increased sensitivity and the joy` of it, shared experiences. She wanted it to go on and on, never wanted to return to rational thought, to the dreadful thought of what might come next. There was only now, and Sam.

When the room stopped spinning, there was a stillness within her so strong she felt it vibrate between them, emanate through the room, hold them in its tranquil, soft grasp. She tried to speak and couldn't, tried to lift her arms to touch him but they wouldn't. There was no strength in her, just complete quiet and exhaustion. Three mind-blowing orgasms in such a short time, all she could do was look up at him, form words with no sound.

Touch. Hold. You.

He was braced over her, one arm between her head and shoulder, so she rubbed her temple and cheek against his forearm. He saw her words and his arm slid beneath her waist, turned them carefully so he stayed within her as he shifted them onto the bed and settled himself full upon her, that hard male body warming, protecting and sheltering her own.

Let me lose consciousness before you decide to leave, she thought, *so I can believe you're the most wonderful dream I've ever had.*

He pressed a kiss to her lips, nestled his jaw against her cheek and ear. "Go to sleep, snow angel," he murmured. "I'm right here, inside you, around you. With you."

* * * * *

She was an early riser most mornings, but Christmas was special. It was ironic, since she'd never had anything particular to look forward to on this day. Still, as if the inner child never lost hope, when dawn touched its rosy fingers to her window and caressed her face, she woke to a frosted windowpane and the promise of a sunny, snowy day. A good day for snowball fights and snowmen. To make snow angels.

A breath tickled her ear and remembrance came with awareness. Awareness of a body spooned around her, an arm firmly around her waist, a male palm cupping her bare breast, stroking it.

"Merry Christmas, Constance."

She closed her eyes against the flood of tears and his hand rose, the forearm pressing her back against his chest as he cupped her jaw, stroked her throat until she turned her head up for a kiss. "Christmas is a time to be happy, angel."

"I am. *I am.* Oh, Sam." She turned to her back to look at him as he raised to an elbow, still holding her firmly. "Thank you. Thank you so much. Even if it's only for last night. Thank you."

His eyes darkened. "I'd say too many guys have made sure you keep your expectations low, haven't they?"

Not just men had done that, she knew. Life had. But this holiday was about the miracle of the unexpected. The anger in his expression raised a tiny hope that maybe such a miracle had happened for her.

"I wasn't planning a one-night fuck," he continued, oblivious to the rapid flow of thoughts going through her head, the happiness welling in her. *He was here. He had stayed. And he was furious that she had thought he would do otherwise.* "I never would have come if that was the case. Is that what you wanted, Constance?"

"No," she managed without smiling, though it was very difficult. "No."

"All right then. Let me tell you what I want from you now." He shifted so he was above her, his body sliding over hers, covering her, his knee nudging hers apart, settling himself between them.

She arched with a guttural moan as he eased himself inexorably into tissues well used the night before, but she could see in his face he was making a point. A claim. And those same tissues, though sore, were moistening for him, responding to him in kind. Accepting him, possessing him as much as he was possessing her.

"I want you to let go, Constance, and believe. Isn't that what Christmas is about?"

"Not belief. Faith, Sam."

Her lips did curve now, and his expression eased from determination to sensual heat as she revealed her feelings. He bent and took her lips in a thorough kiss, then slid down her neck to her breast to take one nipple and suckle her.

"Obey me then, Constance," he whispered against her flesh. "Have faith and let go."

The tug of desire and yearning beneath his mouth pounded deep into her heart and she capitulated. She released her fears and opened herself to the miracle of Christmas, the promise of love. To him.

About the author:

Joey W. Hill lives on the Carolina coast with her wonderful husband, a houseful of animals, and their dauntless sailboat, Shadowfax. She is published in two genres, contemporary/epic fantasy and women's erotica, and has won awards for both.

Joey welcomes mail from readers. You can write to her c/o Ellora's Cave Publishing at 1337 Commerce Drive, Suite 13, Stow OH 44224.

Also by Joey W. Hill:

HOT FOR SANTA

Lacey Alexander

DEDICATION

To my editor, Heather Osborn, who totally rocks!

"Would you like to sit on Santa's lap, little girl?"

Would I ever! thought Amy Finnegan.

But, of course, he wasn't talking to her. Forcing a smile, she reached up to straighten her green elf hat, then took the hand of the child in question. Leading the little blonde girl to Santa's throne-like chair, situated in the middle of the mall, she watched the child climb onto one red-clad thigh.

Oh, to be able to lower *her* ass onto that sexy thigh. She wanted to moan at the mere thought. Her breasts tingled against her elf costume just imagining that the man with the fake white beard had summoned *her*.

She bit her lip, envisioning what it would be like if the two of them were alone here, if her sexy Santa invited her to sit on his lap, and if she chose to straddle him in his big red chair instead. Her pussy went damp when she pictured him running his hands up under her little green dress, all the way to her hips to discover she hadn't worn any panties.

Of course, she *had* worn panties, every single day they'd worked together, but since everything else about the vision was pure fantasy, why not go all the way?

When Santa lifted her dress in front, spying her bare slit, all open and ready for him, he'd immediately reach into those fur-trimmed pants of his, pull out his hard cock, and watch as she lowered her hungry little cunt down on it, taking it deep inside.

"You know what?" Santa's deep voice boomed.

Amy flinched as she was yanked from her fantasy, only to find he was still addressing the little girl.

"You're the very last child to tell me what she wants for Christmas this year before I hop in my sleigh tonight and start delivering toys."

The tow-headed girl looked uncertain. "Will you have time to make mine?"

Santa smiled. "Of course I will, with the help of my trusty elf, Amy." He pointed in her direction. "She's my favorite little helper." He sent her a quick wink, and dear God, even *that* made her pussy pulse.

After convincing the little girl she'd get everything on her list, he lowered her to the floor, told her to be good, and—flashing a grin that looked sexy as hell even behind his snowy beard—told her not to forget the cookies, since he'd need a snack by the time he got to her house.

As the child ran off to her waiting mother, Amy saw him glance to the large, ornate clock suspended from the mall's ceiling. Pushing to his booted feet, he took a few steps toward her. When he spoke, it came out a little less hale and hearty than his Santa voice, but the warm tenor of his tone still heated her up inside. "Well, that's the last one. Looks like I can hang up my beard for good."

She tried to sound just as cheerful. "And I can take off my pointy elf shoes for the last time."

She knew she should be happy about that, but she wasn't. She'd never dreamed she could lust so hard for a man in a Santa suit, but now that it was Christmas Eve and their charity work was drawing to a close, a heavy shroud of disappointment settled over her. She'd looked forward to seeing him every day after work for the few hours they did the Santa gig together in the evening. And during the last month, Saturdays and Sundays had become her very favorite days of the week, even if it meant elf detail from ten to ten. Now, as the final last-minute shoppers dashed past and storekeepers began to lower their steel link doors, she couldn't help thinking how boring her nights would seem from this point on, without even the *hope* he would make a move on her. It was going to be a long, cold winter.

"Have I ever mentioned you make a cute elf?"

Amy's heartbeat tripled as she raised her gaze to his. Cole Bradshaw had been her friend for years and the object of her intense desire for a month, and no matter how many signals she'd tried to send out, this was the first time he'd ever said anything even remotely flirtatious. Well, other than the night a year or so ago when they'd been drinking together at a happy hour and he'd started a surprisingly naughty conversation, wondering what sorts of things she'd be willing to do if a guy asked her to. But she'd quickly figured out he was thinking of her as Everywoman on that particular evening, mining her for information about the tastes of the average girl on the street. It clearly hadn't been personal.

Now she smiled and hoped the warmth she felt on her cheeks didn't equate to a blush. Reaching up, she pulled down his beard to take a look at that gorgeous, masculine face of his — all brown eyes and olive complexion, a dark, sexy, two-day stubble on his chin. "You're a pretty hot Santa yourself."

His grin melted through her like warm syrup. "Listen, are you busy tonight?"

What? Had that last signal actually *worked*? It was Christmas Eve, so most people had plans, but given that Amy and Cole were both from out of town and neither had flown home to see their families this year, the question was logical — and oh-so-welcome to her ears. "Um, I'm having dinner with a friend and her husband, but after that..."

He looked utterly enticing when he raised his eyebrows. "Why don't you stop by my place on the way home? I don't have anything happening, and I hate to spend Christmas Eve alone. If nothing else, I'm sure we can at least find *Miracle on 34th Street* somewhere on cable." In a teasing, singsong voice, he added, "I've got eggnog," as if that would be the factor to push her over the edge.

"Sure. Sounds nice. About...ten-ish?"

He nodded. "See you then." As he began to stride away, he stopped and looked back at her with another alluring wink. "As often as you've seen me in this Santa suit lately, I hope you'll still be able to recognize me without it."

* * * * *

In preparation for Amy's arrival, Cole had plugged in the Christmas tree lights, lit a few candles, and built a blazing fire in the hearth. He'd arranged the special gifts he'd bought for her under the tree, and he'd put his Santa hat back on one last time — minus the rest of the outfit.

Now, as he sat waiting for her, glancing down at his raging hard-on, he hoped like hell he hadn't gone too far, been too bold.

But from the moment he'd understood that Amy had a crush on him, he'd wanted her. He'd wanted her in a way that had nearly consumed him. And sure, they could go the usual route, take the path that began with handholding and gentle first kisses — but somehow, with Amy, he'd wanted more than that, from the start. She was sweet as hell, but he couldn't help wondering if...even hoping...that something darker and more feral might lurk inside her, as it did him. And if Amy *didn't* possess a hot, adventurous side, well, maybe if he was lucky, she would before the night came to a close.

Either way, he longed to arouse her in a way she'd never been aroused before. Already, he wanted to be *different* to her — better than any lover she'd ever had. He'd always felt close to her, always wondered if maybe something beyond friendship could grow between them, and now that he was finally going to pursue it, he'd decided to go no holds barred.

He only hoped she'd be as turned on by his game of seduction as he was.

* * * * *

"What did you bring?" asked Amy's best friend, Kelly, over the cell phone wedged tightly against Amy's ear.

"Cookies."

Amy sat outside Cole's townhouse in her car glancing down at the cookie tin on the passenger seat. She'd been nervous, so she'd called Kelly to shore up her confidence.

"Cookies are good. Now, more importantly, what did you wear?"

"Black jeans, red Christmas sweater."

"No, silly. *Underneath*."

"Oh." Amy let out a sigh. "Well, I wore...plain white underwear and a white bra."

Kelly's voice brimmed with her usual dry sarcasm. "That'll really turn him on."

"Look, through my entire elf career, I wore a sexy bra and panty set under my elf suit every single day, just in case he ever started reading my signals and made a move on me."

"And...?"

"And, well, after twenty-eight days of lacy lingerie, I guess I'm officially giving up."

Even if he *had* told her she was cute today.

Even if he *had* invited her over here tonight.

They were friends, after all, so such gestures meant nothing. And although she'd entertained the idea of wearing a sexy teddy beneath her clothes, just in case she was wrong, she'd stopped herself. She couldn't survive feeling the silk and lace rub sensually against her skin all night if nothing was going to happen.

"Giving up?" Kelly spouted. "*Now*? Why would you give up *now*?"

Amy sighed. "Eggnog and an old Christmas movie don't exactly spell seduction, so even if I felt hopeful when he first invited me, I've now drawn the conclusion that it's only a simple act of friendship."

Yep, she was finally getting it through her thick head that *nothing*—sexual, romantic, or otherwise—was going to ensue between them. It didn't matter whether it was because Cole was on the rebound from a recent breakup with a long-time girlfriend or because maybe he just wasn't attracted to Amy. What mattered was that she'd spent over a month in unrequited lust already, and she wasn't the type of girl who liked to waste a lot of time on the chase. Playing hard-to-get had never been a game she enjoyed, either on the giving end or the receiving—she liked to get to the action as soon as possible. So she'd told herself tonight would *not* be about signals or chemistry or those incredibly sexy grins of his; she was simply spending a holiday with a friend. That way she wouldn't have to be disappointed in the end.

"Okay, listen to me," Kelly said. "How long have you known the guy?"

"Four years." She'd met Cole on the job. She'd been new to both Chicago *and* the investment firm where they worked. Although in different departments, the two of them had interacted enough that they'd become fast friends and stayed that way.

"And how long have you been wanting to get horizontal with him?"

"Well, I suppose I've been attracted to him since the beginning, but it's only been the last month that's felt like pure torture. And for your information, it doesn't have to be horizontal. It could be vertical, at a perpendicular angle, or upside down for all I care."

Only when he'd told her about his breakup just before Thanksgiving had Amy truly admitted to herself she thought of him as more than a friend. And when he'd invited her to be his elf, explaining the money from the Santa photos would go to a local charity, her eager acceptance had only proven to her how much she wanted him. Green was hardly her best color, yet she'd jumped at the chance to be his elfin assistant.

"But it's not going to happen," she added, reminding herself as much as Kelly. "And in fact, my Christmas gift to myself is going to be getting over him, and my New Year's resolution is going to be moving on and setting my sights on someone else."

If she could. The truth she didn't tell Kelly was that she couldn't recall the last time she'd had the hots for someone this bad. It was worse when the guy was already a friend, because that instantly turned attraction into something that was about more than just sex. She really cared for Cole.

And if she sat here thinking sappy thoughts like this for even a minute longer, spending the whole evening with him would be pure torture, so before Kelly could come up with a snappy reply, she hurried the conversation to a close. "I have to go."

"Just one question first."

"What?"

"If you've known the guy for four years and been flirting with him for a month, and this is the first time he's ever suggested a private evening for the two of you, don't you think assuming nothing will happen is...a little hasty?"

Maybe Kelly made sense, but Amy couldn't get her hopes up now that she'd found the strength to make the decision to move on. She answered succinctly. "No."

"Well, then, one *more* question. If you're so determined nothing's going to happen tonight, why were you nervous enough to call me?"

Good question. Too good. She answered with a small growl of frustration, speaking through clenched teeth. "I said I have to go. I'll talk to you after Christmas."

With that, she disconnected the call, shoved the phone in her purse, and got out of the car. Despite Kelly's arguments, she was still determined to put the last few wasted weeks of lust behind her, and with that thought firmly in mind, she tucked her cookie tin under one arm and rang Cole's doorbell.

"It's open. Come on in."

Amy sighed. He couldn't even be bothered to answer the door? It solidified her theory that he saw her only as a friend—a very casual, *mi casa es su casa* kind of friend.

Reaching for the knob, she eased the door inward, surprised to find the lighting so dim when she stepped inside.

The first thing she spotted was the fire blazing in the small hearth in his living room—a toasty welcome from the typical Chicago winter dropping snow on the suburbs outside.

The second thing she noticed was Cole sprawling comfortably in an easy chair. *Wearing nothing but his Santa hat.*

Amy sucked in her breath, felt dizzy. What the hell...?

His cock was even more majestic than she'd fantasized, jutting like a stone column up past his navel and onto his washboard stomach. He absently stroked it with one hand, like he might casually pet a cat at his side, and his eyes twinkled brighter than the lights on his Christmas tree when he gazed up at her.

She could only imagine the look of utter shock on her face. Forcing her opened mouth shut, and shoving her cookie tin onto the nearest table before she dropped it, she simply stood and stared.

"Would you like to sit on Santa's lap, little girl?"

Her heartbeat dropped to her cunt, seeming to pound, pound, pound against the crotch of her jeans. Part of her wanted to ask him if she was dreaming. And part of her wanted to make sure he hadn't started on the eggnog without her and forgotten who he'd invited over tonight. But the biggest part of her knew not to look a gift Santa in the cock, so without saying a word, she crossed the floor toward him.

The fire warmed the room, but Amy knew the heat invading her senses came directly from him, emitted from the sexual glimmer in his gaze, the lazy confidence of his pose, the unspoken power radiating from his tremendous hard-on.

Easing down onto his bare thigh was, surprisingly, just as intimidating as it was arousing. Even as a wave of pleasure echoed outward through her pussy and ass, turning her nipples to solid pebbles against her bra, being so close to him and the magnificent erection between his legs felt like cuddling up to a sleeping lion that might awaken and overpower her at any moment. She hoped he couldn't feel her tremble as his arm slid around her waist, as she draped her own around his broad shoulders.

He looked up into her eyes. "What do you want for Christmas, Amy?"

She couldn't resist meeting his gaze, licking her upper lip, and glancing down at his cock. "That."

His seductive smile sent another surge of wetness through her cunt. "Well, Santa would love to let you have it, hard and deep, but first you have to answer a very important question. Have you been naughty or nice?"

The question made her flush with fresh warmth as she let out a giggle and cast him her best playful look. "Well, I'm afraid I've been a very bad little girl lately."

His gaze never wavered. "What have you done that's so bad?"

"For the past month I've been lusting for you, and wearing lace panties underneath my elf dress just hoping you'd peel them off, and thinking incredibly dirty thoughts about you day and night."

His grin managed to stay unerringly sexy even as it turned a little sheepish. "Santa's sorry it took him so long to figure that out."

"And exactly what tipped Santa off?"

"A little birdie named Lisa told me." The woman, also from their office, took the Santa photographs at the mall. Amy had confided in her one day over lunch, and she was suddenly very glad Lisa couldn't keep a secret.

"Unfortunately, though," he went on, his grin fading, "naughty little girls have to be punished before they get what they want for Christmas."

Amy bit her lip. "Punished how?"

A wicked grin took over his expression as he shifted his gaze to the Christmas tree next to the chair. "Santa has some presents for you to open."

Glancing beneath the tree, she saw four gifts, wrapped in elegant red and gold foil. The sight made her suck in a deep breath. It meant this wasn't an impulsive act on his part—he'd been planning it. She looked back to him. "I hate to break it to you, Santa, but gifts don't sound much like punishment."

"You haven't seen the gifts yet."

A thrilling dart of uncertainty shot from her chest down to her womb. She studied his eyes, which were slowly turning from playful to something more serious and forbidding. When next he spoke, his voice was deeper, commanding. "Sit down on the floor, near the gifts."

Amy didn't move. She really liked it just fine where she was—now that she'd grown used to his imposing nude presence, she didn't particularly want to leave his sturdy thigh.

"Do it," he snapped lightly, making her flinch. Her pussy spasmed as she hurriedly rose from his lap and knelt on the floor next to him.

He pointed toward the nearest gift. "Open that one."

It looked like a sweater box, but she had a feeling it contained something much more interesting. Chills of anticipation ran up her arms and down her spine as she slowly unwrapped the gift, finally taking the lid off the box and spreading the tissue paper inside to find a red velvet corset and a pair of red stockings. Despite the lushness of the velvet, the silver clasps that snapped it shut—along with the silver rings on the garters—said it was lingerie designed for obedience.

Her chest tightened with excitement, making it difficult to breathe. He hadn't been kidding about punishing her. It instantly brought back a part of the conversation they'd shared that one intoxicated evening when he'd grilled her on her tastes in bed play.

"How do you feel about domination and submission?" he'd asked.

Before he'd posed the question, she'd never had any interest in it, but imagining it with him had instantly sounded intriguing, so she'd said, "For a guy I really liked, I'd be willing to experiment with it."

So it appeared they'd experiment with it *together*.

Then again, maybe Cole did this all the time. Maybe he'd mastered being a master, which would mean the only person who didn't know for sure what would happen here was her. Another little shiver edged up her spine, radiating outward through her limbs, as she thought, *Don't act nervous, even if you are. Don't be shy or embarrassed. Embrace this.*

"Go put it on." He pointed to the next room.

Her heart pounded a mile a minute as she gathered the corset and stockings, then stepped into his bedroom and turned on a lamp. As she stripped down to her plain white underwear, she glanced in the mirror above his dresser and was suddenly very glad he'd provided the lingerie for the evening.

Shedding her bra and undies, she wrapped the plush corset around her, securing the metal hooks and pulling the laces tight. A perfect fit, the corset accentuated her hourglass shape and thrust her breasts nearly to her chin. The lush velvet barely concealed her nipples and the garment's silky lining rubbed against the taut nubs, making them harder still.

Next she pulled the silken stockings slowly up her legs, attaching them to the garters suspended from the hip-length bustier. It was only as she glanced toward the mirror once more that she realized she hadn't opened a pair of panties to go with the ensemble. Every pore of her body seemed to tighten at the realization. She dropped her gaze in the mirror to her clean-shaven slit, gaping open to reveal her hungry clit and pussy lips. It looked pretty, and oh-so-ready, and she couldn't wait to show it to Cole.

As she began walking toward the living room, the elastic garters slid against her hips and ass, creating a lovely bit of friction on her sensitized skin. The tight corset hugged every curve, clinging deliciously to her stomach, waist, and breasts. By the time she stepped through the doorway, she felt like the ultimate Christmas toy for Cole—and she didn't even need to be unwrapped.

* * * * *

Cole could have sworn his cock grew another inch at the sight of Amy in red velvet. Her honey blonde hair fell in soft waves about her shoulders. Her luscious breasts, before now just shadows of cleavage or mounds hidden beneath sweaters, were on proud display from her rosy areolas up, their ample curves pushed high on her chest. Between the red straps of the garters, her hot, bare pussy glistened for him. He'd never pictured Amy as the kind of girl who would shave her pubic hair, yet only a small tuft of it remained above the naked lips of her sweet cunt.

Every ounce of his body was super-charged with her acquiescence—now he only hoped she'd agree to *all* his requests. He'd spent the last year with the wrong girl, and when Lisa had told him Amy had a crush on him, he'd at first felt dumb as a stump, but just as quickly had been hit with the feeling that she was the *right* girl. For now, and for a lot longer, too. Her compliance with his sensual game so far bolstered that feeling.

He wanted desperately to lower the red velvet and suck on her nipples, wanted to ram his cock deep into her lovely pink pussy. And it would be all too easy to lose control at the very sight of her, but he had to restrain himself. Holding back would bring them both more pleasure in the end, and God, how he wanted to bring her pleasure.

"Very nice," he said, before pointing to another gift. "Now open that one."

He watched intently as she kneeled by the tree and ripped the paper off the next box, discovering a pair of black leather thigh high boots with four-inch heels. Boots made for fucking. Judging from the slight heave of her breasts within their velvet confines and the instant anticipation filling her gaze, she liked them. She glanced at the side of the box, then raised her eyes to his. "How did you know my size?"

"The same way Santa knows what to get for all boys and girls. Magic." Actually, he'd peeked in her bag when she'd bought a new pair of shoes on their lunch break last Saturday.

She offered a soft smile. "What next?" Her voice came out heated, breathy, her excitement beginning to build just like he wanted it to.

"Bring them to me," he instructed.

Taking the tall boots from her hand, he placed one on the floor in front of her. Curling his hand warmly around her nylon-clad calf, he helped her ease her foot down into the soft black leather. With painstaking movements, he tightened the laces, inch by inch, drawing the boot snug to her ankle, calf, thigh. Tying a bow at the top, he lowered his mouth to her thigh, delivering a gentle bite just next to the garter. She let out a light moan that traveled straight to his cock.

He laced her into the other boot in the same slow fashion, aware that she watched his every move, felt his every touch as he bound her into the leather. When he was done, he lifted his gaze to her face. "Walk over to the fireplace. Let me see you."

As she strolled across the room, the tight, high boots made her shapely legs look a mile long. It might be Christmas Eve, but she sizzled hotter than the fourth of July. Pausing by the hearth to let him study her from behind, she wiggled her bare ass ever-so-slightly, then turned and made her way back, her hips swaying, her eyes filled with unmistakable heat. She stopped directly in front of him and he studied the curve of her cunt, as well as the pink clit jutting out, waiting for attention. Attention it wouldn't be getting for a while yet, according to his plan of slow but intense arousal.

Even so, he reached out, unable to resist gently cupping the nude mound in his palm. She shuddered as he raked his fingertips over the ultra-smooth skin. He pulled his hand away and looked up into her crystal blue eyes. "Only bad little girls shave their pussies."

Her gaze was glassy, sexy, expectant. "Then that proves just how bad I am. I should definitely be punished."

Cole pulled his legs together, his cock still standing at full attention, stretching up over his abdomen. "I'm going to have to give you a spanking, naughty little girl. Bend over my knees."

Instantly, he found her soft curves stretched across his thighs, her round ass centered over him as she used the arm of the chair to support her upper body. Damn, just feeling her heat against him sent another furnace blast of excitement to his cock.

"You've got a pretty ass," he said softly, then brought the flat of his hand down hard across one cheek.

She cried out, a sound he perceived as half pain-half pleasure, and the slight sting to his palm echoed up through his arm, down through his torso.

He slapped her ass again, hard, and this time her cry was definitely a hot groan.

"Tell me you're bad," he ordered.

When she didn't respond right away, he struck her ass again. "Tell me."

"Oh, spank me, Santa," she cooed in an utterly sexy voice. "I've been a bad little girl. Spank me hard."

His cock stiffened even further and he rewarded her with more arousing whacks to her lovely ass, where a red mark had begun to appear in the firelight.

"Oooh, yes, spank me! Spank me!"

God, she was hot. So fucking hot that he was sorely tempted to sink his fingers down between the crack of her ass into her wet pussy, more than ready to feel the slick heat of her warm, tight passage—but no, this was supposed to be punishment, after all, and she sounded like she was having far too good of a time. Her pussy would have to wait.

After a few more nice hard slaps to her luscious ass, he stopped abruptly. "Get up."

When she stood before him again, her eyes brimmed with a new fire, a darkness that told him—oh yes—she was having a very good time getting disciplined.

He pointed to another gift, which she knelt beside and began to unwrap, looking as anxious as a kid on Christmas morning. "Oh…" she gasped softly when she saw the red handcuffs and red satin sleep mask—or in this case, holiday bondage mask. Setting the box aside, she rose back to her heels and turned her gaze on him, as if waiting for his next instruction. He had to hold back a satisfied smile at how deeply and easily she'd let herself be drawn into the game.

"Hand me the cuffs, but first turn your back to me and bend over very slowly to get them."

She pivoted away from him and leaned at the waist to pluck up the red handcuffs, giving him a luscious rear view of her pink slit.

"Very nice, baby," he murmured, taking the cuffs from her outstretched hand. "Keep your ass to me and put your hands behind your back." He locked the cuffs around her wrist—one snap, then two—his stomach contracting with the excitement of subduing her. "Now go sit down on the couch."

Her eyes took on a glassy sheen and her cheeks diffused with rosy anticipation as she settled on the nearby sofa, the firelight dappling her skin. Finally rising from his relaxed position in the chair, he picked up the red mask and walked toward her.

"Spread your legs."

She parted her thighs on command and he dropped his gaze to her pretty cunt. She looked so wet that she had to be soaking the couch cushion with her juices. He stepped between her knees and said, "Now move a little closer to the edge."

Sitting up straighter, she inched forward until he commanded, "Stop."

Her face was at eye level with his cock, only a few inches away. Her gaze locked onto his erection and she looked downright hungry. Damn, she really *was* a bad girl. He'd hoped like hell, but had never really believed she would be so into this kind of foreplay. Her hunger and lack of fear got him even hotter.

He slid the satin mask over her eyes, covering them completely. She sat very still, calm, giving her lip a sexy little bite. He wished he had a camera so he could photograph her like this, so he could freeze the vision and keep it forever—his perfect little submissive, just waiting to see what he would demand of her.

"Open your pretty mouth for me, bad girl."

She parted her lips wide, letting her tongue lay lightly on her bottom lip—clearly waiting for his cock. He smiled. Dirty, wicked little girl.

"There's something I want you to taste," he said softly. "Are you ready?"

She nodded, mouth still in perfect cock-sucking position.

Reaching behind him to the coffee table, he picked up the thick candy cane he'd placed there earlier, sliding it slowly onto her waiting tongue. Beneath the red satin, the corners of her mouth turned up in a small grin as a sound of amusement escaped her throat.

He leaned near her, whispering "Suck it for me."

As her lips closed firmly over the stick of candy, his cock jolted. He slid the candy cane deeper into her accepting mouth, once, twice, three times, and when he slowly pulled it back out, she flicked her tongue over the end of it so sensually that he almost felt it at the tip of his erection.

Setting the candy cane aside, Cole reached out, stroking his hands through her hair, repositioning himself so that his cock was dangerously near the heaven of her lips, tinted dark candy red from the peppermint stripes. He heard his own breath come faster as he wrapped his fist around the base of his shaft, nudging the head lightly against her mouth.

She opened for him, but he pulled back, away — punishing himself as much as her.

Her smile gone, she whimpered in frustration.

"You want this, baby?" he purred. "You want this cock in your mouth?"

"Mmm, yes."

He considered teasing her some more, making her work harder, making her beg, but he didn't think his body could take it. So he steadied his hard-on level with her face, then eased it in.

Her moan of delight as her wet lips closed around him made him tremble. Damn, she was good. He slid his cock smoothly, deeply into the recesses of her warm mouth, watching how calm she remained, calm but determined, leaning forward to take even more than he offered. He moaned and pushed deeper, deeper still, until well over half of his erection was buried between those pretty red lips.

He pulled in his breath slightly as a cool, tingling sensation echoed through his hard-on — from the peppermint lingering in her mouth, he supposed. He'd never felt anything like it and it added infinitely to the pleasure rippling through his body.

His cock pulsed like mad, and for a few seconds he thought he might explode, but then she backed off, falling into a warm rhythm, taking it in, sliding back on it, taking it in, sliding back. "Mmm, yeah, baby," he growled. "Just like that."

Just watching her provided nearly as much enjoyment as her mouth did. He'd never seen a woman appear so voracious, yet so submissive at the same time. His long, deep strokes between her lips soon turned into fucking her mouth — gently but thoroughly. He loved her trust — she couldn't see, couldn't touch, but she trusted him not to push too far, not to give her anything she couldn't handle. "You suck my cock so good, baby," he breathed over her.

* * * * *

Amy let his words fill her senses as much as his enormous cock filled her mouth. One part of her could scarcely believe she could even wrap her lips around his thick shaft, let alone take it all the way to her throat, but by the time he'd slid it in, she'd wanted it so damn bad she hadn't even thought about being intimidated by his size. She'd just accepted it, reveled in it, swallowing as much of him as she could.

Not being able to see increased her sense of how big he was as she relished every solid inch that moved in and out of her mouth. Having her arms trapped behind her back was at once frustrating and exciting—it took away her control, yet she *wanted* it that way, wanted him to have as much power over her as he wished, wanted to be his Christmas sex slave.

"Do you want to see, baby? Do you want to see what you're sucking?"

"Mmm," she answered around his big cock, nodding. She enjoyed being blindfolded for him, but if he was offering to let her feast her eyes on him, she couldn't bear to turn it down.

He swept the mask away from her eyes and she spied the tremendous column moving in and out of her mouth. She wished she could take more of him, *all* of him, but he was at least nine or ten hard, beautiful inches. After admiring the sight of his hot cock, all silk over steel, small veins curving around it, she lifted her gaze to his, locking on his eyes while she sucked him. The way he towered over her made her feel all the more like his sex slave.

She would have loved to suck his cock all night, but finally, he withdrew his hands from her hair, his shaft from her mouth, which was suddenly tired and swollen upon his retreat.

She smiled up at him. "How do you want to punish me now, Cole?"

At the use of his name—the first time tonight she'd called him anything but Santa—a flash of unexpected warmth passed through his gaze before his sterner look came back, along with another wicked grin. "Turn around."

Amy sucked in her breath at the request, and then turned her back to him, getting to her knees on the couch. *Fuck me*, she thought. *Please fuck me.* She arched her ass toward him.

But he was only unlocking her handcuffs. Like her mouth, she didn't realize her arms were sore until they were free.

Running one hand smoothly over her ass, he said, "Sit back down."

By the time she did so, he was crossing the room away from her, giving her the chance to see his firm, sexy ass for the first time. He knelt next to the tree, plucking up the last small gift. "One more," he said, returning to place the present in her hand. It looked like a tie box, but smaller. Or a jewelry box, but bigger.

Amy's heart pulsed against her chest as she pulled off the shiny paper and lifted the lid. She gasped at the sight of the red vibrator inside. It seemed to vastly widen the boundaries of what might happen now, making her slightly nervous again, even as a thickening hum of excitement rippled through her body.

"Look at me," he said, his voice deep, unyielding.

Somehow, with the vibrator lying in an open box on her lap, it was a little more challenging to lift her gaze. She forced herself to look up and her breath caught in her throat. A lock of dark hair peeked from beneath the Santa hat, dipping over his forehead. His eyes glimmered with determined lust.

There wasn't anything she wouldn't do for him tonight, nothing she wouldn't let him do to her.

And with that thought, she let go of the last little bit of self-consciousness in her soul and turned the dirty girl loose. "Are you going to put this in my pussy?"

Please say yes. She had to have it now—she thought she would die without it. Her poor cunt felt so empty and neglected.

He shook his head. "This is a punishment, remember?" He quirked a grin. "Even if you *have* liked it so far."

She bit her lip. "Then what are you going to do with it?"

"*I'm* not doing anything with it. *You* are."

He pushed the shiny, smooth phallus into her hand and a fresh frisson of heat trickled down through her body. He wanted her to fuck herself with it while he watched.

Despite her eagerness so far, Amy wasn't usually quite so brazen as she was being with Cole. Any other night in her life, any other man, and she'd have probably said no. But with him, she didn't even hesitate. She was his bad girl. His sex slave. He inspired her to shed all her inhibitions. She *wanted* to fuck herself for him.

So by the time he'd lounged back in his easy chair, still fully erect, she'd lifted one high-heeled boot onto the couch, bending her leg at the knee, giving him a full view of her open pussy.

When she looked down, her slit was gaping, wide and pink, all her folds glistening wet.

Raising her gaze to his, she found his eyes glazed, his expression dark and lustful.

He never said a word; he didn't have to.

Amy twisted the end of the vibrator and a buzzing noise filled the air. Then she poised it at the lips of her cunt.

The smooth red cylinder slid in effortlessly, all the way to the hilt.

"Fuck," he whispered, his expression awe-filled.

Licking her upper lip, she began to move the vibrator in and out of her wet opening. She'd never let a man watch her pleasure herself before and she'd never thought she wanted to, but having his eyes on her made every ounce of her body tingle with delight.

The stimulation inside her pussy filled her with pleasure, but...oooh, her poor clit ached, begging for attention. Using her other hand, she reached down to stroke her middle finger across the protruding pink nub. Mmm, yes—she let out a sigh of relief at her own touch, moaning as the searing heat spread through her cunt and out through her body, her arms, legs. "Oooh, yeah," she purred.

"Baby, you're so damn hot," he said in a low, dangerous voice. "But don't come yet."

She knew from experience she was capable of more than one orgasm. "Why? I need to."

He simply shook his head, a stern warning. "No."

She didn't ask anything more, even as tempted as she was to ignore him and finger herself to ecstasy. She clenched her teeth and forced herself to stop touching her clit—for him. A sound of frustration left her throat, ceasing the sweet pressure on the hungry little nub at this point was pure torture.

"Good girl," Cole said, leaning back a little deeper in his chair. "Now fuck that pretty pussy for me some more."

* * * * *

He could get lost in watching her, Cole thought, in watching that vibrator disappear into her wet pink cunt. Just above where the red shaft sank so deep, her clit jutted out, swelling bigger than it had been when she'd first come out of his bedroom. He wanted to lick it, ease her ache, but not just yet. It was killing him, but in the long run, he knew stretching out her anticipation would bring her deeper pleasure.

Since his own patience was waning, though, he made a split-second decision. "I think you've been disciplined enough, so now I'm going to give you your *real* Christmas present."

She withdrew the red vibrator from her pussy, peering up at him with a sexy smile. "What is it?"

He grinned, and spoke slowly. "A long, hard Christmas fuck."

A look of pure joy stole over her face as she said, "Mmm," then leaned back on the couch, her legs spread for him.

Cole couldn't wait another second, and he couldn't move slowly any longer, either. Each passing moment that he wasn't buried inside her was becoming agony. Pushing up from the chair, he reached the couch in just a few long strides and, positioning himself between her thighs, glanced down. Her beautiful pussy beckoned, parting for him like a pink sea. Her inner lips remained unfolded from the vibrator, her passage a dark opening that needed to be filled with every inch of his hard, burning erection. Without further delay, he shoved his cock deep into her warm, wet cunt, releasing a mighty groan.

When she sobbed beneath him, he stopped, gasping out, "Are you okay?"

"Mmm, yes," she whimpered. "So good, so big."

The words made a smile of sexual pride unfurl across his face. "I'm glad you like it, baby."

"Your big cock is making me crazy," she purred up at him, lifting her hips off the couch to meet his next stroke.

It was all he could do not to growl. "Aw baby, *you* make *me* fucking insane with excitement."

Sliding his hands up the plush velvet at her sides, he closed his fingers over her ample breasts, kneading them through the soft corset.

The firm, massaging touches made her moan deeper, louder, made her pump her pussy against his cock harder. Fuck, she was able to take him so *deep* in that hungry little cunt and he slammed into her with more and more power as she met each solid thrust.

Curling his fingers into the top edge of the velvet, he pulled down slightly, revealing her nipples. God, he instantly wanted to feast on the gorgeous pink beads. Still fucking her, he flicked his tongue over one hard pebble, making her bite her lip as she watched. Then he lowered his mouth fully onto the peak, sucking on it as eagerly as she'd done with his cock. She whimpered and moaned and gripped his hair between her fingers to hold him there as she arched her chest, forcing more of her soft breast into his mouth.

He continued plunging his cock into her juicy opening as she struggled against him, pushing, grinding. He fucked her long and hard and deep, as he'd promised, and he was almost amazed he didn't feel near explosion. He could only assume his promise to her was somehow allowing him to keep control even as intense pleasure blanketed his whole body. And he knew it wouldn't have felt this way if he'd just fucked her from the beginning. Together they were gleaning a deep pleasure wrought from anticipation, from drawing out their lust.

"Fuck me from behind," she pleaded suddenly, her voice gone ragged.

"What?" It caught him off guard. She'd been so obedient up to now, even when he'd insisted she quit fingering her clit. But this new demand from her, when he'd least expected it, sounded good.

"Fuck me from the back! I feel it deeper that way. My pussy feels fuller."

He couldn't help taking advantage of the opportunity. "Beg for what you want."

"Please, Cole, fuck me from behind. *Please!*"

The hot little whimper in her voice was enough for him — hell, who was he kidding; he couldn't have resisted giving her what she desired in that moment if he'd tried. Every ounce of his control had disappeared.

After he drew his cock out, she got to her knees and turned over, bracing herself on the arm of the couch. "Now," she pleaded.

Spreading the cheeks of her ass with his hands, he slid his slick erection back into her warmth.

"Oh God," she moaned at the entry, and he could have sworn her pussy actually took him in deeper this way, seeming to swallow his whole length in a heartbeat.

"Is it good?" he asked, pushing in tight.

"So fucking good," she breathed. And as he placed his hands on her hips and began to move in and out of her warm, deep cunt, she panted, "My g-spot loves your cock, baby."

He could only growl in reply, her words making him pummel her pussy harder.

"Yes! Yes! Fuck me hard!" she shrieked.

He grunted with each harsh stroke he drove into her, loving how well her cunt swallowed him, savoring the way she cried out now with each stiff thrust.

"Oh, God! Faster, faster!"

As Cole fucked her — *slam, slam, slam* — he felt like he'd died and gone to heaven. He'd only dreamed of a girl who loved to fuck the way he did, who loved the intensity, the hard heat, who wanted him to ram his cock into her wet pussy as hard and fast as he could. She was so receptive to him that he wanted to somehow give her more. Glancing down next to his knee on the couch, where she'd abandoned the vibrator, he suddenly knew what else he could offer her.

"You want more, you naughty girl, you?" he whispered near her ear.

"Mmm, yes. Please." She sounded desperate.

Taking up the vibrator even as he continued to slide his cock in and out of her, he slipped the red shaft into his mouth to get it wet, tasting the salty juices her cunt had left behind. Then, using his free hand to part her ass a little more, he positioned the vibrator's blunt point at her tight little hole and slowly began to push it in, using short but firm thrusts.

Beneath him, she let out a moan of surprise. "Oh, are you...are you...?" The tiny fissure began to expand, to accept the tip of the vibrator. She moaned again.

"I'm fucking your ass with our little red toy."

"Oh God." She sounded doubtful. "That thing isn't so little. And I've never..."

"Shhh," he told her. No, it wasn't little, but he thought she could take it. God knew she'd taken everything else. He sensed her body wanting this, needing it, without her even knowing. As if to confirm the thought, her asshole spread a little wider, taking the thickest part of the vibrator inside.

"Oh..." she whimpered beneath him.

"Does it feel good?" He continued gently fucking her pussy even as he pushed the second shaft deeper.

"Mmm...oh God...yes."

Soon he was sliding the vibrator in and out of her sweet little asshole in the same rhythm he fucked her cunt.

* * * * *

The pleasure of being doubly fucked was nearly overwhelming to Amy. She screamed out at each and every thrust, feeling as if her pussy and ass might come apart at any second—but oh God, it was good. She couldn't believe she could endure a double penetration—she'd never been fucked in that opening before and had never expected to be, let alone at the same time a huge cock pierced her cunt.

Pound, pound, pound—the two shafts entered her, filling her beyond all comprehension, making her so weak it was all she could do not to collapse beneath the weight of such heady bliss. And just when she was beginning to wonder how much longer she'd be able to stand the incredibly thorough fuck, Cole pulled his cock out of her.

"Wh-what are you doing?"

His voice was softer than before. "Giving you something you need even worse."

She didn't move an inch, aware he still held the vibrator in place in her ass. It felt strange, new, to have nothing in her pussy, but something so big and prevalent in the opening behind.

Slowly, he maneuvered himself onto his back, continuing to hold the toy inside her, until he slid his head between her thighs. Amazingly, he was still wearing his sexy Santa hat, reminding her of how this delicious holiday seduction had begun.

Smiling up at her, he dragged his tongue across her clit. She flinched, the move driving the vibrator into her ass a little deeper, which sent another jolt of pleasure to the distended nub—God, it was like a sensual game of ping pong in her nether region. She was more prepared for his next lick, though, so she sank into it, pushing her swollen clit into his mouth, no longer nervous about propelling her ass farther onto the vibrator.

"Can you turn it on?" she purred, realizing for the first time that she could have still more sensation back there.

"Oh yeah, baby," he growled, clearly excited by the request, and a second later the shaft came to life, humming pleasantly in her super-tight passage.

Talk about heady pleasure. She had to grit her teeth to withstand the heavy, filling sensations that buzzed through her as he licked her clit and fucked her ass at the same time. She threw herself into it even more, wanting all the joy she could soak up, pushing her pussy against his busy mouth, rocking back against the vibrator in her ass. "Oooh, yeah," she moaned as her asshole clenched around the humming tool.

She looked down into his warm brown eyes as he sucked her clit and found him watching her. She licked her lips while she tweaked her sensitive nipples between her fingertips, sending thick bursts of pleasure through her chest and downward. Reaching to spread her pussy wider for him, she used the first two fingers of one hand while the other hand massaged her weighty breast, still half covered in luxurious velvet. The snug corset moved against her body, making her feel as if she were being caressed *everywhere*.

"Lick me, baby," she whispered. "And keep fucking my ass. I'm getting close. So close." Mmm, yes, the desire was twisting tighter and tighter inside her, hurtling down the delicious path toward satisfaction. "Oh yeah, close, baby," she breathed. "So fucking close. So...oh, God, I'm gonna come. I'm gonna—" A super-charged orgasm like none she'd ever known roared through her, breaking off her words with a tremendous moan. She let out ferocious cries with each hard pulse of a climax that was so strong, so intense and strange, that it was almost painful even as it delivered the ultimate pleasure.

Finally the frenzied contractions waned, leaving her limbs shaky, her body spent, yet...

Oh God, this never happened to her. Never. She was *still* excited. She'd had plenty of multiple orgasms, but it always took a little time to reinitiate her body, to get her pussy hot again. Already now, her cunt was hungry, her clit aching, her entire body humming with electrical currents even though he'd just withdrawn the vibrator. And this new arousal brought with it a fury, a hard craving that overcame her weakness and transformed her into an aggressive animal, a woman who needed more of him and was going to take it. No more little sex slave tonight. Cole had had his fun, his turn at domination— now it was time for her to call the shots.

"Sit up," she said gruffly, backing off of him and grabbing his arms to hurry him along.

The moment he complied, she lifted one knee across his lap and pushed his shoulders back against the sofa. A glance down at his cock revealed he was still thoroughly hard for her, so she wasted no time, rising up on her knees and lowering her needy pussy down onto the engorged shaft.

Oooh, yes—her pleasure compounded with each hard inch she took inside. When she sank her weight onto his hips, swallowing his entire cock into her cunt, the sensation was nearly overwhelming, this particular position making his shaft feel even larger. It was as if he was stretching the boundaries of her pussy, forcing it to accommodate something much bigger than it had ever held before. She clenched her teeth, caught between pleasure and pain, adjusting to the massive pillar impaling her. "So big," she whispered.

"Can you handle it?" His tone conveyed a sexual challenge.

"Of course I can handle it. I love it." And she did. Even if this position took some getting used to with him, she adored his big cock; the mere sight of a tool so large was enough to get her wet, *keep* her wet, *forever*.

Slowly, she started to ride him as her pussy grew accustomed to how immense he felt inside her now. And soon she was rocking, fucking, moving in tight little circles because, that quickly, she sensed another orgasm on the horizon, and her clit was begging her to rub it against the base of his cock. He cupped the sides of her exposed breasts, raking his thumbs across the taut pink nipples as if playing an instrument.

Both of them were panting when she said, "This is just like a fantasy I had, except we were in your big red Santa chair and you had on your Santa suit and I had on my elf dress."

Cole grinned. "That's so hot, baby. But this is better."

"Why?"

His eyes twinkled with mischief. "Because here, I can do this."

She cried out in surprise as the vibrator met her ass again. This time he slipped it in much easier, again filling her in two holes. He began sucking her nipple, drawing it hard into his mouth, as he fucked her ass with the toy and her pussy with his big, beautiful cock.

It was too much, too much sensation to withstand, but on the other hand, maybe it was just enough because—oh yes…oh God! The waves of pleasure broke again, hard and furious, pounding through her like hot heartbeats centered in her cunt. "I'm coming! I'm coming, Cole!"

She rode the climax out, nearly overcome with the way he pleasured all the sensitive spots on her body at once, and this time, when the orgasm faded, she really *was* spent. But she managed to keep riding him, stirred to fuck him even harder when he yelled, "Aw, God, Amy...me, too!"

As he pumped his cock hard up into her, she went still, and when the pulsing sensations vibrated against the inner walls of her cunt, it filled her with a whole new kind of bliss. He groaned with each burst, and she loved having taken him so deep into pleasure.

When his moans diminished to panting, when his body turned still beneath her, she placed her hands on his cheeks and kissed him. Their first kiss.

She had a feeling it would be the first of many.

* * * * *

An hour later, Amy snuggled naked with Cole on the couch beneath a blanket. They nibbled at the cookies she'd brought and drank eggnog while *Miracle on 34th Street* blared from the television in black and white, sending a new glow across the dark room to vie with the firelight.

Setting her glass aside on the coffee table, she cuddled against his broad, sinewy chest. "I'm glad you invited me over for eggnog tonight," she said with a playful smile.

His grin was just as teasing. "Maybe we can do this every year."

"Mmm, a whole new reason to look forward to Christmas."

Cole gave his head a lazy, confident tilt. "Well, maybe it doesn't have to be only at Christmas. As long as you have the urge to be naughty, you can have me all the time."

Beneath the cover, her pussy began to tingle anew. She pulled back from their cozy embrace just enough to brush her beaded nipples against his well-muscled stomach. "I'm getting the urge to be naughty right now."

"Mmm," he moaned, setting aside the tin of cookies. His hand disappeared beneath the blanket to graze Amy's inner thigh. "Do you know how long I've been waiting for a girl who likes playing the kind of game we played tonight?"

She shook her head.

"Too long, baby. Far too long. And to think you were right here all the time. I had no idea how hot and sexy you could be, Amy. But it's the best Christmas present I could possibly get."

She wanted him again, desperately now, so she pulled him into a long, slow kiss, her tongue sparring gently with his as his fingers sank softly into her slit. Her pussy began to swell with delight.

"Do you know what the moral of this story is?" he asked.

She shook her head and watched his grin widen.

"Bad little girls get nothing but Cole for Christmas."

About the author:

Lacey Alexander is the pseudonym of an award-winning author whose romance novels have been published by Harlequin and Kensington. Additionally, over forty of her short stories and articles have seen publication. Lacey lives in Kentucky with her husband of fifteen years and she loves being a full-time writer. When not creating romance and romantica, she enjoys crafts, American history, and travel, and she particularly likes incorporating her favorite destinations into her work. She is an active member of Romance Writers of America and Novelists, Inc.

Lacey welcomes mail from readers. You can write to her c/o Ellora's Cave Publishing at 1337 Commerce Drive, Suite 13, Stow OH 44224.

Also by Lacey Alexander:

Hot In the City: French Quarter
Hot In the City: Key West
Hot In the City: Sin City
Hot For Santa!

ELF SONG

Samantha Winston

"Christmas in the Sugar Plum Fairy's castle has been a magical moment ever since the Sugar Plum Fairy performed a ballet for the Nutcracker Prince. It started when a young mortal girl, Clara, freed Prince Branagh from the Nutcracker spell cast upon him by a wicked magician. Since then, he comes each Christmas to see us perform and to take part in the Christmas feast."

Melle watched as the guests followed Miss Gwen, the dance instructor for the fairy ballet troupe, around the castle. She had overheard Miss Gwen's speech at least a hundred times already, and if she heard it one more time, she would shove a candied apple down Miss Gwen's throat. Miss Gwen had started practicing her speech in August, and by November, most of the people in the kitchen where Melle worked and where Miss Gwen insisted on practicing her speech, wanted to skewer her with a carving knife.

Melle set to work chopping dates. Thank Mistral, Miss Gwen had finally gone out of earshot. Melle's hands flew, and soon the dates lined their trays, ready to be coated with sugar and spices. A glance at the wall showed the date—December twenty-third. The prince would arrive tonight in his sleigh, in secret, as usual.

She'd love to get a glimpse of the prince. She'd never been able to before, always claiming to be too busy in the kitchen with the feast. But this year she'd decided to see him. Those who had, said he put all the men in the castle to shame. She wanted to see for herself. She didn't dare tell anyone though. They would only make fun of her, Melle, the kitchen elf, trying to catch a glimpse of the Nutcracker Prince—a prince from the fairy kingdom, heir to the throne of Hivernia.

Carefully, Melle carried her trays of dates to the drying cupboard and slid them in their holders. Then, looking around to make sure no one saw her, she grabbed her shawl from its hook, slipped out of the back of the cupboard and through the window leading to the pantry. After that, it took only a minute to tiptoe down the holly and ivy-decked hall, across the frosty courtyard, and into the main building.

Bright-leaved holly with red berries hung in gorgeous swaths along the banisters, mistletoe sprigs dangled over doorways, candles dipped in golden glitter lit the hallways, and the castle echoed with Christmas carols and laughter.

The dancers would be in the ballroom, rehearsing with the musicians. The kitchen staff would never miss her, she'd volunteered for clean-up duty, not cooking and serving. Besides, it wasn't as if she got noticed a whole lot.

The Sugar Plum Fairy would be in her quarters, along with her court. From what Melle had heard, the Nutcracker Prince arrived in the evening for the dance, stayed for dinner, then left the next morning at dawn to be at his uncle's palace for the family's traditional Christmas Eve dinner. If she hid in his guest room, she would get her chance.

Her heart pounded and she shivered with fright as she slipped into his room. The poinsettia flowers she'd arranged sat on the mantel. She'd twined holly and ivy together with sugared pears and apples to create a stunning centerpiece on the table. But if anyone caught her in here now, she'd be banished from the palace.

The Nutcracker Prince was a mysterious man, secretive and silent, and his aunt, the Sugar Plum Fairy, had decreed he be left alone. Some said he'd been terribly wounded in his fight against the Mouse King. Others said he'd never gotten over losing Clara—though he'd been just a lad when the adventure had happened. Clara had gone back to her land, and with the evil magician dead, the door had sealed forever between the two worlds. For Clara the adventure had been nothing but a dream, but for the prince it had been a terrible trial, ending with the final battle against the Mouse King. He'd freed the land from the tyrant king's grip, but some said that he'd lost his will to live in the process.

Melle rubbed her head, suddenly tired. The battle had taken its toll on her life too. From archer in the elf militia, she'd gone to assistant cook and maid in the palace. But it had been her choice, a way to get away from the stress of facing her elf kin and seeing her pain reflected on their faces.

Why think of the past at all? She could not call her family back from the dead, why dwell upon the pain? Better to think of the present. She straightened her shoulders and looked around the room. It needed warming.

The winter's chill seeped into the room despite the heavy curtains and thick rugs. So, she would light a fire in the fireplace. Surely the prince would appreciate a cozy fire?

After the fire blazed merrily, she hid behind the curtain, curling up on a cushion in the casement of the window. She wrapped her shawl around her shoulders and cuddled into its softness. The fire's warmth reached her and she yawned, rubbing her eyes to try to stay awake. It seemed too great an effort to keep her eyes open.

* * * * *

Myst and Glyf tossed their narrow, white heads and neighed loudly. They picked up their pace, trotting faster, the sleigh behind them silently gliding through the falling snow.

Branagh lifted his head and peered through the gloom. Although he wouldn't admit it, his shoulder ached painfully, but the sight of the castle appearing out of the gray lifted his spirits. All year long he looked forward to these few days when he left his parents' palace and paid visit to his subjects by himself. Christmas, for him, brought very mixed feelings.

It meant the end of the crippling spell that had frozen him in nutcracker form, the end of the evil magician…and the end of his archenemy, the Mouse King. It had also brought him Clara to whom the evil magician had given him—in his nutcracker form—as a gift. The magician had thought to get rid of Branagh once and for all. But Clara had fallen in love with him and ended the spell. Then he'd gone back to his land and fought the Mouse King and won. Yet when the battle ended, he lost Clara for all time. After the victory celebration and the Christmas festivities, she'd gone back to her world, and he'd stayed in his. Christmas time was a time of joy and sorrow for him, but now, most of all, a time of peace and quiet.

His aunt, the Sugar Plum Fairy, knew more than anyone the hurt he'd suffered at the hands of the Mouse King. She'd tended his wounds and had made Clara and him welcome in her palace after the battle. To hide his infirmity, she made sure that his sleigh arrived in secret by a back entrance to the castle. As his horses trotted under the arched doorway, she stepped out of the shadows and took their reins.

"How are you, my dear boy?" She patted Myst and Glyf, and then pretended not to notice as he stumbled getting out of the sleigh, his bad leg buckling as he stepped down.

He caught Glyf's harness and stayed upright, feeling a hot rush of frustration. A crippled fae prince—was it any wonder he preferred to stay hidden?

"Branagh, I shall take you to your room. Tarquin will care for the horses and Darwi will bring your bags." His aunt turned and strode towards the palace.

Gritting his teeth with the effort, he stretched his stiff legs and followed her into the castle. After a good rest, he would be able to fix his glamour in place. The spell concealed his infirmity and made him appear perfectly normal. But fatigue made it impossible to keep up, so he hurried through the empty hallway to his room. "Thank you, Aunt Serena," he said, taking her hand and kissing it.

"Would you like to come to my rooms and relax for a while? You're here early this year." Her voice ended on a slight questioning note. She'd certainly heard his parents' decree and wanted him to tell her about it.

He adored his mother's sister. But he couldn't talk to anyone about it. Not just yet. "Thank you, I'll rest here. Don't worry about me, I'll be fine."

Her pale, delicate eyebrows lifted, but she said nothing. With a nod, she left for her rooms, which always teemed with giggling young women, flirting courtiers, genteel ladies-in-waiting, and of course, all the most trendy and fashionable people of the land. He'd always felt so out of place at court, even his parents' court. No wonder he'd left in search of his own adventure, and how unfortunate that he should have fallen into the clutches of the evil magician.

He opened the door to his room and stopped. The fire had been lit, and pleasant warmth greeted him. With a contented sigh, he stood and warmed his hands in front of the chimney, feeling the ache in his shoulder and knee subside a bit. A knock sounded, and old Darwi came in with his bags. The elf disappeared into the dressing room to hang up the clothes. Just as quickly he reappeared, threw Branagh a quick glance, nodded in satisfaction towards the fireplace, and left the room. Branagh locked the door behind him to keep out any curious wanderers. With the palace full of guests, best to keep the door locked and the key in a safe place.

Branagh turned back to the fire, and a faint whiff of cinnamon spice caught his nose. Looking around the room for the source, he saw nothing, so he shrugged and went to the bathroom to run a bath. He adored the huge, copper, claw-footed tubs here and the bathrooms were vast, with thick plush towels and wonderful handmade soaps. Not that his own palace lacked refinement, but his aunt took elegance to the limit. Invitations to her Christmas celebrations were coveted throughout the land, and his place of honor in the dance hall was jealously desired.

He peeled off his tunic and shirt, stripped off his boots and leggings and left everything in a heap on the floor. Then he climbed into the tub, sighing as the warm water enveloped him. Steam rose, and in the mirror facing the bath, he saw his reflection. As always, without the glamour, it showed a pale young man with light brown, haunted eyes and a twisted shoulder. With the glamour spell, he became what everyone thought a prince should be—straight as an elm, with a confident gaze and no limp. Here though, he could let his guard down and be himself.

The warm water loosened his muscles and he felt himself relaxing. He rubbed a bit of sandalwood soap onto a cloth and washed his legs and shoulders, and then he knelt and washed his cock. It surprised him by growing heavier in his hands, and a pang of desire made him groan aloud. What he'd give to have a fair maiden kneeling in front of him, oblivious to his wounds, ready to take him into her eager mouth or sex. There came another whiff of cinnamon, and then the sound of the door handle turning quietly.

He paused, and then in silence, he eased out of the tub and peered into his bedroom. There, staring worriedly at the door, stood a small elf woman. She wore elf garb, not as colorful as fairy dresses, but possessing a simple beauty, a shawl the color of night fringed with silver and a dress of forest green, made of softest leather that hugged her breasts and hips before flaring into a long, supple skirt. A sprinkle of sugar on her dress spoke of her job in the kitchens. Her hair caught the firelight and held it in its auburn depths, but he couldn't see her face or tell what she looked like.

What matter? She was there. She'd obviously been sent by his aunt, who knew about a man's needs. But an elf? Far shyer and more serious than fairies, elves seldom strayed from their forest home. Hmm. Perhaps his aunt had a good idea. An elf would be a welcome diversion, and more importantly, an elf would keep his secrets.

He stepped further into the room. "Why keep your clothes on? Take them off now, that I may see you better."

At his voice, Melle whirled around. She'd thought to creep out of the room, but the door had been locked.

She'd woken to the sound of running water. Her heart had nearly stopped. She'd come to see the prince. She just hadn't counted on getting such a good look. But she'd taken a deep breath, tiptoed to the door, and peeked in. The most magnificent man she'd ever seen lay in the steaming water, his hair tousled, his eyes shadowed with fatigue. Then he'd knelt in the tub and taken his cock in his hand, and as it had hardened, her whole body had been hit by a spasm of desire so strong it nearly sent her to her knees. What would it be like to feel that cock sinking into her wet cunt, driving into her body in a hard, steady rhythm until she sang in pure delight?

Reality hit her like a frozen snow bank. A fairy prince, heir to the throne, didn't make love to an elf woman. Bowing her head, she crept to the door and turned the handle. It didn't open. Someone had locked it, and the key was nowhere to be seen. Panic iced her spine—she would be banished for sure! Then a low voice from behind her said, "Why keep your clothes on? Take them off now, that I may see you better."

She froze in her place, staring. He stood, naked, water dripping from his body, the firelight turning his skin to molten gold. Her knees trembled. His deep, purring voice had struck a chord in her. What would it sound like when he cried out in pleasure? Gooseflesh prickled on the back of her neck.

"I said, take your clothes off. Don't be shy. Did my aunt send you?" He smiled and she saw his body waver a bit, as if he tried to cast a glamour spell. A glamour spell? Why would he need one? She saw then that one of his shoulders dipped a bit, as if in pain, and that his right leg sported a vicious scar from knee to ankle.

Lifting her eyes, she noticed he stared at her, his eyes hooded with obvious desire. He didn't look angry at all that she was in his room. In fact, his eyes had a predatory gaze, as if he watched a choice morsel. She lost the power of speech as he approached. Her heart thudded so hard her body shook. Gently, he took her chin in his hands and tipped her head up.

"Such a shy creature you are. No, don't say anything. I prefer silence." He stroked her cheeks with his thumbs, his fingers cupped under her jaw. "What incredible eyes you elves possess. We fairies can be jealous of no one but elves, for you far surpass us in beauty."

Melle gave a start. Who was he fooling, *she, beautiful?* His words fell as if from honeyed lips and, entranced (perhaps she had been caught in a spell!), she tipped her head up for a kiss. She'd never wanted anything as badly — not food, not water, not even sleep. A kiss, she wanted a kiss, and then she would die happy. Her toes curled in anticipation.

A spark danced in his eyes and he bent, brushing her lips with his. At his touch, a shock seemed to leap from his lips to hers. Had he felt it? He gave no sign, but his eyes darkened and his mouth grew soft. A whimper escaped her as her nipples began to tingle and a terrible craving grew in her belly.

He kept his hands on her face, holding her to him, his mouth suddenly more insistent. Her lips parted beneath his probing tongue and she felt his velvety touch as he drew his tongue teasingly along the inside of her lips. He tasted of wintergreen, with a hint of spice and mulled wine. Fire followed his touch, and longing. He moved closer still, and the tip of his penis touched her belly. He hesitated, then pressed it a bit harder, letting her know just exactly what he wanted. Its rounded tip burnt like a firebrand.

Fire burned in his eyes too. Honey-colored in the firelight, they gleamed golden as a lion's eyes and just as hypnotizing. His stare burned into her as he thrust his tongue slowly into her mouth. At the same time, he brought his whole cock into contact with her belly, sliding closer until he pressed against her, thigh against thigh, his thick erection like an iron bar between them.

His tongue found hers and began a subtle dance. Teasing with the tip, he thrust it in and out of her mouth, slowly working it deeper, until their mouths seemed melded together and she couldn't tell where his lips left off, or where her tongue began. Her breath came in gasps now, she felt as if she could hardly breathe. His breathing deepened as well, and his cock flexed against her belly, igniting another fire, this time deep inside her cunt. A spasm shook her, and a surge of wetness flooded her passage.

When he lifted her dress, she moved back and opened her legs to give him access. Her silken shawl slid from her shoulders and pooled at her feet. She kicked off her deerskin moccasins and unbuttoned her dress, pulling her arms out of the sleeves — somehow without letting go of the prince — letting it slip off her hips to the floor. Naked, she stood for a minute, trying to catch her breath. But the sight of Branagh's golden body, glowing incandescent in the firelight, stunned her. Her heart pounded so hard she thought it would crash right out of her chest.

She shouldn't be doing this, but how could she not?

Swiftly, he dipped his hand between her thighs and found her aching cunt. She drew breath with a hiss as his fingers pushed into her slick, swollen flesh. Sharp tingling followed his fingers' movements. He teased her gently, his rough fingertips skimming against her clit until she thought she'd scream. Deeper! She clutched at his wide shoulders, her hands slipping on damp skin, as she tried to press him closer.

He gave a soft moan, and then slid two fingers into her heated passage. An echo of his moan tore out of her belly and rose to her throat. Spasms of longing loosened her muscles to let his fingers in deeper. Faster now he stroked, pressing, searching. Twisting and gently rubbing, as if feeling for the spot that would give her the most pleasure. And...oh yes, there!

A song throbbed behind her lips as his touch sent waves of heat through her body. Molten honey ran through her veins, her body strained towards him, and a shockwave of pleasure shook her from head to toe.

Then he drew a shaky breath and pulled his hand away. As he pulled his fingers out of her body, liquid ran down the insides of her thighs. A primal, musky odor filled the air, along with the scent of sandalwood and cinnamon spice.

An ache of pure emptiness nearly sent her to her knees. Now! She wanted him now! It had been too long, far too long! After her husband had been killed in battle, she'd wanted no one—no one until now. The memory of his lovemaking woke her senses, brought tears to her eyes, and cracked the ice around her heart. Something struggled in the deepest depths of her soul, something desperate to live again, to feel, even if it turned to pain.

She had loved before, and she would love again. The song of the elf swelled in her throat.

He must have sensed her urgency, for with a violent thrust, he plunged his cock between her labia, driving it into her tight passage with two great thrusts.

A cry of sheer pleasure burst from her lips, and she tilted her head back and let herself melt into his strong embrace. His arms held her tightly and he buried his face in her neck as he pounded into her, his hips driving like pistons. Wrapped in his arms, Melle reveled in the sensations rushing through her. His hands, so hard and yet gentle, cupped her buttocks, keeping her in place. He kissed the vulnerable skin of her neck, and his eyelashes brushed her cheek. His cock, long and thick, speared her and withdrew in a steady rhythm, spurring her towards the pinnacle of pleasure. Over and over, he plowed into her, lifting her senses higher, ever higher, until she felt she could go no higher and not shatter.

His cockhead hit her womb with each long, hard plunge into her. Pain merged with pleasure until her muscles clenched, and then a flutter began in her belly. Her cunt pulsated wildly as a blinding orgasm ripped through her and a high, pure note left her throat as she began to sing.

Elf song! The sound wrapped around them and bound them together. Each long spasm in her cunt echoed in a note rising from her throat. Part of her soul left her body in the song, part of her heart. Ripples of music washed over her, shivering down her back and legs, wrapping around their bodies in an almost visible cloak of music.

A small part of her tried to stop it, but the song swelled, grew in force, blinding her with its intensity. All her longing, all her pain and joy at finding a new partner revealed itself in her song, a song unlike any she'd heard since her beloved had died.

Branagh thought his threshold for pleasure had been reached. But that was before this evening. He'd had sex, but not like this. Not without speaking, without hesitating. He'd always felt dissatisfied, even as he accomplished the act. Nothing had ever grabbed him and shaken him as much as this shy, yet uninhibited woman. Her body seemed made for his hands alone, his cock drove into her heated pussy as if guided by fate, her eyes, so cool one minute, blazed with desire the next. She needed no speech, her body spoke for her. Her kisses set him on fire, her lips as sweet as spiced honey. Her hands clutching at his shoulders urged him on, faster, harder.

Coherent thought fled, all sensation gathered in his loins and started to build. Soon, all that mattered was his cock, driving to her womb, and each second, each minute seemed to lengthen and then crystallize, hardening in his loins.

She began to quiver, her cunt clasped his cock in a frantic throbbing... And then she began to sing. Music burst from her throat in a symphony of emotion. The song pulled him into her orgasm, pushed him over the brink. As he spilled his seed into her body, each long, powerful burst of seed accompanied her song. His body and hers became one. He lost himself in her sensations, or rather he joined her. She sang their passion, and the wall he'd so carefully built around him broke with the sharp crackle of shattering ice.

Elf song. He'd never heard it, only rumors of its enchantment. Now he knew the stories to be true. There had been pure joy in that song, yet an echo of pain had shaken his bones. Hot desire surged through his body at the clear notes, and each time he'd ejaculated, the music seemed to draw it out until it lasted forever. When it stopped, she fell beside him, her body shaking, and he slumped onto the floor, too exhausted to stand or keep his glamour in place.

His heart thudded painfully against his chest. What must she think of him, now that she'd seen his deformity? She'd destroyed his defenses in an instant...and yet...in their place a deep peace settled. He gathered the strength to open his eyes, and he saw her staring at him pensively. Stripped of his glamour, he had the impression she weighed him in her gaze. "What is it? Haven't you ever seen a —"

She put her hand lightly over his lips, hushing him. "Why do you use the glamour with me?"

He frowned. Surely she could see that he needed to hide his misshapenness. "A fairy prince must be perfect." He narrowed his eyes. "How did you know I used the glamour? No one else has ever seen me use it."

"Elves can see through glamour. Didn't you know that?"

"No, I didn't." Truth be told, he'd never thought about it. Magic surrounded the fae like the air they breathed. Elves' magic centered on nature, he knew. Other than that, he didn't know too much about elves. They kept to themselves. He turned over and winced as pain shot up his arm.

She gave him a shy smile. "You don't need the glamour, you're quite handsome enough without it. I see how your shoulder pains you. Lie on the bed, and let me rub the ache away. I have not the spell of beauty, but I have good hands and can take away much of your pain. Why did you not ask for help before?" She helped him to his feet and eased him onto the bed.

He lay on his back and she went into the bathroom. He heard the sound of splashing in his bath, and when she came back, she had a towel wrapped around her body and her hair looked damp. She held up a washcloth. "Don't move, let me clean you."

He raised himself on his elbow. "Tell me the truth. My leg and my crooked shoulder don't bother you?" He held his breath.

Now that her haunting song had broken the walls around his heart, he had to know.

"No. They are scars from a battle you won against great odds. You should be proud to show them."

Proud? He'd never thought of it like that. Always the scars had been a humiliation, proof of the indignity he'd suffered at the magician's hands and the fight with the Mouse King. "If I hadn't been so foolish as to leave the palace, the magician would never have captured me. I would have been strong enough to face the Mouse King."

"The story would never have been the same." She slid onto the bed and touched his shoulder then his knee. "You would never have met Clara, and perhaps the battle would have gone otherwise. Your rage to vanquish was tied to your love for Clara. Without it, perhaps you would have lost everything."

"I hear your words in my heart." Unbearable pain mixed with joy. The same notes as in her elf song. They stirred him in a way he thought he'd never be touched again.

Softly she drew the cloth over his belly and thighs, wiping away the signs of their lovemaking. Then she took his cock and tenderly laved it with the wet cloth, stroking it until he found himself hardening again.

She looked at him, her eyes sparkling. "What's this? You're still aroused?"

"You excite me." He gave a lazy grin. "What is your name, elf?"

A shadow seemed to darken her eyes, but she gave a smile. "Melflouise. Everyone calls me Melle." Her voice had a little catch in it, a faint roughness that stirred the hairs on the back of his neck. The sexiest voice he'd ever heard.

"Melle. It suits you. Soft, yet determined. No, don't stop. I want you to make me hard. I want to make love to you again, Melle. I want to love you all over. This time I'll know your name, and I will shout it as I come." He lowered his eyelashes. His heartbeat pounded in his chest and throbbed in his cock.

Her hands must have some magic, for at her touch, it seemed a spark leapt out and touched his head then traveled straight to his cock, stiffening it almost unbearably.

Elves had a wild, enthralling beauty that fairies adored, and their eyes...he could stare at their eyes forever and never grow tired of them. Her dark red hair, cut short, curled around her head. Her pointed ears tempted his hand to caress them, and her full mouth must have been made for..."Suck me," he ordered, raising his hips suggestively. "I want to see your lips on my cock."

She looked at him, and his breath caught in his throat. Such eyes! Melle's eyes were pure gray with frost over them, like the shimmer of snow on dark ice.

"I will be glad to, but first, turn over so that I may ease your pain."

"Fine, but don't tarry, pretty Melle. With each touch of your hands I'll be thinking of your mouth sliding over my cock." He gave a low growl, and then turned over, his hard-on pressing into the bedcovers. He heard the swish of her towel slipping off, and then she slid her thighs on either side of him, settling her naked buttocks on top of his. Her pussy, with its neatly trimmed, curly pubic hair, tickled his ass. He moaned as he suddenly felt the hot touch of her labia brush against his skin as she leaned forward.

"Relax," she breathed in his ear. Her hands rubbed his sore muscles, concentrating mainly on his twisted shoulder, pushing and easing it into place. He knew she could never make it better, but already the constant pain lessened.

"That feels wonderful," he murmured, as her hands kneaded his sore muscles. His cock gave a massive jerk as she pressed her breasts against him, sliding them up and down the top of his shoulders. Her nipples hardened, skimming his back like hot pebbles. As she leaned forward, her legs opened and her damp pussy came in contact with the sensitive skin on his ass. He closed his eyes, imagining his cock sinking into that wet heat.

Shivers trilled down his spine as she scraped her fingernails along his back.

He swallowed hard. He couldn't touch her, his cock was buried in bedcovers, not flesh, and he couldn't even kiss her in this position. He concentrated on her breasts teasing him, her hard nipples like small fingers on his back, and her cunt—hot now, and wet and getting more slippery—as she moved her hips back and forth. He clenched his ass, driving his cock harder into the bed.

"All right," she said, getting up. "Roll over."

He did, his cock pointed stiffly at his belly. He gripped her wrists and pulled her to him. "I want you to suck me."

She knelt between his knees and lowered her head.

"No, not like that. Turn around." He propped a pillow under his head and pulled her hips towards him. "Open your legs. Put one knee on each side of my head."

She did, and now he had a view of her magnificent cunt positioned right over his face. Excellent. He grabbed her ass with both hands and pulled her down to him. With a groan of delight, he thrust his tongue into her cunt, pushing in and out as if using a cock. Her flesh hugged his tongue, and he licked upwards until he felt the little bone-hard protuberance of her clit.

With a little cry of delight, Melle bent forward and took his cock into her mouth. Her lips slid over it, while her tongue tickled the hypersensitive spot right behind the head. She touched his balls with her fingertips, stroking them with light feather-touches. Her nipples drew across his belly and a nerve jumped in his groin. His balls contracted as she tickled, while her hot, hot mouth pulled and sucked his cock. He grabbed the covers in his hands. He had to anchor himself on the bed or he'd fly right off it.

His cock grew harder, and at the same time, juice flooded her pussy, running down his chin. He reached over her buttocks and holding her tightly, used his thumbs to spread her pussy wide open. Her clit stood up, straight and hard. He nibbled on it with his lips, and with the tip of his tongue he thrummed it fast and hard. Pointy, it rubbed against the tip of his tongue, vibrating as she writhed against him. Another rush of liquid honey surged from her pussy, and he lapped it greedily, now thrusting his tongue deep into her passage. Honey and spice, salt and musk—her taste and scent captivated him. More, he wanted even more of her. He wanted to bite her flesh, mark her for his own.

Her lips tightened on his cock and she grabbed its base with both hands while at the same time, she used her tongue in swirling motions while sucking voraciously. The steady pull of her mouth nearly made him lose control. He wanted to explode into her mouth, but not yet, not so soon. First he wanted, no, he needed, to hear her sing.

He flicked her clit with his tongue, and then plunged it deep into her cunt, going back and forth between her tight, throbbing passage and her hard clit. He used his fingers to penetrate her, pushing her up higher so he could watch. Her juices coated his fingers and he nudged his forefinger against the tight rosebud that was her ass. A little cry escaped her, and a new flood of wetness welcomed this touch.

Oh, she liked that did she? He pressed harder, and slipped past the tense ring of muscle. Her ass clamped down on his finger and she uttered another loud moan. An urge to make her his, all his, to possess her in all ways took hold of him. Heat enveloped his finger, a tight, deliciously wicked heat. He pushed harder, encouraging her to accept him. Both passages suddenly relaxed and opened, and his fingers plunged to the hilt. Wild shivers shook him at the sight of his fingers dipping in and out of her slit and her ass nearly pushed him over the edge. He clenched his teeth and managed to contain his orgasm until she leaned hard against him, a wave of pulsations rushing from deep within her and shaking her entire body.

A high note poured from her throat, and vibrated against his penis. Her hands wrapped around him tightly, her mouth fastened to his cockhead, while her song trilled from the tip of his cock the whole length of his body.

Like a crystal glass, broken by the highest note, he burst. Crying her name, he bucked against her, thrusting into her mouth as he came. He poured his seed into her, while she gasped and pressed her cunt even harder against his fingers and mouth.

His whole body shook with the force of his orgasm. It lifted his hips skyward, his muscles straining as he shot stream after stream of his seed into her avid mouth. Greedily she closed her mouth around his jerking cock, milking him dry while he held her cunt firmly to his face, his roar as he came muffled by her swollen flesh.

* * * * *

Chest heaving, he looked at the woman curled by his side. An elf. He'd just had the most incredible sex in his life with an elf. The unexpectedness of it, his sudden devouring passion and her total acceptance stunned him.

She lifted her head and looked at him, her eyes bright. "You are incredible."

"I was just thinking the same about you." He touched her lips gently with his finger. "Such a talented mouth. I can't understand why you're not the toast of the court."

She lowered her eyes. "I have no wish to become the toast of the court. We elves are not like you. We are not as...free with our charms."

Did she regret that, or did she disapprove? He wished he knew. "I know, you think us frivolous and decadent." He shrugged. "But we are all different. I prefer to satisfy my needs in private."

"I would love to satisfy your needs in private whenever you wish." The sparkle had returned to Melle's eyes and he felt absurdly happy. His bubble burst a second later. He had to get ready for the night's entertainment, and regardless of his delight in Melle, there was still his parents' decree.

With a muffled curse, he rolled over and got out of the bed.

"What is the matter? Does your shoulder still hurt you?"

At the mention of his shoulder, Branagh realized he hadn't thought about it, or his glamour spell. The strain of keeping his spell in place had evaporated.

Tentatively, he rotated his shoulder, feeling the muscles loosened and hardly any pain. He looked at Melle, and saw the worry in her eyes. "No, it feels much better, thank you." He paused, and then nodded towards the bathroom. "I have to get ready for the festivities. Would you accompany me tonight?"

A red flush stained her cheeks. "I'm sorry, I cannot."

"Why?" He frowned. Any woman in the palace would be falling over herself in an effort to have an invitation from him. *Oh right, as if you ever wanted to ask anyone.* The only woman since Clara he wanted to accompany him was refusing him.

Had she just slept with him to satisfy her curiosity? A shiver of trepidation ran down his spine. No, he'd felt something with her that he'd never experienced before, and she had sung! But there wasn't time to dwell upon it. He shook his head. "Never mind, you don't have to explain anything. Why don't you stay here though, and I'll rejoin you later, after the fete. Would you like anything to eat? I can have one of the kitchen staff send you something."

"I am kitchen staff," she said dryly. But a smile played about her full lips. "I'll be glad to stay here and keep your bed warm." Her eyes grew dreamy. "I can't believe you want me to stay."

By the snows of Mistral—she had doubts of her own. Doubts he'd have to overcome. "Of course I do." He cocked an eyebrow at her and gave a lascivious grin. "You suit me perfectly, Miss Melle. I'll have to thank my aunt for her Christmas present."

She opened her mouth to speak, but he needed to hurry. "Whatever it is, it will have to wait," he said, entering the bathroom and closing the door behind him.

He washed quickly, then dressed in the clothes he'd hung in the adjacent dressing room. Finest leather pants and a linen shirt, an embroidered, red coat went over that, and then he pulled on his riding boots. No time to fuss with his hair. He hated fuss anyway. He ran his hand through his curls and then as an afterthought, glanced in the mirror.

A tall fae prince stared at him gravely. The lines of pain had vanished from his face, and his eyes had lavender shadows not from suffering, but from a good, long round in the sack. His lips looked faintly swollen from hard kisses, and there was a love-bite on his neck. He grinned at his reflection and shook his head. His grin faded though as he thought of his parents' decree and what it meant for him…and for Melle. His clenched his fist. Damn! Why did he have to meet her now? Why couldn't he have met her years ago, or never?

He turned away from his image and stood for a moment, head bowed. How could he escape a royal command? He couldn't. That's all. He stepped out of the dressing room into his bedroom and gazed at Melle. She slept. Softly, he leaned over and kissed her lips. She didn't stir, even when he drew the covers over her shoulders and put another log in the fire so she wouldn't get cold.

The empty corridors echoed with his footsteps. He hurried, for he must already be late.

The banquet had already started, but his aunt didn't reproach him. As he entered the long dining room, a crier announced him and he stood a moment, to give everyone time to gawk their fill. Guests filled the room, and he recognized most of them. His aunt's table stood on a raised dais, and he saw his two cousins, Rath and Lother, and other important members of his aunt's council there. Who was the stunning fairy woman dressed in purple who sat next to his cousin, Rath?

His aunt patted the chair on her right. "You must have been exhausted. I gave orders not to disturb you. Did you have a good rest?"

A rest? Is that what she called it? He took her hand and kissed it. "Wonderful, thank you."

"This is Princess Yvattia," said his aunt, and he bowed to the beautiful woman on his right.

As usual, everyone stared at him openly, and some waved. He gave a nod towards the guests sitting below and, after shaking hands with everyone at the table and greeting his two handsome cousins, he sat.

"You look tired," said Rath, spearing slices of smoked ham and melon. "Have a good trip?"

Before he could formulate a reply, Lother asked, "How're your parents?"

"Everyone is well. They send their greetings and hope to see you soon." Branagh grinned at Rath. "The trip was hellish, as usual. When are you going to clear out that forest?"

"When hell freezes over." Rath paused, smiling brightly at the princess next to him. "Princess Yvattia is from North Umberland. We've decided to marry, so you'll have to abandon your hermit ways this summer and come to our wedding. I expect you to eat, drink and be merry, and not hide away somewhere all alone." He grinned and reached behind Yvattia to clap Branagh on the back.

Yvattia's sweet smile reminded him of Melle's. "I am so pleased to finally meet you, Prince Branagh. Rath has told me so much about you."

"I'm sure he has. I only hope he didn't scare you too much." Branagh took some melon and tried to look interested as everyone spoke of the latest gossip and festivities. His mind kept straying to the woman he'd left in his bed. He wished she'd have come with him. He would have loved to have her here, at his side, just as Yvattia sat next to Rath.

As the evening wore on, Yvattia and Rath exchanged amorous caresses, and Branagh saw Rath slip his hand beneath her bodice to stroke her breast. Her nipples hardened, poking against the silky, violet cloth, and a flush appeared in her pale cheeks. Rath gave a wicked grin as he saw Branagh watching.

"She's hot as embers," he said. "Watch. She loves to share too."

As soon as he said this, the lights dimmed in the dining hall and soft music started to play. The curtain rose and the ballet started. The troupe pirouetted onto the stage and began the beautiful ballet.

Branagh had his eyes riveted on his cousin, though. He watched Rath as he unfastened Yvattia's robe in order to expose one of her breasts. Her cream-colored skin flushed with pleasure as Rath tweaked her nipple. Her breathing quickened and she moaned softly.

Elsewhere in the room, guests fondled their partners. During dinner, it was never overt,. That would be considered crass. But after dinner, when the lights had dimmed and when the ballet had started, barely stifled sighs and moans sounded among the tinkle of crystal and silverware. Bared breasts were a common sight then, as were guests disappearing beneath the table to pleasure their partners. Hands dipped between spread thighs, cocks sometimes surged out of pants, coaxed by hands or mouth.

Yvattia sighed deeply as Rath's hand vanished below the table. She pushed her chair back, giving Rath clear access and also giving Branagh a view of her legs opened wide. Her dress bunched around her hips as Rath deftly parted her blonde pubic hair and dipped one finger into her swollen cunt. She grabbed his hand and pressed it harder to her. Rath chuckled as he pushed two fingers into her slit and wriggled. Running her tongue over her lips suggestively, Yvattia reached over and grabbed Branagh's hand as well. Rath made room for him, pulling his fingers out of her cunt with a sucking sound.

Branagh, never one to deny a lady pleasure, slid his fingers into her wetness and she moaned and opened her legs wider. "You too, cousin."

Rath joined him, thrusting his finger in and out of her sex, and gave him a wink. "She's about to come," he mouthed.

Branagh could feel it, too. Her clit vibrated beneath his thumb, and the muscles in her passage swelled and tensed. One after the other, they pumped her heated cunt, Branagh pushing in while Rath pulled out. Their fingers slipped and slid together, until Yvattia grasped their wrists and held on. Her hips suddenly jerked and her cunt twitched, then contracted painfully hard around his finger. She uttered a high cry that blended into the sound of the orchestra's flute.

Rath gathered his betrothed into his arms, holding her trembling body to his chest and Branagh turned away to give them some privacy.

"Why Branagh, have you at long last decided to take part in the festivities? And what's this? You've finally decided to let drop your glamour? What happened that made you finally decide to join the land of the living?" His aunt's words may have been teasing, but Branagh heard a definite questioning note in her voice.

He turned and smiled at her. "I have to thank you for that. The elf woman you sent, Melle, is very special. I wish I'd met her sooner." As his words left his mouth he realized how true they were, and a sharp pang of sorrow stabbed him, for they could never be together.

A muscle twitched in his jaw. He'd never see her again. "Why did you send her, if you knew of my father's decree?" He couldn't keep the bitterness out of his voice.

His aunt looked at him and a frown pulled her eyebrows together. "Melle?"

"Yes, Melle. She waited in my room for me." Anger and regret spurred him on. "Why today? Why did she have to come into my life now? You could have introduced us before, or never let her near me."

"An elf?"

"I know. Who would have believed I'd…" He broke off and brought his fist down on the table with a crash. His plate broke in half and the guests looked up as conversation stopped. Shocked silence descended over the dining room, but a red fury submerged him. "I will not follow the decree. As soon as the dinner is over, I'm leaving for home. My father will listen to me." His voice rang out over the crowd.

"Like when you left the first time, only to be captured by the magician?" His aunt, he realized, could snarl as fiercely as an ice bear. She waved her hand and the broken shards disappeared from the table. "It seems you are good at breaking things. But this decree shall not be broken." Embarrassment washed over him, but just for an instant. Then his frustration returned.

"I'm no longer a hot-headed adolescent." He narrowed his eyes. "I *will* have a say in my future."

"But an elf! They have never ruled the fae, they chose the forest, leaving us the responsibility of ruling and protecting this land."

A loud murmur sounded through the crowd and his aunt stood and faced them. "Would you accept an elf as queen?"

Shouts of 'Never!' and 'No!' echoed through the hall.

Heart pounding, Branagh pushed his chair back and stood before the assembly, making no attempt to hide his wounds with the glamour. Icy fury filled him. "Don't belittle her for what she is. The elves fought as bravely as the fae. Besides, her heart belongs to me. By Mistral's snows, by Thaw's flowers, I swear it's true!"

His aunt drummed her nails on the table. Even in the dim light, Branagh could tell his words had upset her.

"What is it?"

"Would you wager your future on that?" She stared at him, her eyes bright with malice. "Would you let me test the elf and find her wanting?"

"What does she have to do?"

"Declare her unconditional love for you, in front of all."

"And if she does?" He leaned over the table, refusing to be intimidated. She might frighten some fae—but he'd fought the Mouse King, and by Mistral, he'd fight her if he had to.

"We summon your parents and challenge the decree."

Could it be possible? Was this a way out of the decree? "Yes. I accept. What do I have to do?"

"Nothing. Wait here." She stood up and left, walking quickly.

Branagh watched her leave, fighting a prickle of unease. She left to go get Melle, and would certainly bring her into the hall. Would his pretty elf fail him? No, he knew she loved him. It had poured out in her song, and his bones still vibrated with it. Truth had been in her song. Now they needed time, time to heal, time to get to know each other. But would his father let them? Could he challenge the decree and win?

"Are you sure of yourself, cousin?" Rath asked worriedly.

"Very sure." Branagh ignored the shocked looks some of the guests gave him and turned back to the ballet. On stage, men and women in filmy garb still twirled and leapt, their movements flowing beautifully in time to the music.

Suddenly, the vast dining hall and stage became dark as the torches, lamps and candles all blew out at once. An uneasy murmur swept the hall. Branagh frowned. What could this be?

A pale glimmer appeared in center stage. It grew in brightness until it showed a room. With a start of surprise, Branagh recognized his room, and in his bed slept Melle. Her face in repose was as pure as an angel's. Another whisper sounded, this time appreciative. Fairies loved beauty, and Melle's naked body curled in the covers made a stunning sight.

As he watched, the door burst open.

"Wake up! Get out of that bed! What do you think you're doing?"

Someone shrieked in her ear, and Melle's eyes flew open. Shock took her voice away, and she sat up, gaping at the Sugar Plum Fairy, sparks of fury in her eyes, standing at the foot of the bed.

"Answer me. Who gave you permission to come into this room?"

Melle clutched the covers to her chest, too horrified to speak. What could she say? Her heart crashed against her ribs and her stomach clenched in fright. "No one," she finally managed to stutter.

"I suppose you think he loves you now," the fairy spat, leaning over so that her nose was inches from Melle's. "Did he tell you what his parents decreed last week? Did he?"

"No." Melle managed a whisper.

"He is to marry the Princess Sapphire on Christmas day."

The words rained upon her like blows, ripping her newfound happiness to shreds. "I never thought he'd marry me, or that he loved me." Melle found her voice and drew herself up, sitting as straight as possible. She would never give the Sugar Plum Fairy the satisfaction of seeing how she'd been hurt by this news. But the fairy's next words stabbed her in the heart.

"Guards, seize her!"

Melle leapt to her feet but too late to escape the three guards. If she'd been in the forest she might have gotten away, but in the room, her feet hampered by covers, she tripped and the guards caught her easily.

"Take her to the dungeon, put her in chains, and give her a lesson she won't forget." The fairy spun on her heels and swept out of the room, her violet robes floating behind her like purple smoke.

Melle kicked and struggled, but the guards remained impassive as they dragged her to the dungeon. The stairwell seemed endless as it spiraled downwards, and the dark made Melle's very soul shrink with fear. Then the guards flung her against a stone wall, and as one held her tightly, the other two fastened iron chains to her wrists.

To all fae, elf and fairy alike, iron stings worse than nettles. Melle shrieked in pain as the iron handcuffs locked in place around her fragile wrists. Then the guards jerked on the chains and she found herself dangling against the wall. She scrabbled to get her feet under her and shivered as the damp stones brushed against her skin.

"A lesson, said the mistress?" One guard laughed as he uncurled a long whip from around his shoulder.

"Give it to her good. She needs to know what suffering is," another guard said.

Melle knew what suffering was. She'd lost her home and her family in the war against the terrible Mouse King—the same king who'd so grievously wounded Branagh. After the war, she'd found a second home in the palace of the Sugar Plum Fairy. She had thought to bury her anguish and sorrow by working in the palace kitchens. But she'd never imagined she'd finish like this.

The whip whistled through the air and a tongue of fire seemed to flay the skin off her buttocks. Melle screamed in pure agony and pulled hard against the chains. Another slash fell, this time across her back. The sting brought a flood of tears to her eyes and ripped another cry of pain from her throat. Twice more the whip fell, each blow stinging like a sword cut.

"That should teach the elf her place," said a guard in a thick voice. He leaned close to her and whispered, "Next time, stick to your own kind." He put his hand on her buttocks, squeezing hard. Then they left her alone in the dark.

She waited until she no longer heard their footsteps then she tried to wriggle out of the chains and handcuffs. It did no good, and the iron hurt more and more each second. Finally she stopped struggling against the chains and tipped her head back.

"I don't care what anyone says," she screamed to the uncaring walls. "I never would have hurt him. I only wanted to ease his pain!" Her voice cracked and her body slumped, her arms cramping in protest against the pain.

"I swear, I love him," she whispered brokenly. "I sang for him. I gave him my elf song." Tears coursed down her cheeks.

Suddenly the chains holding her vanished, and the stone wall turned into smoke and blew away. She found herself in a small room with just one narrow window, a torch burning in a wall sconce, and the Sugar Plum Fairy standing before her. Flickering firelight made her appear menacing.

"What is going on?" Melle rubbed her wrists where a fleeting whisper of pain faded. The pain in her back left her as well, as if the whipping had never taken place.

"My nephew is precious to me." She paced back and forth in front of Melle, her voice as sharp as cut glass. Crimson sparks of anger seemed to follow her swirling robes, and then she stopped and pointed a trembling finger at Melle. "I want only the best for him."

"And I suppose the best would never be me," Melle spat.

"Why should my nephew interest you? Why, you don't even approve of us! You call our festivities licentious and immoral."

"I never..." Melle's voice trailed off. Perhaps she had, on occasion, mentioned fairies' behavior as wanton. Had it been jealousy at seeing the other women's excitement? She blinked away humiliated tears. "No one ever invited me," she whispered, an agony of embarrassment washing through her.

"Probably because you are an elf." The fairy waved her hand dismissively. "My nephew must marry someone who will be an advantage to him and to the kingdom." The Sugar Plum Fairy glared at her, her eyes flashing.

"He can choose for himself, can't he?"

The fairy shook her head. "Alas, no. He is heir to the throne. Have you forgotten?"

Shock rendered Melle speechless for a second. "I'm sorry. I didn't think. Of course, he is prince, not just any man." She knew she spoke the truth. There had never in the history of Hivernia been an elf ruler. And yet, elves and fairies married and had children. They shared many traits and some of the same blood and ancestors. One people had embraced all magic and had become fairies, the other had turned to nature. Her chest felt suddenly hollow, however, she lifted her head proudly and met the Sugar Plum Fairy's gaze. "I will leave the palace. He need never know where I've gone."

"Where will you go, Melflouise? Your family is gone, is it not?" The fairy spoke softly.

"I have distant relatives in the west. They may take me in. If not, I can enroll in the elf guard. Once I was a fair archer."

"I know. You fought bravely, as did your husband and parents during the war…"

"Stop! I beg you, say not another word." Melle stared at the darkness outside. Snow fell, glittering as it fell past the lighted window. She would miss the palace, and Branagh…her heart contracted. How could she leave without a farewell?

"Would you see him one more time?" The fairy's voice was gentle.

"Yes." The word came spontaneously. She blinked, and then nodded slowly. "Yes, I would see him."

The fairy waved her arm in a large circle, and a sphere of light left her fingertips and grew. It lit up the stage, where they stood, and it lit the dining room where a thousand guests sat in stunned silence.

Prickles of consternation rushed over Melle's naked body. Her nipples hardened and her naked skin tingled with gooseflesh, but she stood squarely, her chin lifted in defiance.

A sigh ran through the crowd. In the strange light, everyone's eyes seemed to sparkle like diamonds. Then someone sniffed loudly, another person uttered a muffled sob, and she realized that tears filled their eyes. One by one, they got to their feet.

"Melflouise Fairnight, Archer of the Vinewood militia. Do you love Prince Branagh?" The Sugar Plum Fairy's voice seemed to rock the very foundations of the palace.

"Yes." Melle straightened her shoulders and faced the crowd squarely, seeking the one she loved. She saw him almost immediately. He stood out among all others, his eyes bright, his expression one of wonder. Four disheveled guards held him fast. A rent in his tunic and a cut on his face showed he'd been struggling.

"I had to keep him from leaping to your rescue," the fairy chuckled, nodding to the guards, who stepped back.

"I don't understand." She couldn't tear her eyes from Branagh.

Freed, Branagh leapt over the table and scattered guests in his haste to reach her. Once at her side, he took her in his arms, holding her so tightly she could hardly breathe. "I don't understand either," he said huskily, "but when I saw the guards take hold of you, I nearly went mad." He nuzzled her throat. "I care not that you are not of fairy blood. An elf is what I want, and you are what I need. Melflouise, I love you too. I will give up my throne for you if I must."

A roar sounded from the crowd. "No! Prince Branagh!" At the same time, a clap of thunder flung open the doors. Into the hall strode the king and queen of Hivernia. Snow glittered on their silver-fur cloaks, and around them frost swirled in a shimmering mist. "Give up your throne? I think not." The king's voice raised the hair on the back of Melle's neck. "You will marry Princess Sapphire and forget this woman. She is an elf, and elves have always left ruling to the fairy king. I won't change my decree."

"She is my chosen one," Branagh said, his arms cradling her in a protective circle. "I will not follow your decree and marry the Princess Sapphire. What other choice have I but to abdicate?" An icy wind seemed to chase his words around the vast room.

"So be it. Leave now." The king's voice betrayed no emotion at all, but Melle felt a tremor run through Branagh's body while stunned whispers swept the hall.

"No!" she cried, and tried to pull away. When Branagh would not let her go, she turned to him. "You can't give up your inheritance for me. Let me go, I beg you."

"Never!" His voice stopped her in her tracks. "If you must leave, we leave together."

She'd never been so terrified in her life. Lightning and thunder played about the roof of the hall as father and son faced each other. The guests cowered in their chairs, while the queen rushed to her sister.

"You would leave all this behind?" The king swept his arm wide, and a clap of thunder shook the hall.

"With pleasure." Branagh's voice dripped pure ice. He took Melle's arm and pulled her out of the room, slamming the door behind them.

Once in the empty corridor, Melle twisted out of his grasp. "What are you doing?"

"Did you lie? When the chains bound you and the whip cut your back to ribbons, did you lie?"

She shook her head, tears flying from her eyes. "No. But I can't let you throw away your life for me."

He took her chin in his hand and tipped her head up to his. "Throw it away?" A strange look crossed his face and he shook his head. "Nay, tonight I take my life in my hands and I live it. I stop hiding behind glamour, stop trying to be perfect, someone I am not. You opened my eyes, Melle. I leave now, and you are coming with me."

Melle hardly felt her feet as they walked to his room. While he tossed his clothes into his bag, she found her clothes and put them on—her best dress and her mother's fringed shawl and her archer moccasins, relics of a past life. Dressed, she hesitated. If she ran away now he might stay and claim his rightful place. She had no right taking that away from him. She put her hand on the doorknob.

"Will you leave me, Melle?" She whirled around. His eyes flashed at her. "Well? Will you run away from me?"

Lifting her chin, she met his brooding gaze. "Not if you tell me again you love me. You've said you wanted me, and that you're taking me with you. But do you love me, Branagh? I need to know, because when we cross the threshold, I want to be bound by more than just infatuation and misfortune."

"Fortune's fools," Branagh said, his low voice a shivering caress. "Is that all we are? I think not." He knelt at her feet and took her hand. "Melflouise Fairnight, I love you. I long to hear your elf song again, each night and day of my existence. Will you stay by my side, Melle?"

She closed her eyes. Images of her husband assailed her and the terrible pain of his loss tore a sob from her throat. But in front of her a man knelt who would assuage that pain. She knew it. Her future weighed heavily on her shoulders, but she would trust her own strength. "Yes." One tear slid down her cheek.

"I know how you feel. I too have loved and lost, but that doesn't mean we can't love again... Or that we won't lose again," he added in a quiet voice.

* * * * *

Sparkling gusts of snow, borne upon a harsh wind, stung their faces. Trees leaned, their branches whipping across the sides of the sleigh as Branagh urged the horses faster through the forest. Myst and Glyf picked up their pace, sinking to their knees in the drifts. Clouds scudded across the moon, making shadows to race the sleigh.

"Where are we going?" Melle's eyes gleamed from under her hood in the pale, silvery light cast by the full moon.

"I know of a place with shelter for the horses and we can stay in the sleigh. Tomorrow we'll go north. There are people I know. We can stay with them until I figure out what to do. Rest now."

While Melle dozed, warm and snug in her furs, Branagh guided the horses along a winding path, taking the trail he'd discovered as a youth through the deepest part of the forest. At the foot of a great cliff, a dark cavern beckoned. A cavern was large enough to hold a sleigh and two horses. Branagh always kept fresh fodder and firewood handy, for he stopped here often. He jumped out of the sleigh as they arrived, but Glyf and Myst knew the way and trotted into the echoing cavern. Branagh unharnessed them and spread their hay on the floor. Then he broke the ice in the spring so that they might drink. Afterwards, he built a fire in the hearth, a ring of large stones with two flat ones placed like a bench.

Melle woke then, blinking as the flames lit the cave. "How lovely," she breathed.

It was lovely. Stalactites and stalagmites hung from the ceiling or grew from the floor in glittering splendor. A frozen pool shimmered in the center of the crystal cave, while the firelight warmed the air and cast mysterious shadows into the depths of the cavern.

"Come, sit by the fire." Branagh took her hand to help her out of the sleigh.

The smile that had blossomed in her eyes froze on her face. Glyf and Myst let out terrified neighs and bolted from the cavern. Branagh whirled.

And came face to face with an ice demon, its fangs bared in fury. Taller than a man, the nearly transparent ice demons usually leapt upon their prey and tore them with long, razor-sharp claws. This one snarled, pale blue light running through its strange, icy body. Standing still, they resembled ice statues, but when they moved, their bodies flexed and twisted, as if ice water had suddenly come to life. And they hated fae and elves with a passion.

"Melle, my sword's in the sleigh!" He picked up a rock and hurled it at the creature to keep it back. The demon snarled and lunged towards him, teeth snapping wickedly.

"Here, Branagh!" Melle tossed him his sword and he caught it. The leather-wrapped guard slapped into the palm of his hand and he swung the shining blade at the demon, catching it on the leg. Blue ice-blood spattered from the wound and the demon howled.

"Get out, and don't come back, and I won't have to kill you," Branagh ordered. He didn't think the monster would listen, they never did. You'd think—he dodged another swipe of the creature's claws and slashed its arm—they'd learn. But no, they never quit, they only knew to fight to the death. This one was no different, and it snapped and scratched, eyes shooting sparks of rage, until he could get close enough to deal it a deathblow.

As he cleaved the demon's head off, the beast slashed upwards with a clawed foot. He dodged, but his bad knee buckled, throwing him a hair off balance. Instantly, searing pain exploded in his hand, and ice shot up his arm, freezing his chest. The ice demon died, its body disintegrating into a flurry of ice-crystals, but an ice crystal had lodged in his hand.

Stinging pain blinded him, and chills made it impossible to breathe. He reeled, trying to keep his feet, but the pain drove him to his knees.

Arms held him. A sweet voice called his name, but he saw nothing.

"Melle," he whispered as he sank to the ground. Why did he have to leave her like this? Couldn't the fates have given him another chance? He tried to fight against the blackness and cold, but knives of frost stabbed him, the pain making coherent thought impossible. When the darkness came, he nearly welcomed it. By Mistral, if only he'd been quicker...

* * * * *

Huddled in the sleigh, Melle wished for her bow and arrows, but she'd long since put them away. Why would an ice demon be so close to the palace? She hated those beasts, but hadn't seen any for years. That one came here now boded no good. They kept to the far north, in normal times. What had chased it south? She frowned. Ice demons feared next to nothing. Whatever had driven it from its territory had to be terrible indeed.

Branagh kept it at a distance with his sword—by Mistral he could fight! Her blood sang as he parried and blocked the creature's blows, keeping it on the defensive. Its bite could kill in an instant, and its claws were razor sharp. Poison ran in its veins. Luckily its intelligence was limited, and it snarled and snapped at the sword, while Branagh maneuvered for the kill. The deathblow came unexpectedly, and the creature probably didn't know what had hit it. Its head flew across the cavern, its body exploding in a scintillating shower of frost.

"Well done!" Melle flung herself out of the sleigh and rushed to Branagh's side. "What is it? What's wrong?" Fear laced her words, for Branagh stared at her unseeingly, the color draining from his face. She flung her arms around him, but he staggered, and then fell to his knees. His head lolled against her shoulder. His breathing was labored, and his body shivered uncontrollably.

"What happened?" she begged, cupping his face in her hands. His eyes had turned black with pain and he didn't seem to hear her. Frantic now, she laid him on the cave floor and searched for a wound. His chest and legs seemed fine, and then she caught sight of his sword hand. "No!" she whispered. It had turned blue and when she touched it, cold penetrated her very bones. An ice crystal from the demon had lodged beneath the skin and poisoned his body. She had very little time to save him.

She needed the power of the fire and of the earth united, and as an elf, the magic of nature would help her gather those things. But she needed assistance, and for that she had to call her kin. Were any around? Would they come when summoned? She ran to the cave entrance and sang into the night. "By the stars and by the moon, I call for aid. By the glen and by the grove, I call. By the snow and the frost, I call you this winter's night. I, Melflouise of the Fairnight clan, do summon help."

The words and music would have gone unheard by human ears. But the song rose through the treetops like a harsh winter's wind, like the sound of ice falling from the branches.

Her muscles tensed as she waited, eyes probing the night. Then a slight sound alerted her and she stepped out into the snow to greet three elves that came out of the night like shadows.

"Melflouise Fairnight. Too long has it been since we heard your song," said the tallest elf. His black hair fell like a raven's wing over one eye, for he'd lost it during the war. He put his bow down and hugged her. "Too long has it been, though my pain has not lessened."

"I know, Llewellyn." Melle could hardly bear to see her dead husband's twin, but at the same time her heart sang—he had great powers of healing.

His companions embraced her as well. "We've missed you, sister." Her brothers, Merlin and Sebring, had grown since she'd seen them last, and she realized with a pang how much she'd missed them.

They looked at her warily, and she knew that her leaving had hurt them. She had no time to explain, though she longed to hold them in her arms and tell them everything. "I'm so glad you're here," she said, fighting back tears.

"Why have you called?" Llewellyn asked, his good eye flashing in the starlight.

"Prince Branagh has suffered a wound from an ice demon and I fear for his life."

The three men looked at her, and she saw curiosity in their gazes, but they said nothing. As one, they strode into the cavern and knelt over Branagh's still body.

"Merlin, we will need balsam, and Sebring, you must find wintergreen and a handful of earth from under a yew tree." Llewellyn looked up at Melle. "We may not be able to save him. Someone should go to the palace and warn the fae." He broke off and shook his head. "It will not be easy to explain, and they will not appreciate one of us breaking the bad news."

"I think we'd better try to save him first and bring him back to the palace with us, if we cannot," said Merlin, getting to his feet and putting his bow and quiver on the sleigh. "I saw two horses not far from here; they trembled with fear, but have found shelter in a clearing. I shall fetch the balsam and the horses."

He left without a sound, and Sebring kissed Melle on the cheek and whispered, "Don't worry, we will save your lover. I see how you ache for him. Never fear, Llewellyn will do all that is in his power." Then he too left, slipping out of the cave into the night.

Melle hardly dared look at Llewellyn, just the sight of him hurt. Softly, he touched her shoulder.

"I loved him too," he said gently. "He is gone now, let him go, please. When you left to shut yourself up with the fae, it tore your brothers apart. You were the only one they had left. Now, you must come home. Bring your lover, if you wish. He will be welcome as one of ours."

She nodded, too overcome to speak.

"Your life is with this man now," he said. "Sing for him. He needs you."

Melle's heart lurched at the sight of Branagh. So pale, so cold now. Could they save him? "Earth magic, I summon you," she sang, laying her hands over Branagh's wounds. "Mother Earth, bearer of life, come heal this man." Her voice grew in strength, and then Llewellyn joined her. "Mother Earth, we conjure you."

Sebring came in and put the handful of earth on Branagh's chest. When he pressed upon it, a soft glow emanated from his hands. He placed the branch of wintergreen on Branagh's lips and blew upon it softly.

Tears gathered on Melle's lashes. She sang the healing song, while Llewellyn and Sebring passed their hands over Branagh's body.

Then Merlin came with Myst and Glyf, and the balsam. He singed it in the fire, and laid the burning branch directly on Branagh's hand.

The four elves sang together now, and Melle's heart swelled in gratitude for their goodness and their acceptance of her love. "Fire magic, we beseech you, come and heal this man. By your purifying powers, cleanse the poison from his hand."

The song ended and silence washed over them. Drained, Melle sagged against her brothers' shoulders. They put their arms around her, and heads bowed, they waited while Llewellyn pressed his hands to Branagh and murmured the spells of healing.

When he finished, Llewellyn stood and leaned heavily against the sleigh. His angular face reflected his exhaustion, but he smiled at Melle. "Don't worry, we didn't fail. Look, already your lover's heart beats stronger and his cheeks are flushed with life."

Melle blinked and the tears she'd barely held in check spilled down her cheeks. Branagh's face came sharply into focus. "Greetings from the land of the dead," he said, his voice a mere whisper.

As if she'd been a puppet held up with strings and they'd been cut, Melle slumped over his chest. "Branagh! You're back! Praise Mistral!" She couldn't let go of him, even when he groaned and sat up.

He flung his arms around Melle and squeezed her tightly. "In the darkness, a song called to me and lured me out of the pain. I heard your voice, Melle, and knew I would be saved."

Melle found her breath and leaned back. "Why do you close your eyes, Branagh?"

"Is my hand still there?" He sounded frightened still.

"Yes, can't you feel it?" A pang of worry stabbed her.

He opened his eyes, glanced at his hands, and then grinned crookedly. "I didn't want to look." Flexing his hand, he shook his head. "I was so afraid you'd had to cut it off. That's the only way I know to stop the poison.

"I thank you," he said, looking at her kin. He got to his feet, swayed, and then caught Melle's arm to steady himself. "Prince Branagh at your service. I owe you a great debt."

"I am Llewellyn Fairnight, and these are Melflouise's brothers, Sebring and Merlin Winterhelm."

"I see the resemblance between you and Melle," Branagh told her brothers. "Fairnight? Are you related to Melle then too?"

"Her husband was my twin. How are you feeling now?" Llewellyn asked gravely.

Melle heard the anguish in Llewellyn's voice. He and his twin had practically breathed as one. Even now, he must feel as if half of his body had been cleaved off. But he'd never run off, as she had. He'd stayed, and taken care of her brothers.

Gratitude and shame warred in her mind. But part of her whispered, *you had to leave. Llewellyn has always loved you, and you would have destroyed him had you stayed.* A violent shiver ran through her body.

There. She'd faced it. The true reason she'd had to leave. If only she could make Llewellyn and her brothers understand. But how could she?

Then Branagh's eyes met hers and the warmth and love in them melted the frost in her heart. He was the one for her.

"I'm afraid the poison has chilled me to the bone." He grinned, but it looked strained, and his hand tightened on Melle's.

Llewellyn nodded. "The fire needs more logs, I will get them. Melle, take Branagh to the sleigh and warm him beneath the furs."

"We will take the horses and ride to the palace. Help will be here by daybreak," said Merlin.

"I doubt that—I gave up my title and kingdom for Melle and my father banished me," said Branagh as he crawled into the sleigh. Even though Melle covered him with all the furs he shivered violently.

The three elves looked startled, and then Sebring said, "It won't matter. When he finds out you are hurt, your father will forget his hasty words."

"Besides, strange things are afoot," said Merlin. "The ice demon is only one happening that has caught our attention. The fae will have to listen to the elves for once. Our ears are closer to the forest and we hear much."

Afraid Branagh would take offense, Melle started to admonish her brother, but Branagh kissed her. "Peace," he said. "Your brother speaks the truth. Let them go to the palace. Even if my father won't have me back, he should know about the ice demon and listen to the elves." He broke off, and to Melle's relief, he gave an easy grin. "If you hurry, you'll catch the end of the festivities."

Her brothers leapt onto the horses' backs and without saddle or bridle, streaked off towards the palace. Llewellyn disappeared into the darkness to get more wood, and Branagh pulled Melle into his arms.

"I don't want to let go of you."

"Then don't." She leaned back into his embrace.

"Thank you for saving me." He paused. "Your husband's twin is quite handsome."

"Not as handsome as you." She felt a weight lifting from her soul. She'd loved her husband, but a new life had begun and her love now belonged to the fae prince by her side. "You mustn't be jealous. I love only you."

His eyebrows rose in comic surprise. "Fae are never jealous. I simply made a statement. He is handsome, and you know it. As for loving me, I have no doubts on that subject." He kissed her, his lips lingering on her temple. "You know, coming back from the dead has a strange effect on me." Branagh's voice tickled her ear. At the same time he reached down and stroked her inner thighs. She stiffened, and then let him push her thighs apart with his strong hands. He snuggled deeper into the furs and pulled her buttocks to him. She could feel his hard cock rubbing against her.

"I have a confession to make," he whispered. "I hope you will not think me horrid, but when you hung by your arms, naked in the dungeon, I dreamed I stood behind you holding a whip. When I hit you, you begged for more."

"In your dreams, Branagh." But even as she spoke, thinking about Branagh standing behind her with a whip brought a flood of wetness to her cunt. He drew his finger along the inside of her swollen labia, touching the dampness, and he chuckled.

"Can you feel that?" His erection jutted against his breeches, and Melle swallowed hard as a jolt of heat rocketed through her. She couldn't suppress a moan. Branagh didn't have to ask her. She reached down and undid his pants, releasing his erection. Then, careful not to disturb the covers, she wiggled out of her dress, straddled his thighs and pressed herself down upon him, impaling herself on his hard shaft. The sensation of his flared cockhead sliding into her nearly made her faint—the fae had cockheads that flared enormously when aroused, almost like mushroom caps. She sank to the hilt, and she felt the swollen head hit the back of her womb.

"Can you control the shape?" she asked, trying to speak without moaning in pleasure.

He flexed his thighs, holding her by the waist, driving his cock even further into her body. "I can, yes." His voice sounded no steadier. He gave a shudder, and she felt the tip of his cock swell inside her, scraping the sides of her vagina. Oh by Mistral! His cock, rock-hard and swollen, pulsed with desire inside her cunt.

"More!" she cried, then gasped as the edges of his flared cockhead caught on her ribbed flesh and quivered. Moisture ran down her legs as she creamed with pleasure. She braced her hands on his thighs and moved up and down on his lap, seeking to appease the hunger she felt deep inside her. Melle's breasts ached and a terrible longing grew in her cunt. She wanted him to quicken his pace, and she wanted it to last all night.

Contractions rippled through her belly as she drove herself as hard and as fast as she could up and down his shaft, rocking the sleigh with their movements. Her orgasm pulled a trill of elf song from her throat, but she wanted more. Branagh still thrust into her, and her body still burned with need for him.

"I need to come again," she said, writhing. "Please, make me come again."

"Hush, be still. You won't peak so high. You can't so soon after an orgasm. But I can bring you down slowly, and give you another. Let me show you." He lifted her up off his erection.

As he slid out of her body, she groaned in frustration. Then he turned her around so that she faced the cave entrance. "Relax, let me take you somewhere you haven't been before." Branagh's seductive voice didn't prepare her for the feel of his cock pressed against her anus. Wet with her juices, his cock slid slowly into her body, slipping past the tight ring of muscle before she could even gasp. His cockhead felt smooth and narrower, without the wide flare.

"Now, lean back." Bit by bit, he penetrated her ass, stretching her flesh, until he was fully sheathed within her. Huge waves of excitement threatened to cut off her air supply. She could only whimper as new sensations shook her body from the soles of her feet to the top of her head.

Then Branagh slid his hands down her throat to her breasts. He pinched each nipple, gently pulling on them until they hardened, then one hand dipped between her legs and he drove his fingers deep into her cunt, searching for the place that pleased her most.

The muscles in her vagina grew harder and rippled, and she gave a little cry. There, he'd touched it. His fingers pressed against the ribbed wall inside her, and there came a hard jolt of pleasure just before the tremors started. Her body tightened then relaxed, and a rush of thick liquid surged from her vagina.

Suddenly she caught sight of Llewellyn coming back into the cavern. "Wait, Branagh!"

"I can't." His voice ragged, Branagh clasped her tightly as he came, his seed spurting into her. He buried his face in the crook of her neck, his hands clutching her as his cock jerked, echoing the deep quakes she felt inside her belly. As hot seed surged into her buttocks she had the impression her entire body filled with the essence of her lover.

Another rush of heat flooded her body. All at once, thrumming started in her cunt and spread like wildfire through her veins. Her heart nearly pounded out of her chest, and her vision went black as an orgasm ripped through her like a cyclone. She couldn't stop to save her life. Elf song poured from her throat, fast and furious as her own orgasm submerged her, rising like a giant wave and crashing over her. Long, hard, wrenching shudders ran through her as her voice made the crystal cavern ring with sound. It left her panting and slumped against Branagh's chest like a limp rag while the echo of her song lingered in the cave.

Self-conscious, she raised her eyes and looked at Llewellyn. Instead of the sardonic stare she expected, all she saw in his gaze was a naked longing so intense it knocked the breath out of her. He put the wood down with hands that trembled. Melle felt an answering quiver in her belly.

Branagh pulled out of her and nuzzled her neck. Sliding his hands beneath her bodice, he fondled her breasts. "Llewellyn has quite the hard-on," he whispered. "Aren't you going to put him out of his misery? I expect to share you. It's our way."

"It's not our way, though perhaps someday I will accept your offer." She turned and put her hand to his cheek. "I need to speak with him. Will you be all right here?"

He nodded, his amber eyes shadowed with fatigue. "Go to him. I'll be fine here beneath the furs, where I can still feel the warmth of your love."

She waited until his eyes had closed in sleep, then she wrapped her shawl around her, stepped out of the sleigh and made her way to the fire, where Llewellyn sat, his back to her.

"I know why you left," he said, his voice so quiet it seemed part of the night. He turned to her, his face half in shadow.

"You always faced things head-on. I never could."

He paused, his good eye glittering in the firelight. "You're stronger than all of us. I would have made you miserable, and your brothers were old enough to understand why you had to go."

"Yes, but do they?" Disquiet made her heart pound. "Did you tell them why?"

"That I would have died to make you mine? That I needed you like the air I breathed and the water I drank?" His voice trailed off and he shook his head. His hair swung, revealing the dark hole where his eye had been. "No. I never told anyone. But when Elloran died I only wanted to bring him back. Becoming him was the only way I could imagine.

"I'm sorry I drove you away, Melle. I'll never forgive myself for that. Your brothers came to me, not the other way around. They are like you, too sensitive to others' pain."

"You didn't drive me away. I left because of you, yes, but because of me too. I knew that if I stayed I would have turned to you, and I would have made you into Elloran. You are not Elloran, you are Llewellyn, and deserve a life of your own."

He gave a laugh, or maybe it was a sob. In the flickering light, she couldn't read his expression. "It took me years to understand. Now I am Llewellyn, and the sight of you still feels like a knife in my heart. No," he said, putting his hand on her lips. "It's not like before. Now I see my brother's wife, and I feel his loss. But at least I've come to comprehend I can never bring him back."

"No, we can never bring him back. Nor any of the ones we lost." Melle kissed his hand then held it tightly. "I am so glad you are here, Llewellyn. And seeing my brothers has lightened my heart."

"Love has lightened your heart." He looked down at their fingers, entwined, then gently pulled away. He gave her a crooked smile. "Branagh is a fine man, and you will be very happy together, I can tell. Come as soon as you can. My door will always be open."

"Thank you, Llewellyn. I will. Tell my brothers to expect me before the next full moon. We have much to catch up on."

"Peace, Melle. May Mistral light your way." He got up, stretched like a cat, then left the cavern as quickly and silently as he'd come. The vast cave seemed to echo after he left, as if it too felt his absence keenly.

Melle added more wood to the fire and sat a while. It would take a while for the sharp edges of her emotions to dull, but Llewellyn had set her mind at ease. Though he looked at her with hunger in his eyes, she knew his brother's loss had ceased to torment him. He would heal and find someone else. She sighed and rubbed her eyes. Fatigue made her lightheaded, but peace had stolen into her soul.

She undressed and washed in the spring. Elves might be impervious to cold, but she knew the fae needed their warmth. She dried in front of the fire before crawling into the sleigh and curling up in Branagh's arms.

* * * * *

The sound of hoof beats woke him. He opened his eyes, still groggy with sleep. Furs covered him, Melle lay in his arms, and a faint ache in his hand told him that it hadn't been a dream. His cock stiffened as he remembered Melle's lithe body writhing in pleasure and the tight, hot feel of her ass. But then a trumpet sounded and he sat up instantly awake.

His father stood in the cavern's entrance. Darkness still showed at the mouth of the cave, but Branagh saw that a faint line of gray marked the horizon where the dawn would come.

"I have come to apologize," said his father, before Branagh could utter a sound. "I was wrong to cast you from your home, and if you will forgive me, I wish to..." His voice died away as Melle sat up.

Branagh put his arms around her protectively and kissed her. "Apologies accepted. You owe one to Melle, too. And I won't change my mind. Melle is my chosen one."

Gently but firmly, Melle pushed away from Branagh. Naked, she stood before the ruler of Hivernia.

"I am an elf, and never has an elf taken the throne of Hivernia," she said in a clear voice. "I cannot change what I am, but my love for your prince is part of me now and will never let go of my heart."

His father looked at her, and for a second it seemed a shadow fell over his eyes. But then he nodded gravely and said in a ringing voice, "Melflouise Fairnight, perhaps it is long overdue that an elf sits on our throne. For generations, fairies have ruled this land. We need new blood, strong elf blood. The peace in our kingdom is threatened. Uniting the fae-blood thus can only make us stronger."

Melle looked at him and a faint expression of alarm flickered across her face. "Will you elaborate?"

"Not here. Shadow calls to shadow, and this discussion needs daylight and clear heads." His father shifted on his horse and Branagh saw fatigue etched on his features. He must have ridden all night long to get here.

Branagh stepped from the sleigh, rubbing the soreness from his hand. "We will accompany you to the palace, sire. And we will discuss this when the sun is bright, and shadows aren't listening. Whatever the danger, we will confront it together and win."

"Thank you, son." His father's shoulders slumped and relief flooded his voice.

Melle still stood, her chin lifted proudly. Her strength and kindness shone from her like a bright glow from within. He had no doubts she would make a remarkable queen for his people, and they would grow to love her almost as much as he did.

Branagh took her hand and looked deeply into her eyes. "I love you, Melle, for your courage and your compassion. Will you be my queen? My kingdom needs you, and I need you."

A quiver ran through her body, but her gaze never wavered from his. "Yes."

Branagh wrapped his arms around her, filled with a joy so keen it hurt. He looked towards the future, and all he could see was brightness. The shadows would be chased away by all the fae united.

* * * * *

Melle woke and blinked as the pale light, reflected off sparkling snow, dazzled her eyes. Snow drifted along the windowsills and frost designed glittering arabesques across the glass.

For a second, she forgot where she was, and which day it was. She didn't recognize the rich tapestries hanging on the walls, or the soft flannel sheets hugged to her skin. Then a faint chuckle alerted her and she turned her head. Branagh pulled himself onto his elbow beside her, his face lighting up in a wide grin. "For a minute, I thought it had all been a dream."

"It wasn't though. Last night you gave up your kingdom for me, you fought an ice demon and you nearly died."

He pulled her to him and nuzzled her neck. "But I'm still alive, thanks to you, and you're still here. And someone lit the fire. I bet if we pull the bell rope, someone will bring us breakfast in bed. What do you think?"

"I think it can wait a while." Melle pushed a lock of hair out of his eyes. "You look like a dissolute lion."

"And you look good enough to eat." He leered at her and grabbed her nipple with his mouth, tugging hard.

"Easy tiger." She giggled when he flung the covers back and reared over her. His erection jutted towards her thighs, its tip nearly purple with need. He flared the cockhead out and a rush of hot moisture soaked her cunt. Need, intense and sudden, nearly made her cry out.

"I thought you said lion." Then he gave a growl and pushed her legs apart with his hands. "Lion or tiger, I want you right this second, Melle."

Her cunt gave a massive twinge and she raised her legs, wrapping them around his waist to draw him to her. "Well then hurry!"

He groaned as he thrust into her. "This is going to be a quickie."

"That's fine with me." Already spasms shook her body as his cock stroked into her, its motion almost frantic. He flared his cockhead even more and a mad pulsing began in her belly. "Oh Branagh!" She tossed her head from side to side on the pillow, conscious only of his cock filling her to nearly bursting and the huge tremors rushing through her.

She shot up to the heavens and burst, elf song spilling out into the morning light as her body convulsed around him. Her song joined them in a way more binding than any ceremony and united them forever.

Slowly she floated down to Earth to find herself wrapped in Branagh's arms, his face in the crook of her neck, his breath hot on her throat.

"I think I'm going to die of exhaustion way before our wedding," he said in a hoarse voice.

"When will it be?" Melle opened her eyes. The room had stopped spinning, and her heartbeat slowed to almost normal.

"Tomorrow." Branagh rolled off her and laughed. "Why wait? We'll have a Christmas wedding at the Sugar Plum Fairy's palace, is that all right with you?"

Melle's heart swelled and she lay her head on his shoulder. "A Sugar Plum Fairy Christmas wedding. It sounds like the start of an amazing fairy tale."

Branagh kissed her tenderly on the lips. "Yes, one that ends with 'happily ever after.'"

About the author:

Samantha welcomes mail from readers. You can write to her c/o Ellora's Cave Publishing at 1337 Commerce Drive, Suite 13, Stow OH 44224.

Also by Samantha Winston:

CHRISTMAS ANGEL

Lisa Marie Rice

Naples, Italy
Christmas Eve, 2003

'Guarda o' mare quant'è bello,
Spira tanto sentimento'

Look at the sea, how beautiful it is,
How it moves the heart

-Old Neapolitan Song, Torna a Sorrento

A full moon shone brightly over Mount Vesuvius, casting an exquisite shimmering veil of silver over the Bay of Naples. Cruise ships lit from stem to stern with bright twinkling lights made their stately way across the bay like floating Christmas trees. The moonlight reflected off the calm bay sketched a pearly-white path to forever.

It was the most beautiful sight Nicole Caron had ever seen, and she'd traveled the world and seen her share of them.

The terrace of the French Consulate in the 17th century Palazzo Loredana was right on the bay itself, affording a view of Vesuvius, the bustling brilliant glittering city of Naples and the isle of Capri, a distant glimmer strung out on the horizon like a necklace of diamonds.

It was heartbreakingly beautiful and exactly as Alessandro had described it a year ago in Amman.

She'd laid in bed with him, her head on his broad chest and listened to his deep rumbling voice as he described his Naples.

She hadn't been listening all that closely, to tell the truth. She'd just had the most explosive series of orgasms in her life and any kind of exertion other than breathing and smiling seemed insanely ambitious. Nonetheless, his deep voice was hypnotic as she listened to what he had to say.

Some.

Just enough to get an impression of a glittering city by the bay, beautiful and lively and sparkling.

At the time, Naples had been the last thing on her mind, or what passed for a mind in the time she'd come to think of as 'The Alessandro Period'. Like an art historical period studied in college. From the 17th of December 2002 to the 24th of December 2002.

As historical periods went, it was short. Only a week, but a week that had rocked her world. She'd fallen wildly in love and had been brutally abandoned, all in a week. Seven days.

There was even an Italian film on it. *'Sedotta e Abbandonata'*. *'Seduced and Abandoned'*. 1964, director Pietro Germi. She'd seen it during an art film festival in her sophomore year at Brown, when she'd fancied herself an intellectual, dressing entirely in black, with a dyed white Susan Sontagian streak in her dark hair.

At the time, she'd been so sure of herself. So certain that romantic love was dead, a figment of oppressed female imagination. Modern liberated women didn't *do* love; they did conversation and sex. She'd dated Howard Morgan, another intellectual, that year. They'd spent endless hours talking, going to the movies and having very bad sex.

The last she'd heard, Howard was curator of a major museum in Texas and was on his fourth marriage.

To her surprise, Nicole hadn't stayed in academia. On a whim she'd sat for the Foreign Service exam, aced it, and had found herself in the diplomatic corps at the age of 25. Postings in Haiti, Peru and Jordan had followed. All hard posts. Career makers. With hazardous duty pay and opportunities for advancement.

All in places where a single woman had to watch her step.

Turned out sex and the single girl were unspoken Foreign Service no-nos.

Taking a lover meant—always—a security concern. 'Locals' were generally off limits. Single female foreign service officers were prey—considered by all the other male foreign service officers in the tightly knit diplomatic community a highly prized fuck. A single female officer would never endanger her career by making a fuss over being treated badly and she would be gone in two years, anyway. Which made them targets for all the married scumbags in all the embassies in the entire world.

Sex had been more trouble than it was worth.

Nicole had safely negotiated the shoals of singledom in the Foreign Service, feeling smug about resisting temptation and concentrating on her career, which she wanted to crown with an ambassadorship in twenty years' time. So she'd kept her nose clean and very close to the grindstone.

Until Amman.

Until Alessandro.

He'd caught her in the Christmas season, at a party thrown by the Italian Embassy in Amman. If there was an embassy in the world that could make being in a poverty-stricken, dusty charmless city chic, it was the Italian Embassy.

One step into the premises, after having negotiated three security perimeters in evening dress and stiletto heels, and it was like being in a little dream world designed by Versace. Designer premises, designer clothing, designer food. After spending a 12-hour day negotiating with the Jordanians and Syrians over textile quotas and human rights abuses, Nicole had been ready for some playtime.

She'd arrived alone, as usual. Though there had been offers—an attractive single woman in the diplomatic corps is never without an offer of an escort, especially in Islamic countries—she'd opted to arrive alone, chauffeured by the Embassy driver, an endearing African-American who'd befriended her and whom she suspected was the resident CIA officer.

The food had been good at the Italian Embassy, the wine better, the conversation a little on the insipid side. Nicole had been about ready to call Mike to drive her home when a deep voice behind her had said, "You look exactly like the angel on top of my family's Christmas tree."

She'd turned in surprise and her heart stuttered.

He was gorgeous. Out and out gorgeous, a heartbreaker of a man. Tall, broad-shouldered, dark-haired, dark-eyed. Olive-toned skin, perfect features except for a slightly crooked nose, which saved him from pretty-boy looks.

"I'm not an angel," she replied.

"I'm happy to hear that," he'd said, a deep dent appearing in his cheek, the male equivalent of a dimple. He spoke excellent English with a slight but highly sexy accent. "It makes things more promising."

She'd been taken totally unawares, cut off at the knees by her attraction. She hadn't even noticed time passing until they were the last guests left. They'd talked for five hours straight.

She hadn't called Mike after all. Alessandro had driven her home, followed her right up to her luxurious penthouse apartment paid for by the Embassy and had proceeded to strip her, in between deep, drugging kisses. Then he loved her until dawn, spending almost the entire night inside her.

The next day, Nicole worked in a fog of sleeplessness and sensuality. At moments when she needed to concentrate, she'd be utterly blindsided by a sensory memory. All it took was her blouse brushing against her nipple and she'd suddenly remember—could almost *feel*—Alessandro's mouth tugging at her nipple, licking and sucking. One of her countless orgasms had been from that alone—his mouth on her breast. She'd cross her legs and be instantly reminded of Alessandro's mouth there, too. And then—God!—his penis, talented and tireless.

He was very large and it had been a little uncomfortable the first time. He'd risen up on his elbows and looked down at her in shock, a lock of dark hair falling in a curve over his forehead. "Nicole, *carissima,* you're not — ?"

She'd smiled and shook her head at him. Of course not. She'd gotten rid of her virginity on her seventeenth birthday, on principle.

But Alessandro still hadn't moved. He was deep inside her, huge and hot and burning. His dark eyebrows gathered in a slight frown. "When was the last time you made love, *cara*?"

The question threw her. Though the foreplay had been long and luscious, she was still adjusting to the feel of him inside her, internal muscles working to accommodate him. Tendrils of pleasure were starting to work their way outwards. It was hard to pay attention to what he was saying.

"*Tesoro,*" he'd murmured, pressing more deeply. "When was the last time a man was inside you?" His dark eyes were magnetic; she found it impossible to look away, impossible to remember even one man she'd slept with while looking at Alessandro's fascinating face an inch above hers.

"*Ummm...*" Who was the last man she'd had sex with? No one in Amman, of course. Not in Lima. Not in Porte au Prince. So it must have been while she was taking the Foreign Service exams. That smarmy SEC lawyer, scrawny and hairless, the one who always wore white suits like a cut-rate Tom Wolfe. That was it. The one with a marshmallow for a penis. What was his name?

How could she think of the lawyer's name when her arms could barely reach around Alessandro's broad back? When his dark chest hairs rubbed against her nipples, still wet from his mouth, exciting her almost beyond bearing?

"Six — "

Alessandro rotated his hips and she could feel herself opening even more to him.

"Six years ago," she gasped. "Maybe more."

"*Dio.*" He'd closed his eyes a moment, as if in pain, then started thrusting heavily. She'd climaxed so explosively she'd burst into tears.

She'd never had sex like that. Hadn't known sex like that was possible.

After she'd reassured a frantic Alessandro that they were tears of joy, he'd loved her embarrassment away. All through the night.

She sleepwalked through her duties, waiting impatiently for five o'clock when Alessandro said he'd pick her up.

Sure enough, there he'd been, at the security entrance, waiting for her. Tall, broad, elegant, even more insanely attractive than in her memory.

Alessandro della Torre. All day, she'd run through the few things she knew about him, little snippets of information she'd gleaned between the bouts of soul-shattering sex.

He was 35, four years older than she was, Neapolitan, never been married though he'd come close with the daughter of a family friend. They'd both heaved a sigh of relief when they separated.

He spoke superb English and French and had a smattering of Arabic and Russian. German, he'd confessed with a smile, had eluded him entirely. He'd made her shriek with laughter when he did a deadpan imitation of Fraulein Hupper, an amazingly ugly German teacher.

He had a law degree but had never practiced law, having gone into the Italian Foreign service at 25, the same age she'd entered. He was higher than she was in his country's hierarchy, the deputy Ambassador with a trade portfolio. He was an ardent promoter of his country's food and wine, but thought French literature was better and enjoyed American movies. He liked Italian soccer, American football and English tennis.

At the time, it seemed more than enough knowledge to fall in love, though later, with bitter hindsight, Nicole realized that she never got to know anything else about him. He'd been very sparing with personal details. She knew only the most general facts, what would be available on a CV. She hadn't thought to dig deeper. She had somehow convinced herself he was the love of her life, her soul mate. She thought they'd have the rest of their lives to get to know each other.

And, of course, there was the biggie; the real reason she didn't know more. They'd spent most of their free time in bed. He was such a stupendous fuck, talking was the last thing on her mind.

She used the crude term in her head, to reduce the experience to mere sex. It had helped a lot after the first searing pain had started to subside. When she no longer cried all night, but merely woke up after a restless night with tears drying on her face. When she was able to eat again.

She tried to put it all in perspective in the painful months afterwards, though the parts didn't fit. Angular, jagged memories that didn't mesh at all. The Alessandro she'd known, who'd loved her so thoroughly and so well. And the Alessandro who'd left without a word.

She'd spent every single free second with him after that first incandescent night, most of it in bed, though they hadn't always restricted their sex to the bed. There'd been the kitchen table, her enormous terrace, the bathtub, the huge Persian carpet in the living room.

At times, almost drugged with sex, she wondered dazedly whether she was subconsciously making up for the past few years of enforced celibacy.

The sex had been so overwhelming, she hadn't even realized she'd fallen in love until it was too late.

Alessandro had to be away on the 24th of December, Christmas Eve, which wasn't a holiday anyway in an Islamic country. He said he'd be back that evening. With his suitcases. He was moving in with her.

Christmas Eve found her anxiously preparing a gourmet candlelit meal in her brand-new silk negligee. She hadn't been wearing underwear, which would have been pointless around Alessandro, anyway. He'd ripped several pairs of expensive La Perla panties in his haste to be inside her.

He was supposed to arrive not later than 7:30. She'd been in a frenzy of delight since the late afternoon. Cooking madly, spraying perfume on herself to get rid of the smell of cooking, straightening the cushions, taking another bath, keeping the bathroom door open so she could hear him come in, pacing through the house...

By 9 she'd calmed down a little. Alessandro had been detained, that was it. Though it was very strange that he didn't call to say he'd be late.

The food turned from lukewarm to cold, then congealed.

The candles guttered, then went out.

By midnight she started to get worried and at two in the morning she was sweating with fear. Anything could happen in the Middle East, all of it bad. A car bomb, a terrorist attack, a suicide bomber. She switched on CNN. Nothing unusual. The Internet yielded nothing overtly dangerous, either. Nicole wanted to call Alessandro but realized with a sudden chill she didn't know his home number. Or his address.

His cell phone wasn't on.

By morning, Christmas Day, she was in turn frantic and angry, in a bewildering whiplash of emotions. The Italian Embassy was closed, with only a lowly secretary on duty to answer the phone. She was no help, and indeed, seemed not to recognize Alessandro's name.

Nicole spent Christmas day and the next day in her negligee, compulsively watching TV and checking Google News. When she finally went back to the office on the 27th, she felt as if she'd been in a war, frayed nerves sparking and sputtering.

She must have called the Italian Embassy a dozen times in the next few days. Though Nicole knew for a fact that everyone at the Italian Embassy spoke excellent English, she somehow couldn't manage to communicate with anyone in any meaningful way.

And then the Ambassador, Count Stefano Volpi, called her personally, at home. And in his gentle, aristocratic way, he managed to let her know that there was no Alessandro della Torre working at the Embassy and even if there were…it was better to leave him alone.

Count Volpi's call came on Friday evening and Nicole huddled on her couch with the cordless in her lap for twenty-four hours after that, frozen with shock. The Count's voice had been gentle, but firm, and quite clear in the message he managed to convey.

Don't bother Alessandro again.

How had she got it so wrong? Alessandro hadn't been the love of her life. He'd been a good — very good, incredibly good — fuck. That was all. They'd had a brief affair, and he'd moved on.

Pity Nicole couldn't move on as well.

She became stuck in a groove of grief and sorrow.

Nicole sleepwalked her way through her job. There was a major diplomatic scandal that broke out in the new year, lasting all spring. A ring of low-level diplomats funneling millions of dollars of illegal arms in diplomatic pouches into a region already bristling with arms had been unmasked in a sting operation. There'd been two smugglers uncovered in the U.S. Embassy itself, dozens more in other embassies. Everyone in the Embassy ended up working 12-hour days trying to cope with the fallout.

Nicole did the best she could during the day, then came home to her cold empty flat with no appetite for dinner and knowing she faced a restless and sleepless night.

She lost weight. She would catch colleagues at the Embassy falling silent when she walked by. Though socializing was part of the job, she simply couldn't accept any of the invitations to concerts and receptions a woman in her position received as a matter of rote. There was no lightness in her any more, no ability to chat at a cocktail party.

That summer, Nicole decided she needed to find herself a lover. Maybe what she was mourning wasn't Alessandro but sex. He'd awakened her to her intensely sexual nature, then left her dangling. It hadn't been love, it had been fucking and now she needed to get back into the saddle, as it were.

There was no shortage of candidates. Nicole chose carefully. It couldn't be someone in the diplomatic corps, which would be fouling her own nest. It couldn't be someone who lived in Amman, she wasn't in any way looking for commitment.

She finally found the right man. The physical opposite of Alessandro, too. Medium height, slender, blond and blue-eyed with sharp pale features. David Anderson, a visiting businessman from the Midwest, representing some company that manufactured farm machinery. A big company and he was high up in it. Best of all, he didn't live here. She could have a short affair, fuck another man, get Alessandro out of her mind and body and move on.

Nicole allowed herself to be wooed. David spent several evenings over very expensive meals trying, in the flat nasal tones of the Midwest, to impress her. He was even interesting, in his wholesome way. His eyes lit when, one July evening, she invited him back to her flat for a nightcap.

Nicole was almost angry at David's careful foreplay. She wanted a fast and furious fuck, mindless sex that would make her forget herself and—above all—forget Alessandro.

David was determined to turn it into lovemaking. He was a very good kisser but she didn't want kisses, and she finally just turned her head to avoid them. He tried to arouse her with careful caresses but Nicole didn't want that, either. All she wanted was for him to fuck her, hard, in the dark. The hell with foreplay.

She was relieved when he finally mounted her, kneeing her legs apart.

This was what she wanted. A man's weight on her, a man's penis poised to enter her. Fast, hard fucking.

Except that the shoulders she clutched weren't broad. His chest was almost hairless. When she reached for his penis to guide him to her, he was nicely erect but small and narrow.

He wasn't Alessandro.

Even in the dark, she couldn't pretend he was Alessandro.

Every muscle she had tightened. Her entire body closed in on itself in rejection and David couldn't penetrate.

When David levered himself up on his forearms in surprise, Nicole suddenly pushed him off her and ran into the bathroom. She locked the door, slid down to the floor in the dark and rested her forehead on her knees, shaking with deep tremors. She fought against it, arms crossed tightly around her midriff in an attempt at control, but it was no use. She finally gave in to bitter, helpless tears.

She wept in silence, in the dark, grieving for her lost love, her lost womanhood, her lost soul…

When, finally, she found the courage to go back, swollen-eyed, into the bedroom, David was gone. He'd quietly put his clothes back on and left the madwoman's house.

The next day at work, two-dozen yellow roses arrived for her. Two-dozen yellow roses in Amman in summer were a minor miracle and must have cost a fortune. David's note was short and very sweet: *I'm sorry it didn't work out.*

That was when Nicole realized she had to leave Amman if she was to keep even a scrap of her sanity.

She was due for a new posting anyway. She was high up, with a good reputation, a rising star. She had some leeway in choosing. Friends back at the State Department told her what her choices were: Kabul or Harare.

The choice was clear. Another poor dusty desert Islamic city would only remind her of Alessandro. Better war-torn Africa. She chose Zimbabwe and started boning up on the tormented political history of East Africa.

To her horror, however, when she opened the envelope with her new assignment, she read: Consulate in Naples, Italy. Nothing she could do—phone calls to Washington, increasingly frantic letters, contacting everyone she knew who had some pull at State—none of it made any difference at all.

Though she'd fought the posting with every atom of her being, she fell in love with the city from the first day. She'd landed on an early November morning, sunny and warm, and had spent her first day walking the streets, dazzled at the beauty and liveliness.

Maybe, just maybe, she thought, it would be Naples, of all places, that would heal her wounded spirit.

Certainly this view over the bay was enough to soothe the most troubled soul.

The faint sound of music from the baroque quartet playing in the ballroom filtered out into the terrace, but Nicole had no desire to return to the reception. Though it was Christmas Eve, it was warm outside, a gentle breeze coming off the bay. One of the cruise ships sounded its bass horn and the ferryboat to Ischia answered in a treble toot. She thought she could hear laughter on the wind.

Christmas Eve.

A full year had gone by since Alessandro.

For the first time in a long time, hope stirred faintly in her heart. If she could survive one year, why then she could survive two, three, four. At some point in the future, an entire day would go by without thinking of Alessandro. It wasn't much to look forward to, but it was more than she'd had this past year.

Music billowed out from the big double doors as they opened. So someone else wanted to enjoy the unusually balmy evening. That was fine. It was a big terrace and Nicole knew she carried an aura of solitude about her. No one would bother her. Maybe she'd just spend the whole evening out here. Let the entire diplomatic community get to know her as an eccentric loner.

Footsteps. A man's footsteps behind her. Nicole could feel her back muscles stiffen. Couldn't he see she wanted to be alone?

"*Signora.*" A young man's voice. "*Questo è per Lei.*" This is for you, ma'am.

Nicole turned to see the young waiter in 17th century livery. He was holding a silver salver. On it was a painted wooden angel. Curious, Nicole picked it up and the waiter disappeared.

How odd.

She turned the angel in her hands. In the short time she'd been here, Nicole had realized that Naples specialized in Christmas and nativity scene figures. Entire narrow streets were given over to artisans crafting the lovely figurines of *papier machè* and wood. It was a centuries-old tradition and antique figurines fetched thousands of dollars. The churches had exquisite nativity scenes with hundreds of shepherds and Magis and baby Jesus', three-dimensional works of art.

The angel in her hands was an antique and beautiful, the loving work of an artist craftsman, perfect in every detail, from the lovely oval face to the billowing folds of her white satin gown. Nicole stroked the cheek and smiled.

"I told you she looked just like you," a deep voice said and Nicole froze. As she lifted her eyes, the hairs on the nape of her neck rose. The hands holding the angel started trembling.

She could barely make out the figure in the shadows, but she'd recognize that voice anywhere, even in hell.

"I'm so happy to see you, *cara,*" the deep voice said. Alessandro stepped out of the shadows.

Her fingers were too numb to hold on to the beautiful angel and it slipped from her grasp. A wild wind sounded in her head and her knees buckled.

Alessandro cursed and sprang forward. He'd planned it all so carefully, the setting, the timing. He knew it was going to be tricky, knew he wouldn't have much time to make his case, but he hadn't counted on Nicole fainting.

He caught her just as she fell. He staggered.

She'd lost a lot of weight but so had he. He was barely back on his feet. Though he'd carried her with ease in Amman—had gloried in carrying her in his arms to bed—he could barely manage to hold her now.

But with his dying breath, on his knees, he could carry Nicole.

Nicole was *his*, to love and cherish to the end of time.

He needed a place where they could be private and he knew where. He was familiar with every single inch of the French Consulate. It had been in the della Torre family for two hundred years, named after his great, great, great-grandmother, Loredana della Torre, and had been sold only twenty years ago to the French Foreign Ministry to serve as their Consulate. He knew its nooks and crannies and knew where they could find privacy.

Alessandro carried Nicole into the Sala Della Regina—the Queen's Room. The room where the future Queen of Italy, Margherita, accepted the proposal of the King of Savoy.

There was a Recamier couch, basically a queen-sized bed. He carefully placed Nicole on it, then turned to lock the door. No one would bother them, he knew.

He was sweating with exertion as he returned to Nicole, sliding on his knees by her side.

All his life he'd been strong. His current weakness was a curse, bearable only because it meant he was alive. For too many months he'd hovered in that twilight area between life and death.

"Alessandro?" Nicole whispered. Her eyes moved over his face, unfocused.

"Yes, *amore mio.*" He tenderly moved aside a heavy lock of dark shiny hair to run the back of his forefinger down the side of her face. Her cheekbones were more prominent, the skin more delicate, infinitely pale. She looked fragile. Too fragile.

Together they'd put back on the weight they'd lost over the past horrible year. They'd stuff each other with food in bed. Food and sex, the eternal healers.

Nicole would go back to being the glorious woman he'd first met a year ago in Amman. Nothing, however, would ever turn the clock back for him. He'd carry the scars on his body for the rest of his life.

Nicole blinked, then opened her eyes wide. She had the most beautiful eyes Alessandro had ever seen. Cat's eyes, green and intelligent. She blinked again, awareness returning with every passing second. The expression in those gorgeous eyes turned from bewildered, to astonished, to cool.

"Alessandro. Well. This is a...surprise." Her voice was firm now, and she was trying to sit up.

In a sudden electric rush of understanding, Alessandro knew if she got up now, she'd walk right out of the room and out of his life. He would lose her forever.

No. His entire body rejected the notion. Nicole was his, body and soul. He needed to claim her body as his, now. The hell with explanations, he needed her body. Her soul would follow.

He kissed her. At first to shut her up but, after a second, he lost himself in the kiss.

It had been exactly this way the first time he'd kissed her, in his car outside the Italian Embassy in Amman. It had taken every crumb of self-control not to strip her in his car and make love right there in his Alfa Romeo, like a horny teenager. God knew she made him feel like a horny teenager. He hadn't been deprived of sex at all, yet he had fucked Nicole during the one-week fate had allotted them as if he'd spent the past 20 years alone on a desert island.

He held her head, licking his tongue into her mouth. Her taste hadn't changed.

The first four months, he hadn't been able to eat and had had to be fed with constant IV lines. The memory of the taste of Nicole's mouth had sustained him.

He could feel the warfare going on in her body, mind trying to reject him, heart opening to him.

Yes. Her heart was his, too. All of her was his.

Alessandro deepened the kiss, rejoicing when she returned it. He made love to Nicole's mouth, as he'd made love to her breasts and her butterfly.

Nicole had been charmed when he'd told her that the name used by Italian kids for the female genitalia was *'farfalla'*, butterfly. They'd joked about her butterfly, about how well suited it was to him, about its moods and whimsies.

He knew Nicole's butterfly like he knew his cock. Everything it wanted, everything it desired, what made it purr, what turned it off, what made it tick.

It was ticking now, he could feel it, though he wasn't in her yet.

He wanted to be inside her butterfly as fast as was humanly possible.

Only recently was he able to even think of it. His cock had been dead meat for nine long months. He might as well have had a cylindrical piece of wood between his legs. Then in September, when he was first able to sit up unaided, a very attractive nurse had washed him and his cock had stirred. She'd been an intelligent woman and it amused her. She knew perfectly well that an erection, even a half-assed one, was a major accomplishment for him, a man who should have been dead in the ground nine months before. She'd smiled, given him an extra long swipe over his rising cock and left.

Alessandro hadn't wanted the nurse, he'd wanted Nicole. The erection had been an automatic response of his body, one he wouldn't have given a thought to a year ago. But right then, it had been a fucking miracle. The very first sign that maybe, just maybe, he might be able to get his life and Nicole back.

It was as if the hard-on were a signal that his body was coming back from the near-dead. The next week, he stood up on his own for the first time, and the week after, he started walking. Up and down the hospital corridor, it was true, but walking under his own steam.

That was when he'd first started making plans to get Nicole back, calling in favors. Now that he knew he wasn't going to die, he wasn't going to be a useless, impotent invalid, he could start dreaming again. Hoping and planning to put the shattered pieces of his life back together.

He'd moved mountains to ensure that Nicole be posted to Naples.

The Americans owed him, and he'd made sure they realized it. His former boss had called in favors with them, too.

So Nicole had been in Naples, his city, breathing his same air, for about six weeks now. He hadn't wanted to make his move until he was sure he could stay on his feet for more than an hour at a time.

Right now, he didn't have to be on his feet, he was lying next to Nicole and his cock had sprung to full life. She excited him as no other woman ever had and no other woman ever would.

"*Cara, dolcissima*," he murmured against her mouth. She'd loved it when he spoke Italian to her. He bit, lightly, her lower lip, rejoicing when she shivered.

She'd loved everything he'd ever done to her. Her hot responses drove him wild. She drew in a deep breath to say something and he covered her mouth again.

Now wasn't the time for words. Words would come later, together with explanations. Now was for the magic their bodies could create.

Kissing her deeply, Alessandro lifted Nicole so he could unzip her ball gown, an elegant confection of emerald green silk, the color exactly matching her eyes. Hands trembling, he pulled the bodice off her shoulders and down to her waist. If she wanted to protest, he wouldn't let her. He couldn't release her mouth to save his life.

He could tell by touch that she had on one of her expensive lacy bras, the ones that drove him wild. This one had a front clasp and in a second it fell away. Ah, there she was. Round and—yes!—her nipples were hard. With a trembling hand he moved lower, impatiently tearing away her panties—Nicole should never wear underwear around him—and slid his hand there, where he wanted his cock. Right into her butterfly.

She was wet. Nicole had once confessed that she started getting wet the instant she saw him. Which was a good thing because the first fuck was always frantic. He often remembered about foreplay after he was already in her.

This was going to be one of those times.

After a year's absence, Nicole would want wooing, gentle words, explanations. That would all come later. Now, right now, he needed to be inside her, to claim her and in doing so, to claim his lost life back.

A swipe of his hands and Nicole was naked. He couldn't undress, not yet. Not until he was certain Nicole was his again. He wasn't a pretty sight. He had to be looked at through the eyes of love. So all he did was unzip and open his silk briefs. His cock sprang out.

He held her face still for his kisses while he mounted her. He didn't need to guide his cock into her. It knew where to go all on its own.

Alessandro slid into her, into his own little butterfly. Their lips parted as both exhaled on a soft shaky moan at being together again. He dug his fingers into her scalp, into the mass of fragrant hair and shut his eyes so she wouldn't see the tears.

This was what he'd thought of constantly as he fought death. Being inside Nicole again.

He tasted her mouth, her cheeks, the soft spot behind her ear. He inhaled deeply, the smell of her filling his head. He inhaled again and rotated his cock, feeling every centimeter of her tightly clasped around him.

She hadn't been with another man. He'd have smelled it, felt it.

It had been his deepest dread that she would find someone else. That another man would take his place in her bed, and in her butterfly.

How any man could keep his hands off her, once he saw her, was a mystery to him. He'd been blown away, the first time he saw her at the Embassy Christmas party in Amman. The lovely new *Americana* all the men had been talking about. She carried an aura of remoteness and mystery about her, elegant inside and out, as self contained as a cat.

Discreet inquiries informed him she was unattached and had been for some time. Such a beautiful woman could be unattached only out of choice, because she was picky.

And she was. His beautiful Nicole was finicky and fastidious about everything — what she ate, what she wore, what she read, the music she listened to, who she frequented. It was just one of the many things he found fascinating about her.

Alessandro was a man of instinct. He trusted his head and his heart and his cock and all three proclaimed to him, loud and clear, *this is the one*. They'd only had a week, but he knew he would never be tired of her. She fascinated him on every level there was.

The idea that some other man was with her, talking to her, laughing with her, fucking her, while he was chained to a hospital bed, had kept him awake more than the pain.

He had to be certain, had to hear it from her.

He pressed into her deeply, feeling her sharp hipbones cut into him. Her hips had been soft, generous before. He stroked deeply once, twice, then stopped.

"There hasn't been another man here this past year, has there?" He whispered the words, holding her head tightly. He forced himself to keep his eyes open and on hers.

"No." Nicole's voice was low, steady. Sadness was in her eyes. "I tried, but I couldn't do it."

Her words set him off.

Alessandro closed his eyes in relief, resting his forehead against hers, and started climaxing. He had no control at all over his cock, couldn't hold it back if he tried. His semen jetting into her set Nicole off, too, her little butterfly clutching his cock tightly, milking him.

Alessandro moaned as his hips thrust against hers. There wasn't time for more than a few short strokes and then he had to stop, overwhelmed with the electric climax roaring through him, his entire body pulsing in time with his cock.

He simply rode it out, letting it wipe his mind clear, rejoicing in his first orgasm in a year.

It didn't matter that he'd come immediately. It just meant that he would slide in and out of Nicole more easily from then on. He smiled against her hair. His love had a small little butterfly and the second time they always found it easier for him to fuck her, once his seed was in her.

Nicole's contractions were slowing, her breathing slowing, too, though he could feel her heart hammering under her breast.

It was okay. He breathed deeply, joy coursing through him. It was okay. He was alive and had his manhood back. Even after coming, he was still hard, so his cock worked again.

He could function as a man and he had Nicole back.

Everything was going to be all right from this moment on.

Alessandro finally raised his head to smile down at Nicole and met her cool green eyes.

"Well, that was fun." She pushed at his shoulder. "Now get off me."

* * * * *

Nicole wanted to weep. Her lower body was still climaxing. She could feel herself clenching tightly, rhythmically around Alessandro, who was almost larger than in her memory. He hadn't even bothered to make love with skill, as she knew he could, regulating his strokes, following her rhythms. He hadn't had to. Just seeing him had awakened nerves she'd thought dead. Her vagina — what he'd delighted in calling her 'butterfly' — had no pride at all where Alessandro was concerned. Her orgasm would go on for long minutes, though he'd done nothing to merit it. She felt the spasms of orgasm as if they were remote arcane aspects of her body, having nothing to do with her.

Her lower body was welcoming Alessandro back. Her mind was screaming — you fool!

It was like being torn in two.

Was this to be her future then? For the rest of her days, she'd live celibate and alone, sad and empty, waiting for Alessandro to walk in and out of her life as he pleased. She'd spend a year mourning him, then he'd show up and fuck her and she'd be stupidly grateful and then he'd leave again.

Repeat cycle.

It didn't bear thinking about.

She was still climaxing when she pushed again at his shoulder. "Didn't you hear me? Get off me. *Now.*"

Alessandro was looking down at her, face blank with shock. "What did you say?"

Well of course he was surprised. Bimbos didn't say no, did they? They were grateful for every second The Great Man was fucking them.

She took a deep breath. "I. Said. Get. *Off.*"

He clutched her hips and moved upwards with his penis, in short strokes that touched some secret spot only he had ever found.

Pleasure spiked through her, insidious, burning, electric, her body's curse. Tears sprang into her eyes as she tried to twist her hips to get away from him. She couldn't, of course.

"Be still," Alessandro murmured. He held her hips harder, pumped more quickly. Nicole could feel herself moving quickly into another orgasm. She burned with humiliation, as if she was a cheap whore and he had a ten-dollar bill in his hand.

Her thighs started trembling. She had to stop him, had to, before she came again.

"There's a name for this," she said coldly, holding his eyes. "And it isn't a pretty one."

Alessandro's jaw muscles bunched. "This isn't rape and you know it, *cara*."

"It is when the woman doesn't want it."

Something hot flashed in his dark eyes. "You don't want it?" The tempo of his hips increased, he did something that moved the heavy base of his penis directly against her clitoris and thrust hard. Nicole was caught in the grip of a wild burning storm, shaken from the inside out by the force of her climax. She cried out, her entire world reduced to her body, to her vagina and Alessandro inside her. The contractions went on and on as he kept pumping. She was helpless to stop it; it was as if some malign entity had taken over her body.

She didn't want this. She didn't want to respond to Alessandro as if she was a lock and he was the key. The only key.

She had just now started finding some measure of peace and serenity in her heart and he was breaking it all over again.

To her utter horror, Nicole burst into tears.

"*Tesoro*," Alessandro murmured. She tried to evade him, but he held her head still for his kiss. He kissed her mouth, her closed eyelids, the tears from her cheeks. "*Carissima, amore mio, non piangere.*"

Don't cry, he was saying.

He was right. She mustn't—she daren't—cry. Crying showed weakness and she was far too vulnerable to him. She shut her eyes tightly, biting down on her lips, willing the tears away. She'd shed far too many tears for him, anyway.

It was so hard to think with him on top of her. He was still making love to her, his penis sliding in and out, much more deeply now. He'd shot so much semen into her they were making wet sounds and were probably staining the yellow satin of the couch. They smelled, too, the particular smell of her Diorissima, his soap and their sex. The smells of Amman.

She'd tried pushing at him and twisting her hips. Now she'd try her tongue.

"If you think you can just waltz in and out of my life as you please, you're sorely mistaken, Alessandro della Torre. It doesn't work like that."

He levered himself up, still moving deeply inside her and stared down at her. "I'm not leaving your life again, ever, Nicole, *mia cara*. And I couldn't waltz if I wanted to. I can barely walk."

His face was somber, deep lines bracketing his mouth. For the first time, Nicole noticed how changed Alessandro was. He'd aged a lot in the past year. He was much more pallid than he'd been in Amman. Silver threads swept through his black hair. Though he was still heavy on top of her—he was a big man—he had lost a lot of weight. She hadn't noticed it because he was still dressed, but now that she thought of it, she could feel how much lighter he was than before.

She blinked up at him. There was something in his expression...

"Stop," she whispered, and clutched his buttocks. She couldn't think while he was making love to her. Obediently, his hips stilled. "What are you talking about?"

"I've been in the hospital this past year." His deep voice was sober, quiet. "I barely survived Christmas Eve."

"How—what?" Her mind whirled.

"I don't work for the Foreign Ministry, Nicole," he said, watching her eyes. "I never did work for them. I work—used to work—for the Ministry of Defense."

He knew she'd have received briefing books on her new posting, and she had—five thick tomes on every aspect of Italian political life. And its Secret Services.

"Are you—are you SISDE?" A shadowy intelligence agency, modeled after the American CIA, SISDE was responsible for external security.

Alessandro nodded, then his hard mouth lifted in a half smile. "I knew you were smart. You frighten me sometimes. Stefano Volpi told me he had to call you to warn you off. He was frightened you'd put it together."

"He broke my heart." Nicole shivered as she remembered the shock she'd felt after Count Volpi's phone call.

"Yes," Alessandro said simply. "But it was necessary."

"Were you—" Nicole's mind was whirling as she put the broken pieces of the last year together. "Were you in some way involved in the gunrunning scandal?"

"I wasn't just involved, *tesoro*. I broke it. I was in the Amman Embassy undercover. It was a very rare example of international cooperation amongst police officers and security agents because we knew we had to find out how these arms were entering the area. I had the help of an excellent CIA officer in your Embassy. He was under cover, too."

"Mike Holden," Nicole said. "The Embassy driver."

"*Dio*." Alessandro closed his eyes and shook his head. "Remind me never *ever* to cheat on you."

For the very first time, Nicole felt able to smile. "I would cut your heart out and eat it if you ever cheated on me."

"Beautiful and blood-thirsty." He gave her a quick kiss. "I'm in very deep here."

She trailed her hand up his back in an uncertain caress, aware that her heart was opening to him with every word he spoke. "So..." she said quietly. "What happened?"

"I put out feelers, saying I wouldn't be averse to earning money by looking the other way when my diplomatic pouch was being filled and, sure enough, they bit. On the afternoon of Christmas Eve we were to meet, the gunrunners and twelve diplomatic officers from eight embassies. I was wearing a body wire. We had our men outside, waiting. It was supposed to be a clean operation. I got enough information for convictions and was about ready to leave when a young American intelligence officer got overexcited and made a move. All hell broke loose and I was caught in the cross fire." Alessandro took a deep breath. "I took seven bullets. I lost 3 liters of blood before the medics were able to stabilize me. I barely survived and was in a coma for a month."

"Alessandro," Nicole whispered, shocked. In her deepest despair, in the darkest heart of the loneliest night, Nicole had still felt a little kernel of joy just knowing Alessandro was in the world. "You could have died and I would never have known."

"It's the way of the world, *tesoro*. And before we go any further, I have to warn you that I have scars all over my body. Ugly ones. I have metal pins in both hips and a knee, enough to set off metal detectors. I will forever have a limp. I had to retire from SISDE on a disability pension and am currently without a job." He searched her eyes. "With all of that, can you still love me?"

"Alessandro." Her voice was liquid with tenderness. She caressed his face, the new wrinkles around his eyes, the deep lines bracketing his mouth. "How could you even ask? I could never love another man after you."

"Excellent. Do you think you could possibly live the rest of your life in Naples? I know I'm asking you to quit your job and I'm willing to follow you around the world if you insist, but I warn you, I'd make a lousy househusband."

Living forever in this beautiful city. With Alessandro. There was only one possible answer. "Of course I'll live here with you. I can find a job."

"My darling Nicole. You will find that there is an opening for a very high-level liaison job at the NATO base here and that they will jump to have you. And I will be finally putting my law degree to use. I'm joining my cousin Stefano's law office. It's a very successful one and there's family money. A lot, in fact. So you won't ever want for anything. But neither of us will start work until March. We're going to spend the next three months in bed, making love and eating. How does that sound for a plan?"

She blinked back the tears, her heart overflowing with love and hope. "Sounds...wonderful."

"*Bene*." Alessandro flashed a sudden grin, looking suddenly like a young man. "Then let's move on. Are you still on the Pill, *cara*?" He rotated his hips and Nicole could feel the wetness.

Appalled, Nicole stared up at him. She hadn't even thought of it. She could feel the blood draining from her face. "No," she whispered. "My doctor cycled me off for four months. Oh, Alessandro, what are we—"

"Good." The deep voice rumbled with pleasure. "We have just made a child, my darling Nicole. I want a daughter," he ordered. "Several of them. They are supposed to look after me and pamper me in my old age. That is the Italian way. I might some day want a son. Just one, someone to smoke cigars and play chess with. And while we're talking about children—" He reached into his jacket pocket, the movement pressing him more deeply into her.

Nicole gasped, on the razor's edge of climax. Alessandro grinned wickedly. "Patience, *carissima*," he murmured, amusement in his dark eyes. "We still have some business to conduct and then I'll love you as much as you want. Now pay attention because this is important."

It was extremely hard to pay attention with him so hot and heavy inside her. Nicole completely forgot about her lower body, however, when she saw what Alessandro had in his hand.

A ring. A gorgeous antique ring. A diamond-cut emerald in an elaborate setting.

"This ring has been in my family for a hundred years," Alessandro said quietly. "Every della Torre woman who has worn it has had a long and happy marriage. Prolific, too," he added, lips curved in a wicked smile. "I have to warn you that I have four brothers and they are all going to fall in love with you the instant they see you, so we must get married very soon. Immediately, in fact. My little girl must be born a della Torre."

His voice was teasing, but there were tears in his eyes as he slid the magnificent ring on her finger. Nicole didn't even bother wiping away her own tears, streaming down her face.

"Marry me," Alessandro whispered.

"Oh, yes," she whispered back.

There was an explosion in the air and she looked, startled, out the big picture windows at fireworks exploding over Vesuvius, purple and scarlet and gold. It was midnight.

"*Buon Natale, amore mio*," Alessandro said as he began thrusting.

"Merry Christmas, my love," Nicole answered, her own fireworks exploding inside.

About the author:

Lisa Marie welcomes mail from readers. You can write to her c/o Ellora's Cave Publishing at 1337 Commerce Drive, Suite 13, Stow OH 44224.

Also by Lisa Marie Rice:

Why an electronic book?

We live in the Information Age — an exciting time in the history of human civilization in which technology rules supreme and continues to progress in leaps and bounds every minute of every hour of every day. For a multitude of reasons, more and more avid literary fans are opting to purchase e-books instead of paperbacks. The question to those not yet initiated to the world of electronic reading is simply: *why?*

1. *Price.* An electronic title at Ellora's Cave Publishing runs anywhere from 40-75% less than the cover price of the <u>exact same title</u> in paperback format. Why? Cold mathematics. It is less expensive to publish an e-book than it is to publish a paperback, so the savings are passed along to the consumer.

2. *Space.* Running out of room to house your paperback books? That is one worry you will never have with electronic novels. For a low one-time cost, you can purchase a handheld computer designed specifically for e-reading purposes. Many e-readers are larger than the average handheld, giving you plenty of screen room. Better yet, hundreds of titles can be stored within your new library — a single microchip. (Please note that Ellora's Cave does not endorse any specific brands. You can check our website at www.ellorascave.com for customer recommendations we make available to new consumers.)

3. *Mobility.* Because your new library now consists of only a microchip, your entire cache of books can be taken with you wherever you go.

4. *Personal preferences are accounted for.* Are the words you are currently reading too small? Too large? Too...**ANNOYING**? Paperback books cannot be modified according to personal preferences, but e-books can.

5. *Innovation.* The way you read a book is not the only advancement the Information Age has gifted the literary community with. There is also the factor of what you can read. Ellora's Cave Publishing will be introducing a new line of interactive titles that are available in e-book format only.

6. *Instant gratification.* Is it the middle of the night and all the bookstores are closed? Are you tired of waiting days—sometimes weeks—for online and offline bookstores to ship the novels you bought? Ellora's Cave Publishing sells instantaneous downloads 24 hours a day, 7 days a week, 365 days a year. Our e-book delivery system is 100% automated, meaning your order is filled as soon as you pay for it.

Those are a few of the top reasons why electronic novels are displacing paperbacks for many an avid reader. As always, Ellora's Cave Publishing welcomes your questions and comments. We invite you to email us at service@ellorascave.com or write to us directly at: 1337 Commerce Drive, Suite 13, Stow OH 44224.

Printed in the United States
25900LVS00001B/139-186